The Wayside

CAROLINE WOLFF

The Wayside

BLACK
STONE
PUBLISHING

Printed in the United States of America

First edition: 2024
ISBN 979-8-212-63817-3
Fiction / Thrillers / Psychological

Version 2

Blackstone Publishing
31 Mistletoe Rd.
Ashland, OR 97520

www.BlackstonePublishing.com

To Mom, Dad, and Alex

The hiker and his wife crested the trail to the place called the Wayside. This was morning's thinnest edges, the sky a crystalline pink. A few yards away was a tumble of singed old stones, holding roughly the shape of a mansion destroyed by fire. The chimney and fireplace were intact and charred, knotted in thick ropes of ivy. Beer cans and vape cartridges and a bottle of bad red wine littered the ground. A cheap gold-plated necklace glinted weakly beneath the dead leaves. This was the hiker's favorite place. It was less popular than some of the other trails along the rocky coastline, and on some mornings, like this one, he wouldn't have to see a single other soul. His wife liked it, too, but not as much as he did.

The hiker would relay all of this information later, just in case it mattered.

Upon reaching the summit that morning, he rested on a chair-sized rock. He ate the second half of his protein bar, powdery peanut butter with a sticky vanilla drizzle. His wife walked toward the cliff's edge eight or ten yards away.

That was when she saw it.

"A body," his wife said. "There's a body down there."

The hiker rose from his rocky perch. Did she say something? If she had, he couldn't understand it. She spoke down into the ravine, which made her voice echo, ricocheting between this cliff and the one across the water. When the words returned to him, they had warped into pure sound, losing the hard edges that shaped them into language. This was a natural amphitheater, but an ineffective one. (He would share this information later, too, following an urge to absolve himself of a crime he hadn't committed but which may have been committed near him.)

He asked his wife to repeat herself. Still he couldn't hear her, even though on the way up here they had been in the midst of a conversation and his mind was still full of it. They'd been talking about the kids, the logistics involved in rearing them. Usually, now, they talked about logistics. What time they would be able to pick the kids up from his mother's in Petaluma, and then what time would they make it back home to Santa Cruz, and would they have time to stop by Gessen's farm stand on the way home. Gessen's had the best pumpkins, uniformly vivid and smooth, and it was still early enough in the season that the really formidable ones, the ones ripest for carving, would not have been picked off just yet. The kids were only seven and five, but already they knew to ask for the biggest things. He figured they'd be back down to the trailhead in an hour or so, which would get them to Gessen's at four p.m., right before they closed down at five.

He was just about to share this with his wife when she said something about a body, and everything went silent. He saw white. There was a sharp pain in his back tooth.

The hiker joined his wife where she stood just before the end of the cliff. He put a hand on her shoulder and guided her backward one big step, then two. She obliged without turning around. The hand that held her green water bottle shook; he could hear the liquid churning against the sides.

"A body." She said it again.

He heard her this time. Panic eclipsed her features. His arm latched across her torso, shoulder to shoulder, and he held her insistently against him.

She pointed. "Do you see it?"

He looked down. There was the jagged carpet of rocks that bordered the thin ravine that snaked through the twin cliffs. Amidst the rocks was a pale mass. The mass was clothed; there were a pair of jeans, a wool sweater, and high-top sneakers that were probably once white but were now the shade of an egg dipped in tea. The flesh of the mass was swollen like a balloon stuffed with mud. The water lapped gently against it in a way that reminded the hiker of his daughter tapping her finger against her napping brother's arm, coaxing him to play.

Beneath the hiker's grip his wife's body turned soft and boneless. He released her, overcome with revulsion.

He cleared his throat and forced himself to look away from the dead body sprawled across the rocks.

"I see it," he told his wife. "I do."

CHAPTER
ONE

Kate had no idea that her son had liked a band called Jungle, or Jim Jarmusch's *Stranger Than Paradise*, or Kandinsky, or *Psycho*, or the Cocteau Twins—the swirly shoegaze dreampop band to which she distinctly remembered dancing at the Roxy exactly one time, in '95, the summer she interned at Abrams & Frank in New York. Nor had she known that Jake had liked the David Hockney print that'd hung in his childhood bedroom so much that he'd brought it here, to Paloma College, and mounted it over his bed.

Kate lifted the corner off a poster—the Cure—and noticed that the paint peeled off in strips beneath it. There were so many hints of age and neglect in this apartment—a sink that dripped, a toilet that flushed all the way only with insistence and a prayer—but it was charming, too, and comfortable in its own way, and Kate could imagine her son's pride in it, how he would have tended to it as best he could.

And there was light, and that was what mattered most. Sun funneled through the windows, shot through with motes. The air was warm and sticky like a greenhouse. A bird's-nest fern drooped on the windowsill, its leaves seared yellow by the sun.

She hiked up her sleeves to adjust the band of her Cartier
Tank watch, now imprinted on her wrist—during the divorce,
John insisted that she keep it, and through her hatred she managed a thread of tenderness for her ex—then moved to Jake's
desk, strewn with books. *Classical Mythology, The Complete
Poetry & Prose of William Blake, Introduction to Economics.* The
last was John's influence, Kate was sure. Jake didn't have a head
for numbers. Never did. Inside the drawers, nestled beside a
stack of Moleskine notebooks, she found a Victorinox Swiss
Army knife, its hardwood hilt engraved with an inscription: *To
Jake, love Dad.* She worried the knife between her fingers for a
moment, like a talisman, then slotted it back inside the desk.

The police took his laptop—the source, they hoped, of the
answers she so desperately needed—though they'd assured her
they would return it to her soon. But that was two weeks ago,
and now the initial stun of disbelief had slowly begun to melt.
It had not yet coagulated into total clarity. She believed that her
son would walk through that door behind her, and she would
raise herself to her tippy-toes to press her mouth into his curls—
which still, beneath the stale sheen of smoke and must, smelled
like baby. Still she believed this, even after shoveling dirt onto
his coffin. It was glossy and beautifully curved, like a cello, and
she would never not be plagued by the sound it made when it
caught the dirt. A hollow thud. An *oof.*

She inhaled deeply, so deep, until her lungs strained with
it. She couldn't remember the last time she was so aware of the
air, but now she needed it all the time, and urgently, the way
she once needed cigarettes in law school, and still sometimes
did, when she felt pressured at work, which was almost always.

Then she began to unpack her things from the suitcase at
her feet. It was the biggest one she could find. *Big enough to fit
a life,* she'd told the clerk at Bloomingdale's, who maybe would

have laughed if not for this customer's anemic expression, the nothingness behind the eyes. Kate had left her work clothes hanging in her closet at home in San Francisco, and as she'd packed, she'd realized how few casual clothes she owned—everything silk and wool, smelling of the office's industrial-strength antiseptic—and the guilt had consumed her then, too.

Now she stacked all her clothes in the top drawer, and only that one drawer. She'd brought her makeup case—an amnesiac lapse; she'd really forgotten that she couldn't muster the energy to consider what her face looked like to other people—and now she set it on top of the flimsy IKEA dresser, beside a fishbowl stuffed with BIC lighters.

When she was done, she looked at the bed again. This was the worst part, and unavoidable. The sheets were stirred to a froth and kicked to the foot, like he'd had a particularly fitful night's sleep. Kate believed she could make out the faint outline of his body impressed upon the mattress. Jake had been haunted by nightmares for six months straight when he was a child. Every night he woke up screaming and drenched. The dreams, he had said, were too disturbing to recount. When Jake began insisting on keeping the lights on in his bedroom at night, and then kept falling asleep at his desk during class, Kate had sent him to a child psychologist. The shrink's diagnosis: overactive imagination.

The guy was a hack. Kate didn't need to pay two hundred an hour to be told that her kid was creative.

Eventually Jake grew out of the nightmares, and that was a relief. But Kate now wondered whether the demon that had plagued him as a child had found him in this room, in this bed, and sat down heavy on his chest. And Kate wondered if this time Jake just couldn't find the strength to push it off. If he had simply sunk under its weight.

Her phone buzzed from inside her purse, snapping her out of the mess of her memory. Could've been Bettina, head of HR; could've been Tracy, the company's CEO herself. An only slightly less paranoid thought: What if it was Eliza, the civil rights attorney whom Kate had met on Bumble just before Jake's death? (Another of her serial, half-hearted attempts to forge a meaningful relationship with someone she didn't actually work with.) After swiping herself into oblivion, drunk on pinot noir and resentment for every single dating-app user within a ten-mile radius, Eliza had been the only person of any gender whom Kate had felt remotely interested in. Eliza was also a mother to a teenager, had also been unhappily married to a man for many years, and also identified as bisexual. She counted high-octane heist movies, those Italian hazelnut wafer cookies, and collecting designer silk robes as her top three guilty pleasures. (*Give me Agent Provocateur or give me death*, she'd texted, alongside that winky emoji.) After messaging for a few days, they'd made a plan to meet at Charmaine's for a glass of wine after work.

And then Jake died and Kate stopped responding. Did it count as ghosting if the cause of death was literal death?

No, Eliza seemed too smart to chase a ghost. Tracy was the more likely pursuer. Kate's bereavement leave from Chalice expired a week ago. She was supposed to return to the office shortly after Jake's funeral. But when she returned from the gravesite to her slick, stainless apartment in Pacific Heights, the silence was so deafening, the emptiness suffocating, and for a moment the reality of Jake's death enveloped her fully. The prospect of returning to that office was absurd. Grieving was her job now. It left no room for anything else. Her head, her heart, her whole self yearned for Sutter Point, for the son she had failed to protect. She had to go back to him.

And even corporate couldn't argue with a child's suicide. More accurately: corporate couldn't argue with the death of the child of the general counsel, without whom the firm would have drowned in its acquisition of MogenTech, a Tel Aviv–based tech firm that designed and developed data-encryption software. The deal was pivotal for Chalice—without it, the firm would have to sink years and millions into developing their own software— and Kate was pivotal in that deal.

At least, that was Chalice's attitude last week. Now, Kate knew, the firm needed an answer: *Are you in, or are you out?*

Kate let the phone ring and stripped the bed and buried her face in the fabric. But she couldn't smell Jake in it. These sheets didn't smell like anyone anymore.

———

According to the coroner's report, Jake Cleary died of severe internal injuries, including fractures to each rib, two fractured vertebrae, and bone-fragment punctures to both lungs, the spleen, and the heart, caused by falling or jumping off one of the cliffs lording over the Scotia River. (When Kate googled *falling off cliff* later, in search of information—as if information could retroactively save him—she read one Coast Guard officer liken a jumper's internal organs to scrambled eggs.) The report placed his death somewhere between nine p.m. and midnight on Tuesday, October 10th. His body was recovered on the river shore over twenty-four hours later. If he had survived a few more hours, maybe even a single extra minute, he would have turned twenty-one years old. Kate wondered if there was some significance to this number, how it marked the ceremonial end of one's youth, or the beginning of one's adulthood.

Had Jake expressed fear or regret about no longer being a child? Kate couldn't say; they'd spoken once a week since Jake went up to college two years ago, and recently their conversations were anodyne, bordering on formal. Kate could barely register emotion in Jake's tone. Now she wondered whether her son's detachment wasn't boredom with his mother, impatience to get off the line and go out with his friends, but actually a red flag. A clue.

And when she read the coroner's report, she snagged over the phrase "falling or jumping." The police had asked her: *Did your son struggle with depression? Is there a history of mental illness in the family? Has Jake experienced a recent trauma?* No, no, and no. And she hadn't found a note.

Still, they weren't ruling out the possibility of suicide. Suicide was a pandemic. According to statistics Kate gleaned from the Suicide Prevention Resource Center, it was the second leading cause of death among people aged ten to thirty-four in the United States. Jake nestled right in the middle of that range. His age alone made him vulnerable.

Hence: "falling or jumping." In the gulf of difference between the two words, there was an answer.

But there was another possibility, too. This one crouched on the farthest shore of Kate's imagination like one of Jake's nightmare demons.

What if Jake neither fell nor jumped? What if he was pushed?

The SPPD had declined, and then refused, to acknowledge the presence of this possibility. And with every one of their rejections, Kate paddled closer and closer to that damned shore, hunting in the darkness for the answer to its existence.

She hadn't found the answer yet.

And in the absence of an answer, Kate turned to anger.

———

Anger fueled her now, as she strode across Paloma's campus every day and plunged into the basement of the library, to which she procured a guest pass, and where she flipped through Jake's journals and the stack of diaries he'd left in his desk. Deprived of his laptop and phone, she even read his textbooks. Any source through which Jake might speak to her, to reveal the truth of his death. She placed her fingers over his fingerprints, traced lightly where the green pen smudged. (A sign of distress? Also, that Jake favored green pen over blue or black—that might have been something, too.)

She searched for clues, and then for an answer. She didn't know what a clue might look like, but she believed she would know it when she saw it.

Since unofficially moving into Jake's apartment a week ago—the day after she got the call from Wachs—she had developed this maudlin daily routine, bookended by a cup of coffee in the morning at Tony's, the café just down the block from the apartment, and whatever she could stomach there for dinner. By now, Richard, the owner, had begun to feed her things: chicken soup, a plate of plain pasta, mashed potatoes and gravy. Food for children. She didn't even need to place an order anymore. In a past life, she would have found the coddling thing presumptuous. Now, it was a small but meaningful comfort.

Tonight, Richard chose tortilla soup, which he bore from the kitchen almost as soon as Kate took her usual seat at a table in the corner. Kate initially chose this table for its semblance of privacy, but also its clear view of Main Street to her left, then the whole of the restaurant before her.

Richard set the bowl down on the table, the steaming broth hidden under a thicket of tortilla strips and islands of melting sour cream.

"I threw some extra Monterey on there," Richard said.

"And about a half a carton of Daisy, I see."

"I don't like how you're looking."

"It's called the grief diet."

"Oh, I'm familiar. When Tony died I lost thirty pounds, but of course I gained it all back after taking this over." Richard gestured vaguely around the café. "Why you would leave the care of a restaurant to a former off-off-Broadway dancer, I have no idea. Even if that dancer was your husband."

"One of many reasons why I couldn't cut it as a wife," Kate said. "I'm too selfish to be saddled with another person's burdens."

"What you call selfish, I call good sense." Richard tilted his chin toward the notebook Kate had brought with her today. "Anything interesting in there?"

Kate hadn't told Richard about her secret fact-finding project. The project no one—certainly not the police charged with the real, sanctioned investigation into Jake's death—had asked her to do. But Richard knew that she was the mother of the student who had died tragically two weeks earlier. The woman enduring a living nightmare, and who wore that nightmare like a cloak. Occasionally, in those fleeting moments when her clarity was restored, Kate wondered if she was becoming a fixture in town, a complementary shade of local color. The resident griever. The mere fact of her continued presence on the campus where her dead son lived out his final days must have made her something of an eccentric.

Now Kate looked down at the Moleskine. "This was Jake's journal. It's the only one I haven't gone through yet."

Richard managed a small, sad smile. Then the bells above the front door chimed, heralding Detective Wachs, in for his nightly cup of coffee. He came into Tony's at the same time every day for lunch, and then again every evening, exactly twenty minutes after Kate sat down to her own nocturnal ritual. Kate offered him a smile and a nod and reminded herself that Wachs wasn't actually an enemy, despite the Sutter Point Police Department's stunning lack of urgency in determining why her son died.

Wachs returned Kate's exact gestures, both the smile and the nod, but his were tainted with resentment, dripping in long, luxurious rivulets. *Ah, there's the woman who's been harassing my secretary with daily phone calls checking up on our painstakingly organized investigation.*

Richard left to take the police detective's order, and Kate turned back to Jake's diary.

This, the final of the four diaries she found in his desk, she cracked with a combination of hope and despair. Without his phone and laptop—the gold mine Wachs seemed to be blindly sitting on—this diary was the last real chance she had to find something useful. His notebooks from class conjured nothing other than exactly what they were, though Kate was still moved to tears by Jake's immaculate penmanship, rendered in all caps, which looked so much like John's. (In law school John had set up a side hustle selling his notes from class, equally because they were as thorough as they were beautiful to look at.)

This diary opened in late August, at the beginning of the school year. The earlier three diaries spanned the entirety of Jake's college career, from freshman move-in day up until the previous summer, when he decided to remain in Sutter Point to work as a campus library assistant. (The fact that Jake didn't want to come home had broken Kate's heart a little bit, but in truth, she had been too mired in work to try to convince him otherwise. And even if he *had* stayed home, how much time would they have truly spent together? It was just another twist of the guilt-soaked knife.)

Since engrossing herself in these diaries, Kate had picked up on Jake's patterns. He tended to keep up entries for a few days at a time, then drop the practice entirely for months. But the entries, when he committed to them, were energized and inquisitive. They leaned observational rather than self-reflective. He wrote in great detail of sensory experiences. The sound of a tarp flapping against the neighboring building; the smell of a violet perfume he uncorked on a friend's dresser. Since elementary school, Jake had exhibited a natural talent for writing, and he was firm in his decision to major in English at Paloma, but he hadn't expressed a desire to *be* a writer. Here, in his diaries, it seemed he was trying the title on for size.

But in this diary, Kate sensed a shift in tone. These entries were detached and formulaic. One was a time-stamped list of everything he had done that day: breakfast, class, lunch, class, read, meeting, dinner. In another, he wrote down everything he ate. Another was a list of things he needed to get at the pharmacy. Another, a list of movies he wanted to watch. All told, the entries only covered about twenty pages. By mid-September, Jake was done.

Kate looked out the café's window. The small businesses dotting Main Street had shuttered for the night, their twinkling lights snuffed out. And here in the restaurant, only two other diners remained, a couple silently considering each other over glasses of dark, syrupy wine.

She sat back in her seat, exhausted, as if she'd just performed manual labor. And in a way, she had: Over the past two weeks, she had used all her strength, and all her resources, to excavate the mystery of her son. But Jake wasn't soft, tillable soil. He was frozen ground.

Her bowl of soup sat untouched beside her. She managed a few spoonfuls of it, out of respect for Richard, then paid the check and headed out onto the quiet street.

For the first time since Jake's death, she felt the true extent of her loneliness. How arrogant she had been to believe she could really understand another person, even if that person had come from her own body. People defied understanding. She'd known this even before things got so bad with John, when nearly every morning—even the mornings she had convinced herself that she was in love—she woke up beside her husband and considered his sleeping face and thought: *Who is this person?* And then felt that sinking feeling in her chest.

She reached the door leading up to Jake's second-floor apartment, wondering vaguely what she should do with herself for the rest of the night. Falling asleep naturally was out of the question—had been since she got that call. The call that demarcated the before and the after: the time when she was a mother; and the time when, technically speaking, she no longer was.

Hence the thirty-day supplies of Xanax and Ambien that sat on the nightstand, each bottle steadily draining, and both of which her doctor had prescribed immediately, no questions asked.

She was thinking about the night ahead of her, how she would likely blot it out as soon as she could get to those cloudy amber bottles, when the sound of her name startled her. She turned to find Richard bounding down the sidewalk, brandishing a folded sheet of paper above his head.

Panting mildly, he said: "You dropped this on your way out." He seemed to notice Kate's confusion—all she'd brought with her to the café was Jake's diary and her wallet—so he added, "It fell out of the notebook."

Kate took the paper and unfolded it halfway. There, undoubtedly, was Jake's handwriting.

And here, she thought, was her missing link, and with it a glimmer of hope.

She thanked Richard and returned to Jake's apartment, where she sat at his desk and unfolded the paper, smoothing it flush. The desk lamp enrobed the paper in a circle of light. A date was written in the top left-hand corner: October 9th. The day before Jake died.

CHAPTER TWO

She told me writing would help.

I told her I know that, I did that, but it won't help with this.

She told me writing would be like an exorcism.

I told her: I've seen a possession. What's happening to me isn't that.

She told me guilt is a kind of demon.

But exorcising the demon of guilt requires the purifying power of truth. And I can't tell the truth to anyone else.

She said: You'll still have me.

I didn't say: But you're just one person. You are not enough.

She asked me if I took a blood oath. I think she was kidding, but she didn't look like she was.

I said: There was blood on the ground. There was blood everywhere. We had to scrub it off the soles of our shoes.

She said: If you don't help yourself, then I can't help you. And then she turned away.

But something else is happening here. I've discovered the answer to our most essential question.

> *"What immortal hand or eye*
> *Could frame thy fearful symmetry?"*

Here is my final answer.

There is no god and there is no devil, because that would imply some greater cosmic order.

I used to believe in an order. When I was little I talked to the angels when the demons kept me up at night.

But neither god nor devil could have designed what I saw.

What I saw—that was only chaos.

And under the chaos, there is nothing.

She helped me see that. She helped me to see that there is no recourse.

Kate read the note twice, three times, then four and five and six. She read the note until she had it memorized, the rhythm of it steeped into her head like a song. That penultimate line ran rings around the room, gong-like: *And under the chaos, there is nothing.* It had a whiff of proverb to it, or an ancient text in translation.

Kate couldn't square the writer of this note with the writer of the diaries—especially the last diary, perfunctory as it was, which in no way betrayed this baroque paranoia. What had happened between September 18th, the date of Jake's final entry, and his death less than a month later? What was it that had hounded him over the side of that cliff?

Kate couldn't know what was real and what was symbolic in this letter. But she knew for certain that Jake didn't fall off the cliff. He jumped.

And now she truly knew that something, or someone, had hounded him over the edge.

She. Whoever she was, she held the key to the riddle of Jake's death. Maybe she *was* his key.

Then there were the two lines of poetry Jake had quoted. *"What immortal hand or eye / Could frame thy fearful symmetry?"* The lines were vaguely familiar, conjured echoes of the few English courses Kate had taken in college. She confirmed with a Google search: they were pulled from "The Tyger" by William Blake. Kate looked over at the Blake anthology on Jake's desk, its striated paperback spine and softened, tea-colored pages. Somehow, in her research, she had failed to read this book.

With this letter—this horrific, haunting letter—she felt closer to Jake now than she had over the past two weeks. Maybe even over the past few years, since she'd been promoted to general counsel when Jake was in high school (how silly that title seemed now, how inconsequential) and she'd abandoned him—yes, she felt that she'd abandoned him—for that slick and lonely office. So she didn't know when Jake had morphed from her quiet and contented boy to this person plagued by abject fear, given to grave nihilism. But she felt the truth of his answer to Blake's question resonate deep in her bones. In a way, she had always known it, but Jake's death was proof positive: There was no god and no devil; no good and no evil. There was only chaos. And under the chaos, there was nothing.

She looked at her watch: it was nine forty-five p.m., an hour since she'd sat down at Jake's desk. She refolded the note into a small square and tucked it into her wallet, then stood and stretched side to side, unraveling the tension in her back. Then slipped off her shoes and jeans, swallowed an Ambien, and fell into a deep, dreamless sleep.

Kate woke to her phone trilling and an arrow of light shooting through the venetian blinds. For a fraction of a moment, she forgot where and who she was. This had happened to her every morning since Jake died, and she suspected it was a subconscious protective mechanism. This fraction of a moment was the best part of her day.

She rolled over to the nightstand and squinted at her phone. It was John calling. Unlike Kate, John hadn't exploited his bereavement leave. Actually, Kate wasn't so sure he'd taken leave at all—he'd returned to New York, where he'd moved after their divorce, shortly after the funeral ended. Of course John was devastated by the death of his son; John was emotionally limited, but he wasn't a monster. He was just doing what he had always done when faced with the possibility of emotional wreckage: disappearing into his work.

And disappearing was inherent to his line of work. Though John, whose clients required privacy to the point of deniability, preferred the term *discretion*. He practiced art-and-antiquities law, though not necessarily on the right side of cultural heritage. Kate was almost positive he hadn't gone home at all after the funeral, and instead headed to wherever a client's next collectible of dubious provenance resided. But even when they were married, Kate never knew exactly where he went.

Still, John had texted or called Kate nearly every day over the past two weeks, just to check in. Apparently he felt at least a little bit guilty for abandoning Kate in her grief so quickly, almost literally before the dust had settled on their son's casket. This constant contact was another thing Kate couldn't have entertained in her past life, but which she now found comforting. In many ways, their shared loss had brought them closer together than their shared joy in Jake's birth ever had. And honestly, the latter was what had torn them apart. It was a tale as old as modern marriage: she wanted to work, he didn't want her to work, she returned to work, he turned bitter, she turned bitter, neither expressed their resentments, the resentments grew quietly, like a tumor, and their marriage had grown too frail to withstand it. But it was no less painful for its mundanity, especially with their child—Jake only eight—caught in the crosshairs, then shuttled back and forth between the coasts like some fragile cargo.

"Tell me what you're doing today," John said in lieu of a greeting. He opened most of their conversations this way.

Kate turned onto her other side, away from the light. *Figuring out why our son died*, she thought. "I'll read a little bit," she said. "Maybe go for a run later."

"You're reading? That's good." He paused for a moment. "I changed my will this week. You should contact your lawyer, Katie."

"That's not where my head is right now."

"I know it's not."

"I know you know," she said, "and yet you're still telling me what to do."

"And that's why we're not married anymore."

Kate laughed a little. They rested in silence for a moment, and it wasn't so bad. But soon she sensed John stirring on the other end of the line.

"Hey, could you send me some of Jake's things?" he said. "Some of his books or clothes? A tchotchke, maybe? I'd like to have something of him with me here."

"I can't do that." She responded too quickly, she knew, but she couldn't tamp down the panic that seized her at the thought of breaking down Jake's room, letting go of all the information lying in wait in its unseen corners and drawers. "I still need everything here."

John sighed. "I don't like what you're doing," he said, "and I don't understand how living in Jake's apartment and doing nothing all day can possibly help you move on."

This was where she should've told John that she'd found their son's note. She should've told him that, before the writing of that note, their son had sounded pretty much the way they knew him to be—by which she would mean, not considering ending his own life—and that meant that something had happened over the past month that had obliterated his will to live.

Then she remembered a line from an earlier entry in an earlier diary, when Jake had just arrived at Paloma as a freshman—fresh off a year of quarantine with his mother, no less—and everything was hope and possibility and big ideas, and his heart was so open to all of it. In class one day, his American Lit professor had apparently launched into a tangent expounding the virtues of the recluse writers. Emily Dickinson, J. D. Salinger, Elena Ferrante, et al. *It's very hard to keep creative projects a secret,* the professor had said, then repeated in Jake's green pen. *But keeping an idea secret retains its sacredness and power. The more people you tell, the more its energy diffuses. And before you know it, the whole thing falls apart. These people had the wisdom to understand this, and the discipline to act on it.*

Now just a single wild laugh escaped from Kate's throat. "There is no moving on, John," she said. "I will never move on from this."

———

The run was a lie, of course. As soon as she hung up with John, Kate brushed her teeth, grabbed the book of Blake poetry, and headed down to Tony's, where Richard immediately brought her a cup of black coffee.

She opened directly to "The Tyger." And there, indeed, were Jake's orderly notes, crawling from the margins and into the text itself. The page was overrun with his green pen, like ivy colonizing a brick facade. But before she attempted to decode all the words on the page—Blake's and Jake's both—the diner's glass doors opened, followed by an onrush of wind.

It wouldn't be right to call the appearance of the girl mirage-like, because her presence had some heft to it, a gravitational pull. The café was sparsely populated at this hour—it was ten a.m.; too late for the work crowd, too early for lunch—but Kate felt the room's attention collapse toward the girl. She felt inherently disconcerted, the way her lizard brain clocked strange movements when she walked home alone at night.

The girl stepped forward to let the door close behind her, but she remained near the doorframe. She was young, around Jake's age, and undoubtedly a student. Beneath her oversized leopard coat, patchy at the elbows and pockets, she wore flannel pajama

bottoms and a pair of unlaced Adidas sneakers. Her dark hair was
tied back into a drooping ponytail. She looked into the middle distance. Her eyes were glazed, but they retained a flicker of alertness.

"Can I help you with something?" Richard said from behind
the counter. Kate heard a trace of worry running through his
voice. She considered gently approaching the girl, but she wondered, a little ridiculously, whether the girl would bite.

The girl looked vaguely in Richard's direction, then continued to move her gaze in a slow circle around the perimeter
of the room. When she caught on Kate, her features rearranged
into clarity. Kate noticed the sharp intelligence in her face, and
the layer of fear caked over it, like grime on tile.

"I'm sorry for your loss," the girl said.

A pit opened in Kate's belly. "You know who I am?"

The girl stepped closer to Kate's table. In her periphery, she
could see Richard watching them. "Of course. We all know you."

"Did you know my son? Jake?"

The girl nodded. "You look just like him."

Kate gestured to the empty seat across from her. "Can I get
you a coffee? Something to eat?"

"I can't."

Desperate now, Kate stood and pulled the chair out from
the table. "Please, sit with me. I don't mean to upset you"—
here the girl flinched, and Kate softened her voice—"but I'm
just trying to figure out what happened to Jake. You can understand that, can't you?"

"Jake was a good person." Her hand fluttered inside her
pocket. "I don't agree with what he did, but I understand why he
felt like he needed to do it. The pressure—it was just too much."

Richard came over and hovered a benevolent hand over the
girl's back. "Are you sure I can't get you something? A glass of
water, maybe?"

The girl inched away, back toward the door. "No, thank you. I shouldn't have let her see me here." She scanned the room again, then cracked a perversion of a smile, revealing orthodontically straightened teeth: the universal calling card of financial privilege. Yes, undoubtedly a student. "She's not here," she said, her voice lifting. "But she could be anywhere."

She helped me see that there is no recourse. The line from Jake's note sang out, clear and true. It was absurd to think that whomever the girl was referring to now was the same person to whom Jake had mutely pointed in his note. Needle-in-a-haystack absurd.

But everything was absurd, nothing made sense, and there was no one but Kate to teach her this new language.

Kate offered to walk her home, because she felt protective of the girl, genuinely she did, but she was also desperate not to lose this link to Jake.

Of course the girl declined, and Kate didn't push. But when she left, disappearing down Main Street, Kate couldn't help but feel that she had lost another precious thing.

CHAPTER
THREE

A twenty-year-old woman was found dead of a broken neck in the Thurgood Hall dormitory early this morning. The woman has been identified as Alexandra "Sasha" Williams, a junior at Paloma College. Originally from Essex, Vermont, Williams earned a full merit scholarship to the school, where she was pursuing a bachelor of arts in Biochemistry with a minor in Molecular & Cellular Biology.

"She was planning to go to med school after graduating, and then to pursue cancer research," a friend of Williams's and fellow Paloma student told the Sutter Point Courier. According to Williams's friend, who asked to remain anonymous, Williams's choice in major was inspired by her younger sister, Rachel, who died of leukemia when the girls were both in middle school.

"Everything Sasha did, she did for Rachel," the source says. "She didn't talk about her sister that much. I think it upset her too much. But I could always feel Rachel's presence around her."

Williams's friend also remembers her for her "kindness and brilliance." "She was so full of light," the source adds.

Another student living in the dormitory discovered Williams's body on the third-floor landing below a flight of stairs. "I almost tripped over it," says the student, who also asked to remain anonymous. "When I looked down I thought she'd just passed out, but then I saw that her head was in a really weird place. It looked like it stood out at a ninety-degree angle from her neck."

Williams's death occurred less than two weeks after the death of Paloma College junior Jake Cleary, whose body was found on the Scotia River banks near Newburgh on October 11th. The Sutter Point Police Department is still investigating his death.

Before Cleary, there had been no student deaths on or around the Paloma campus in over thirty years. A spokesperson for the Sutter Point Police Department insists that there is no correlation between Williams's and Cleary's deaths.

"We have absolutely no evidence to suggest that these two students are connected in any way," the spokesperson says. "The death of these bright young people is a tragedy, and we grieve along with Paloma College and the Sutter Point community. But the proximity of their deaths is coincidental."

The spokesperson confirms that the SPPD ruled Williams's death accidental. A toxicology report concluded that there were no controlled substances present at the time of death.

Kate didn't need to consult the photograph running alongside the obituary to know exactly who Sasha Williams was. The knowledge made itself known in the very core of her, the same way she knew that the young woman's presence in the café was, in some way, portentous.

And yes, there she was, run through the paper's grainy

printer: There was the rope of dark hair and the Chiclet-straight teeth. Kate could just make out the pixelated mass of some woods behind her, and how the sun, high overhead, cast a light that made Sasha squint. And beneath that squint was the deep well of intelligence, the kind that made a person lonely.

Kate folded up the newspaper and slid it into the far corner of the carrel. She was no longer the type to believe in coincidences. Despite what the SPPD may have asserted, Kate knew it was not mere coincidence that Sasha died so soon after Jake, and she knew that her death was not entirely an accident, just like Jake's death was not so simple (if such a term could ever apply) as a suicide. Kate just needed to find the evidence of their connection, so that Wachs might see it, too.

And, sure, maybe she needed to prove to herself, in no uncertain terms, that her hunches were more than a delusion.

She looked up from the paper and around the library basement. There were no windows in this room, but down here the rotating populace stood in as a sundial, and from the shadows they cast—the girl who never removed her parka, despite the basement's cranking radiators; the top slice of a shaved head in the carrel adjacent to hers, white and fuzzy like a baby bird—she could read the hour as sometime around eight p.m. Which meant she had been down here, trekking through Blake's poetry, for at least four hours. During that time, she'd received and ignored two phone calls from Tracy's personal cell. She had also failed to penetrate Blake's epic poem *Milton*, even with the help of Jake's marginalia and her career-making tenure of parsing opaqueness in writing.

Then she accidentally made eye contact with the young woman at the desk across from her. Kate thought she'd seen her here, too, though not as consistently as the others. The woman's gaze slid away as she slotted her books and laptop, with great deliberation, into her bag. She'd worn her black plastic-framed glasses like a headband, holding back her long blond hair, and now she fixed them onto her face and pulled on a scuffed leather jacket. She made a quarter-turn toward the exit behind her, but she hesitated for a moment; Kate could practically see the thought bubble emerge above her head.

The woman came back around the table and stood at the end of Kate's carrel.

"I'm so sorry to bother you," the woman said, "but are you Jake Cleary's mother?" She spoke quietly; Kate had to lean in a little to hear her. When she did, Kate noticed a thin gold hoop threaded through her septum.

Kate let out a small laugh—a little humorless, a little not. "I seem to be gaining some fame around town."

"I'm so sorry to disturb you," the woman repeated. "But I wanted to come and pay my respects. I was Jake's Brit Lit TA. I hope it's okay to approach you with this. I just—" She looked away and swallowed, hard. Kate wondered: Should she comfort this stranger for her own son's death? "It's a terrible thing. Jake had such smart and interesting ideas, and he always expressed himself so clearly. He was very engaged in discussions, too. I leaned on him a lot."

"Thank you for saying that," Kate said. "It's comforting to hear people speak so kindly about Jake. It's comforting to hear people speak about him at all." She cast her mind back to Jake's Brit Lit papers, searching for the name in the header. "You're Luna Kline? Recitation section three?"

The woman nodded and smiled down at her hands, where she rotated a chunky silver ring around her middle finger.

"I've been reading all of Jake's papers and notebooks," Kate explained. "His textbooks, too. Anything he's written while at Paloma, or put his mark on in any way, I've read it." This was the first time she'd told someone what she had been doing—at least a tiny fraction of it—and she now realized how ridiculous it sounded. How pathetic.

But Luna nodded gravely, like this was the most reasonable thing in the world. "When my dad died, I did something similar. He didn't keep journals, but I hoarded anything with his writing on it." She pulled up the sleeve of her jacket, then the pale-gray cardigan layered beneath it, to reveal a small tattoo etched inside her forearm. *My girl*, it read. "This is his handwriting. I lifted it from a card he wrote to me for my eleventh birthday."

Then the fuzzy baby-bird head adjacent to Kate rose. The person attached to it took a moment to glare at Kate and Luna before turning to leave.

Luna shoved her sleeve down and tossed a hand toward the exit. "I was just about to get a cup of coffee," she said, her voice lowered again. Tentatively, she added: "Want to join?"

An image of Kate's bedside table floated vaguely before her. There were the pill bottles and the book Joan Didion wrote on grief, its unopened cover stained with coffee rings. And an almost-empty bottle of sriracha sauce that Jake had left there, the travel pack of tissues he'd undoubtedly used in lieu of real napkins. And the chill of the apartment, and the darkness of it, and the bed made up with airtight hospital corners, like Kate's mother made her learn as a child and which Kate, in her Gen X indulgence, never even thought to teach Jake.

Now Kate turned back to Luna. "How about a glass of wine instead?"

CHAPTER
FOUR

Luna led them to a small Italian restaurant on Main Street. It was just across the street from Tony's—from their table near the window, Kate could just make out Richard's slick of black hair—but somehow Kate had failed to notice this place. It was nice in a throwback way, the kind of place with red-and-white-checkered tablecloths and mahogany furniture, and a pleasantly drowsy soundtrack of Sinatra and Louis Prima piped in from unseen speakers. Kate ordered a glass of Chianti, Luna a Negroni.

They sat in silence after they ordered their drinks. Kate briefly wondered why she had accepted Luna's invitation at all. She'd clearly extended it out of pity. Why else would Luna, who couldn't be more than thirty, want to spend time with a basically catatonic middle-aged person? And why did she have to insist on wine over coffee? Wine was the most intimate of all the social beverages. The scene was oddly romantic—the tables were literally candlelit—and the restaurant was populated mostly with couples. Committed ones, too. An abundance of wedding rings.

But Luna graciously interrupted her inner analysis. (*I can* hear *you thinking*, John used to say when she went inside like this, alienating him on the outside.)

"How long will you be staying in Sutter Point?" Luna asked. A rosy flush rushed across her neck. "I'm sorry if that sounded too forward."

"Not forward," Kate said. "I'm immune to forwardness. I always have been, to some extent, but now it's hard to care. Hard to feel anything at all."

"SSRIs might help. I mean, they helped me after my dad died. I was nervous about it at first, because I was only sixteen, but ultimately my mom and the psychiatrist were right to put me on them. I don't think I would've been able to finish high school without that prescription. Let alone get here." Luna gestured to the quaint, moneyed college town outside.

"I'm on an Ambien and Xanax regimen right now," Kate said. "But it's probably time to upgrade to antidepressants. I think I'm already becoming immune to the Ambien."

"Ambien gives me the worst hangovers. Like, blind-and-deaf hangovers. Like my entire body got stuffed with cotton balls, then got run over by a Mack truck." The waiter arrived with their drinks. Luna tapped the side of her orange tumbler with a cherry-painted fingernail. The colors of a sunrise. "This kind of hangover, I can deal with."

Kate took a sip of her wine in solidarity. "I don't have a return ticket," she said.

"So it's a 'be here as long as it takes' kind of thing?"

"I don't know how long it'll take to grieve the death of my son, but yes, that's the idea." Kate realized that she had bristled against that question, and that she'd done nothing to hide her irritation, but what she'd said earlier was true: it was hard to care about anything anymore. Social niceties were the first thing to go.

But Luna took it in stride. "You'll be grieving forever," she said. "It almost becomes a part of your personality. Funny, smart, grieving." Now, Kate laughed. "Time dulls the edge, I promise it does. But for a while, you'll be in a living hell."

"I'm sorry," Kate said. "The loss of a parent is a terrible thing."

"Not as terrible as the loss of a child."

The waiter returned to take their dinner orders. Luna requested spaghetti marinara—"I still eat like a twelve-year-old," she said as an aside—and Kate ordered the same, if only because she knew she should eat something. She considered, absurdly, texting Richard; she hoped he wasn't worrying about why she hadn't shown up tonight.

"What do you do?" Luna asked when the waiter left. "Job-wise, I mean."

"I'm the head lawyer at a software firm in San Francisco. Our product is used by companies to share data across different platforms. Blockchain plays a big part in our work."

"I've never heard of that, but it sounds impressive."

"It sounds more impressive than it is in reality."

"Well, my parents would have loved for me to go to law school. But here I am instead, preparing a dissertation on the motif of dollhouses as a metaphor for female confinement in Victorian literature."

Instantly, Kate thought of Sasha. How her eyes flickered on and off, a candle lit and snuffed in quick succession. "What got you interested in that?"

"I've always been attracted to Victorian literature. Well, since I was ten or eleven. *A Christmas Carol* was the first book I read after wrapping up the Junie B. Jones series. But when I got older and started to become really aware of being in a female body—in high school, I guess—I started paying more attention to all the trapped women in these stories, which basically means all of the women in all of the stories. Mariana in her bower, Jane Eyre at her window. But even though they were trapped by literally every circumstance imaginable, they managed to carve out whole universes inside their own minds."

"They created their own solace. That's a generous thought."

"Sure. Until that solace became a prison."

Kate glanced up at the waiter, already arriving with their plates. She felt a dull pressure in the back of her throat. When she looked across the table at Luna, she was surprised to find that the world had gone blurry, and then, when she looked down at the tangle of pasta before her, that the plate was flecked with tears.

"Oh no," Luna said. "Did I say something to upset you?"

Kate wiped at her eyes with the napkin. "Don't be sorry. I'm just overwhelmed."

"I understand. Really, I do. And now, with this other student—it's just tragic. And so bizarre."

"It *is* bizarre, right? You don't think I'm crazy for thinking that?"

Luna put down her fork. "I don't think anyone is crazy. Reality is inherently subjective."

"You know, I'm starting to wonder if this place is cursed." Kate had already drained her glass of wine; her tongue felt buttery in her mouth. "Something happened to Jake. He killed himself. Technically, he did. But something happened to make him do it."

"I don't know about the cursed part, but these kids push themselves really hard. Or they *feel* pushed. Do you think Jake may have felt overworked?"

Kate remembered what the girl, Sasha, had said in the café. *The pressure—it was too much.* It would have been one of the last things she'd ever said.

"I suppose that could be it. Suicide is rampant among young

people," Kate said, regurgitating what she'd read on the Suicide Prevention Resource Center a few days ago. But she didn't believe her own words. Luna's placating smile suggested that she wasn't convinced by Kate's concession either.

The waiter collected their empty glasses and asked if they'd like another round. They both said yes, no hesitation, and agreed again as soon as those glasses were finished. Time quickly lost its shape as they spoke. Kate talked about Jake. Not his death, but his life—not as the worst thing that had ever happened to her, but as the best. Luna was a good, active listener. She asked questions in exactly the right amount and depth, and offered relevant personal experience as a tool for connection, not instruction. Kate told her this. Luna responded that it was a by-product of being the only child of divorced parents, and then of a widowed mother, who often forgot that Luna was neither her contemporary nor her therapist.

"But I've also been pretty heavily therapized since my dad died," Luna said.

"And medicated," Kate added.

"And I have a Pisces moon, plus a Uranus conjunct an ascendant in Gemini."

Kate laughed. "Apparently Jake was interested in astrology, too. He wrote about it in his journals." She counted on her fingers. "Libra sun, Scorpio moon, Aquarius rising, if I'm not confusing them."

"If you're not confusing them, that's a good combination. Intense, but good."

The Dean Martin song crooning in the background suddenly cut out. Without the ambient noise to keep her afloat, Kate became intensely aware of her exhaustion. She checked her watch: it was just after eleven p.m. They'd shut the place down. They split the bill, which the waiter dropped on their table along with two chocolate coins. Earlier, Luna had diagnosed herself with a sweet tooth, so Kate insisted that she take the chocolates.

"An offer I can't refuse," Luna said, pocketing them both.

Luna walked Kate to her door across the street. Kate thanked her before she went inside.

"Most people don't know how to talk to me," Kate said.

"Most people are afraid of grief," Luna agreed.

"But you don't seem to be."

"That's because I'm not."

Sutter Point was twenty miles from the coast, but still the air was cut with a cold, salty wind. The shops along Main Street were festooned in Halloween decorations. A skeleton hung from its neck on the streetlamp above them, its bones clattering delicately in the breeze.

"Have you been to the hiking trails around here?" Luna said. "I try to go every week to clear my head. And remind myself that there's actually a world outside the library. You're welcome to come with me next time. I mean, only if you want to."

"I do want to," Kate said. The projection of the day flickered before her: tightly lacing her sneakers; making small talk in the passenger seat; reaching a summit; exchanging hushed observations, rooted in reverence, with those firecracker leaves floating down around their feet. It was so quaint, that picture. So normal. So like before.

That was what Luna was offering her right now, and Kate found that she really wanted it. Let herself live in the illusion for a few hours. What was so wrong with that?

A little clumsily, they exchanged numbers—Kate let Luna take her phone, punch in her number, then she instructed Kate to send her a text—and exchanged clumsier goodbyes. Luna's right hand emerged, then dipped back into her coat pocket; Kate resisted the urge to lean in for a hug.

Finally, Kate climbed the flight of stairs to Jake's apartment, and Luna walked east down Main Street, toward the studio apartment near campus she told Kate she'd been living in for the past two years. *A glorified shoebox*, Luna had called it.

As Kate prepared for bed, she found herself thinking about that apartment. It would have pale-yellow walls, she imagined, and a red standing mixer in the black-and-white tiled kitchen. Stacks of hardback books would double as a bedside table. Luna didn't strike her as the kind to be mindful of plants, but for some reason Kate thought of her surrounded by green things. Desert plants, hard to kill. A windowsill lined with tiny cacti, each one flowering with a single brilliant bud. Even though the apartment was small, Kate hoped it had enough light.

Then she placed this evening's newspaper on her bedside table, Sasha's squinting smile facing up, toward her.

CHAPTER
FIVE

Kate's mother had been deeply superstitious. She'd refused to leave the house when the thirteenth dared to fall on a Friday, taught Kate to skip the cracks, and instructed her daughter to hold her breath when they drove past a graveyard, after which they would share a deep, luxurious breath—an early bonding experience. From the perspective of pedigree, Ann's belief in a jealous, impulsive god who doled out luck and misfortune based on inconsequential infractions had actually made sense: Ann had been a Boston-bred WASP, strands of Mayflower settlers braided through her DNA. If Kate climbed high enough up the family tree, she'd probably find some rotten branches who'd made a sport of burning women at the stake—the women who dared to meet that terrifying, remote god.

But beyond her folkloric convictions about spilled salt and ladders, Ann had been conventional to the point of dullness. Paint a picture of a mid-to-late-twentieth-century housewife, and there would be Ann, a glass of icy chardonnay in one hand and a PTA flyer in the other. Once, when Kate was a teenager, she'd come home from school and actually found Ann donning a checkerboard apron, a streak of flour smeared across her cheek like a cute after-thought. A relic from the Rockwellian age. That was when Kate had decided that she would do everything within her power to be the opposite of her mother: she would go to law school. (When she'd arrived at Fordham Law six years later, she would learn that resentment was not an uncommon motive among her peers.)

But a law degree alone wasn't enough to completely render the beliefs she'd grown up with null and void. Nor was the one-two punch of her parents' deaths when Kate was in her thirties: first her mother, dead ten months after an ovarian cancer diagnosis, and then her father three years later, who'd suffered a heart attack so massive it sent him keeling over the lawn mower, which had then proceeded to run demented circles around his body.

Kate still found herself avoiding black cats and ladders and picking up filthy pennies off the street, which she would later surreptitiously drop into Jake's piggy bank.

And now, as she crossed Paloma's grassy quad and headed toward the Thurgood dorm, she credited her singular focus on one of her mother's more unusual superstitions: if you fall asleep with a picture of a specific person on your bedside table, then you'll dream of that person that very night. Kate suspected that Ann had totally invented that one. But Kate had, in fact, dreamt of Sasha the night before. In Kate's dream, the girl stood at the foot of Kate's bed, her head lolling lazily against her shoulder. Kate thought Sasha was napping upright. But when Kate crawled to the end of the bed, she noticed that Sasha's head was almost completely detached from the neck, hanging on by a single frayed rope of muscle and a hank of skin.

Kate woke up, gasping, with the divine conviction that Sasha's death was not so straightforward as a trip down the stairs, just as Jake's death was not so straightforward as a jump off a cliff. It was only a matter of discovering the threads of that connection, then sewing those threads together to reveal the greater pattern. Since her conversation with John, she'd inwardly wondered whether he was right: It *wasn't* productive for her to drop everything in order to linger around Jake's former life. To become a ghost haunting a ghost. But now, her sense of purpose solidified.

Thurgood Hall was a solid cinder block construction, a diluted version of the brutalist menaces Kate and John came across on their honeymoon (then later, separately, on business) in London. Kate always found the architecture ugly—so ugly it had to be a joke—but John, as if just to be contrary, deemed it a paragon of symmetry and functionality, and thus of elegance. The only elegant thing about this building, Kate thought as she approached Thurgood's double doors, was the marigolds planted along the walkway, defiantly sunny against this bleak backdrop.

She tried the doors; locked, as she suspected. She pulled Jake's magnetized student ID card from her jeans pocket. She'd found the card in Jake's desk when she'd first moved into his apartment. Retroactively, she chided herself for initially overlooking this glaring clue: if Jake had left his ID card at home—the ID card he needed to get into any building on campus—then he had no intention of ever returning home. Now she grazed a thumb over Jake's locket-sized picture on the card. He looked rakishly handsome and unbearably young. There was the suggestion of a smile in his upturned mouth, a forelock pushed up and away from his mass of dark waves. The rich brown eyes furred in black lashes. *Bambi eyes*, she'd called him, first to his face and then, when he confessed he'd outgrown the nickname, only to herself.

She touched the card to the electronic lock beside the door. It opened with a little click. A security desk stood on the right side of the spacious entranceway, but the guard merely glanced up at Kate as she buzzed herself through the turnstile. He even offered her a distracted, permissive smile.

Kate didn't know where Sasha's room was, but the article announcing the young woman's death noted that her body had been found on the third-floor landing. That would mean she'd fallen down the set of stairs between the fourth and third floors—which likely meant that her room was on the fourth floor, too. The hunch was a stretch, but she had nothing else to follow. She avoided the elevator bank and climbed the stairs instead, hoping to find some clue or intuitive hit on the way up. She only felt loopy. Pairing wine with Ambien the night before did her no favors.

She shoved open the double doors on the fourth-floor landing and stepped into the hallway. It was long and narrow, its white-painted brick walls punctuated with brightly colored flyers and ten or twelve doors, all shut like mouths. A vending machine glowed, beacon-like, at the far end of the hall. The nubbly gray carpet muffled most sound other than the vending machine's low, steady hum, plus a blow-dryer whining from behind one of those closed doors.

Kate approached the first door. It was labeled with the names of the room's tenants, accompanied by their preferred pronouns. Here lived Peter (he/him) and Cory (he/him), the construction paper proclaimed in purple and blue bubble letters, surely rendered by Floor Four's RA.

The bubble letters punched Kate squarely in the gut. Children lived behind these doors. Who was here to protect them?

Then Kate moved down the right side of the hallway, checking the names as she went. Parker (she/her) and Alex (she/they). Anjali (she/her) and Charley (she/her)—the source of the blow-dryer, its whirring now quieter. Carlin (they/them) and Kade (he/him). Joey (he/him) and Dov (he/him). Tabby (she/her) and Sasha (she/her). That was the final door on this side of the hall. The names were drawn in green and pink.

She began to knock on the door, then hesitated. She reminded herself that its sole remaining tenant had lost her roommate less than twenty-four hours ago. Even if Tabby and Sasha hadn't forged a friendship beyond the convenience of their proximity, that proximity alone was a powerful enough force to forge an emotional bond. An indelible one, too, especially when shaped at this malleable age. And Kate understood that a loss wasn't loss at all. Loss was presence, crushing and urgent.

Kate didn't want to push Tabby under its weight any further, if Tabby was even here at all. Kate imagined that her parents would've scooped her up and taken her back home. That was what she would've done.

Instead, she circled back down the hall to Anjali and Charley's room. At the very least, she knew someone was there.

Kate knocked and the door opened almost immediately. The girl held it open just enough for Kate to see a fuzzy blue sweater, a leg sheathed in a knee-high sock, and a hand wielding a blow-dryer like a billy club. Her dark hair was cut into a pixie with long bangs, now freshly staticked and draped just above her lashes. She peered at Kate skeptically. That was good, Kate thought. Women should not trust strangers, even those who looked harmless.

"Hi?" the girl said.

"Hi," Kate said. She gestured to the poster on the front of the door. "Are you Anjali or Charley?"

"Are you lost?" the girl responded.

"No. Well, possibly. I'm Jake Cleary's mother."

Did Kate drop her dead son's name in order to gain this girl's trust? Or reveal her status as a grieving mother to demonstrate her harmlessness? Not necessarily. Not *specifically*. Still, the girl—this was Anjali, she offered then—seemed to relax her grip on her weapon and let the door open farther. In the room behind her, Kate saw a ring light and a camera on a tripod set up at the foot of one twin bed. Makeup scattered over the white comforter, already stained in the pink, black, and bronze echoes of experiments past.

"I didn't know Jake personally," Anjali said, "but I was so sorry to hear about him."

"Thank you," Kate said. "But actually—and I know this might seem strange to you—I'm not here about Jake. I'm curious about Sasha Williams."

Anjali tensed slightly again. "Why? Did you know her?"

"Well, no, I didn't. But I have this feeling that maybe Jake and Sasha knew each other. Or that they were mixed up in something together. I'm not sure. I could be grasping at straws, of course, but—"

Anjali interjected. "I never saw Jake on the hall, if that's what you're curious about. That doesn't mean much, but it's what I can tell you, as far as Jake is concerned. But honestly, I didn't see Sasha around that much either. Even her roommate said she got kind of distant this semester."

"She *got* distant? So she wasn't that way before?"

"I'd never met her before this year, but yeah, that's what Tabby said. And they've literally been roommates since freshman year. So she would know."

"You and Tabby are friends?"

Anjali shrugged. "We're friendly. Tabby just told me all of this a couple weeks ago, when she came into our room crying one night. We hadn't even hung out that much before, but she was clearly in need of some kind of catharsis. So me, her, and my roommate all had this big heart-to-heart about how hard it is to watch your friends evolve in a way you don't like, then you start to drift apart, and then you stop being friends at all. It's just as painful as a breakup. Even more painful than that,

because in a way you expect your closest friends to be your closest friends forever. No one *expects* to break up with a friend. But
that's what was happening with Tabby and Sasha."

Anjali fell silent. Kate let the rest of that thought fill in on
its own: *And then Sasha died.*

"I know what that's like," Kate said. "I've broken up with
a couple of friends over the years. Really close ones, too. And
I've gotten divorced. Guess which one was harder?"

"I would think the divorce?"

"You'd be right."

They both laughed, which helped puncture the pall of sadness hovering over them both.

"Was there something in particular that Tabby didn't like about
how Sasha was changing? Did she mention that?" Kate asked.

"She said Sasha started spending a lot of time in the library,
but she thought she was actually hanging out with other people.
She didn't want to name names, for whatever reason."

"When was this, exactly?"

"A week or two into the semester. Around early September."

Early September—that timing aligned with the shift in
Jake's diaries.

"And also," Anjali continued, fully thawed of her former hesitation, "this isn't something that Tabby necessarily held against
her, but she said that Sasha started to become anxious and paranoid around then, too. Apparently she started to get really intense
about encrypting all the data on her phone and computer, and
she kept all her personal diaries and some books in a lockbox and
hid the key."

Personal diaries. Kate felt a twinge of recognition—there
could have been a connection between Jake's diaries and Sasha's. (Even beyond the revelation, she had to wonder how many
twenty-year-olds kept physical diaries these days.) And based

on Sasha's visceral reaction to seeing Jake's copy in the café, she suspected that one of the books included Blake's "The Tyger."

"Tabby didn't get to see what was in her diaries, did she? Or what the book was?"

"She didn't tell me that," Anjali said. "But she told me that she was genuinely worried about Sasha's mental health. She thought about going to our RA about it. But, like, our RA is only a year older than us. What could he do that we wouldn't know how to do? And *everyone* is anxious or depressed, and I'm not convinced that this campus is equipped to handle the onslaught of us. This guy I know, apparently his roommate went to one of the school's mental health counselors because he was so depressed he stopped eating anything other than Luna Bars. And you know what this counselor told him? Maybe he should try *running.* So, in reality, either you have parents with the money to find you a good therapist, or a psychiatrist to give you good drugs, or you handle your issues on your own."

Kate felt a throb of guilt so deep she thought she might double over. She *did* have the money to find Jake a therapist, or to find him a reasonable, compassionate psychiatrist with the patience to design a medication regimen that worked for him, not against him, if it did indeed come to that. But Kate couldn't have known that he needed help. Jake revealed nothing to her.

Despite that logic, Kate believed that his death was her fault. Not fully—she wasn't there yet—but in part, absolutely. A mother should know when her child was in danger. A mother must always know. To not know was a failure of biology and character both. Kate wouldn't accept any answer other than that.

"Sorry I laid that all on you," Anjali said then. "I'm clearly dealing with my own issues."

"Please don't be sorry. You've been more than helpful." Helpful toward what end, exactly, Kate didn't say. She didn't quite yet know the answer herself. "And I understand how strongly you feel about what you said, truly I do. But I need you to know that if you need help, then you have to ask for it. And if you don't like what you get, you have to keep asking until you get what you need." Kate smiled a little, softening her edge. "I'm an attorney," she added, by way of explanation.

"It shows."

Clearly Kate had lost Anjali with the unsolicited lecture, but she really didn't mean to be pedantic. She just couldn't leave the girl's cries for help unanswered.

Kate said goodbye and left to mull over what Anjali had told her, passing the security guard—now armed with a foot-sized sandwich, its juices dripping opulently atop a nest of crumpled napkins—on her way back out onto the quad. She sat on a bench facing the library, watching the uneven stream of students float by. A breeze shook loose a shower of dead leaves from the red oak above her. She pulled out Jake's ID card; trancelike, she caressed his face with her thumb.

She'd already surmised that the change in Sasha's behavior seemed to coincide with Jake's, according to his diaries—and where Sasha apparently grew frantic and paranoid, Jake withdrew completely. Both were common reactions to trauma. Four to six weeks later, they were both dead.

Sasha's diaries would've been an invaluable resource (what had she been so frantically hiding from Tabby?), but Kate imagined that that evidence, along with the rest of her personal belongings, would be in the care of her parents. Instead, Kate decided to turn her focus to the other lead Anjali had provided her: whomever Sasha started hanging out with early in the semester. And if Kate's theory about Sasha and Jake's connection was truly sound, then Jake would have run in that circle, too—and for that, she needed to get in touch with Jake's friends. She was ashamed to admit that she didn't know any of his friends' last names. She wasn't even completely sure of their first names; anytime she cast her mind back to their conversations, the names Jake mentioned slipped right through the cracks of her memory. She could blame this on her aural learning skills, pitifully lacking, but which her near-photographic memory had historically made up for. Or she could blame it on the fact that she just wasn't paying enough attention. This was the harder truth, and so the truth that won out.

The obvious option would be to check Jake's social media profiles and see whom he'd taken pictures with, whom he'd followed and tagged. But Jake's Facebook profile was inactive—Facebook was for Kate's generation—and his Instagram account was essentially inactive. He'd only posted seven photos and followed forty-seven people, though close to seven hundred people followed him. Kate didn't think too much on that imbalance. The particulars of Instagram etiquette were too subtle for her to understand inherently, like this generation of digital natives did, and not something she had the time or interest to study herself. She'd created an Instagram account three years ago, because it seemed to be the thing you had to do in order to reaffirm your existence on this planet, but since then she'd only touched it a week ago, to look up Jake.

And if Jake had any other online presence—a TikTok account, a YouTube channel, some impassioned discourse on Reddit—then Kate wouldn't know. That information, along with Jake's friends' names—and literally everything else, as far as her investigation was currently concerned—lived inside his phone and computer.

By this point, she decided, she had waited too long for Wachs's investigation. She needed to get Jake's things back. And if Wachs wasn't coming to her, then she would have to go to him.

She got up from the bench and set out east across the quad, toward the police station, renewed of the energy that

had propelled her toward the Thurgood dorm an hour earlier, and in the crux of that energy she stepped almost directly
onto the toes of a person walking in the opposite direction,
toward Kate, seemingly with equal momentum. Kate bit her
tongue with the force of the collision. She smelled baby powder
and ripe red fruit and then, a half second later, a dash of
leather, like new car seats. When she looked up to apologize,
she was met with a familiar shock of golden hair, which today
was piled up into a high, messy bun. The late-morning sun
pitched a corona around the delicate face, half-obscured by
black plastic-framed glasses.

And when Luna looked up to apologize—she, too, was to
blame for the collision—Kate caught the same flicker of recognition
cast over her, a sensation like two puzzle pieces snapping together.

"Oh my god, I'm sorry," Luna said, pulling a heavy-looking
tote bag farther up on her shoulder. Today, she wore her beat-up
leather jacket over a butter-yellow silk skirt and the same gray
cardigan she wore last night, the top two buttons undone. A
gossamer-thin gold choker gleamed against her collarbone. She
nodded toward the redbrick building flanking one whole side
of the quad. "I'm five minutes late for the lecture this morning, which is absolutely terrible. I'm never late for anything."

Kate looked at her watch: it was twelve forty-one p.m. She
brought forth the snapshot she'd stored in her memory of Jake's
schedule: his Brit Lit lecture fell on Tuesdays and Thursdays at
twelve thirty-five p.m.

"If you're on time, you're late," Kate offered. It came out
more blandly than she'd intended.

"That's my motto, too. Usually."

"What's unusual about today?"

"I *may* have had another drink or two with a friend after
our dinner last night. That would put me at a solid six drinks

total. At one point in my life, I could drink like that on a school
night, but then I turned thirty and my metabolism pretty much
went to shit."

Kate chose to ignore the sharp dart of jealousy when Luna
mentioned another friend. "Wait until you turn forty," she said.

"If I look half as good as you do when I'm forty, then I have
a lot to look forward to."

Kate let out the kind of dismissive laugh she'd always used to
deflect compliments—one of the manufactured, aw-shucks va-
riety that Kate detested in others but couldn't help but fall back
on herself. Luna maintained a calm, steady gaze, not a single
iota embarrassed or apologetic. Kate regained her composure.

"You should've seen me before my son died," Kate said,
"when I actually had a soul animating my body."

"I think your soul seems just fine."

"I used to wear makeup, too. And clothes made of materials other than cotton and spandex."

"Okay, fine," Luna said, smiling a bit. "Maybe you'd look
good in silk."

The conversation had clearly tipped into flirting territory,
a terrain Kate had not really visited in person since last year,
in which she briefly dated a man sixteen years her senior—an
affair that ended with the finality and violence of a car crash,
after a friend of Kate's, who'd had an identical experience with
the same man, revealed that he was married to a woman whom
he loathed and made a sport of deceiving with a steady procession of affairs with younger women. Kate would've ended it
regardless. He claimed to be a close personal friend of Bill Gates,
and he also owned a boat, an unremarkable little pocket cruiser
that he referred to by its name, *Adelaide*, or else with feminine
pronouns and deep and abiding pride, as if he'd built the thing
himself. He referred to that boat a lot. Even more often than

he referred to Bill Gates, or to his three young children, whom he had also kept secret from Kate.

It wasn't clear yet whether this flirtation with Luna was of the sexual-romantic or the burgeoning-friendship ilk, but her knee-jerk response was to deflect both. This was not so different from her usual initial reaction to proffered intimacy, but compounded with grief—her constant, smothering companion—she may as well have flung up an iron shield, studded with spikes.

But when she relaxed a little bit, peered over the shield's edge, Kate actually didn't hate the sparkle and buzz of her and Luna's rapport. Actually, it was a relief from all the heaviness in her life. It was a reminder of who she had been before, and how that person—the one who'd expanded in the face of the light, rather than shrunk from it—still existed inside of her.

And now, when Luna looked down at her phone to check the time, Kate found herself coveting her attention.

But before Kate could scrounge some pithy response to Luna's comment, Luna said, "Where are you heading so quickly?"

"Just to Tony's for a bite to eat," Kate said. She liked Luna, but she still didn't trust her enough to tell her she was going to the police station to try to beg or barter for her son's laptop. "I haven't eaten since last night. I'm actually feeling a little lightheaded."

"I won't keep a woman from her lunch." Luna glanced anxiously at her phone again, but she made no move to leave yet. "Are you doing anything tomorrow? I'm way overdue for that hike."

"I think I can clear some time in my packed schedule," Kate said. They agreed to meet in front of Kate's apartment at nine the next morning; Luna would supply the coffee.

With that, Luna peeled off toward the English building. Before she turned in the opposite direction, setting off to find Wachs again, Kate watched as Luna's heavy bag bumped against her thigh, hiking her skirt higher with each step.

That moment's small pleasure was short lived. Kate's phone rang. John was calling her.

"You missed me already?" Kate said. A sad attempt to re-capture that bygone levity. Kate and John had spoken on the phone just two hours ago, with nothing doing. That he was calling her again so soon after could only point to bad news.

"I have a piece of news," he said. Kate threw up her hand, the one that wasn't holding the phone, in an *I told you so* ges-ture. But she was alone on the street, and there was no one to tell except herself. "I got in touch with the landlord today. We're listing Jake's apartment."

Kate paused and lowered the phone. She tried to take a deep breath.

"Why didn't you tell me this morning?" Kate asked when she picked the phone back up.

"There was nothing to tell this morning," John said. "I only got in touch with the landlord after our conversation. Thinking about you wandering around that apartment all day, surrounded by Jake's things . . . it's not okay, Katie. It's not okay for you, and it's not okay for me. So I decided to pull you out of it."

"And you didn't think to loop me into this decision before you made it?" Kate asked.

The question was mostly rhetorical, as Kate was not surprised. Angry? Yes. Disappointed? Well, not exactly. John did what John wanted, and so often that had meant nudging Kate to the side of the road so that he could push ahead. Historically, it had only been after Kate was facing backward, in the wrong direction en-tirely, John an ever-shrinking spot on the distant horizon, that she'd even understood that John had thrown her out with the roadkill. John was selfish—that was just who he was. His ruth-lessness could be helped about as much as the fact that he was a lefty, or that he thought cilantro tasted like licking a bar of Dial.

And Kate had divorced him precisely because of it. She had legally gotten the fuck out of his way. The prospect of once again becoming collateral in John's decisions—it was exasperating. Infuriating.

But Kate no longer had the fight in her.

"I know this is hard for you," John was saying now, "but I promise it's for the best. The guy is optimistic that he can get another tenant in there within the next two weeks, even though we're well into the semester. Apparently there's been some plumbing issue in the dorms and kids are scrambling to get off campus. I'm going to see what I can do about prorating the month's rent."

But Kate was barely listening. Instead, she was counting.

Two weeks. She had two weeks to find out what happened to Jake. She supposed she could always find another apartment to rent in Sutter Point, but it just wouldn't be right. Jake's apartment was the beating heart of the investigation. There, surrounded by his things, his detritus, the imprints of him . . . That was how Kate kept him close. Kept him alive. Could hear his secrets, if only she was able to press her ear a little deeper into the ground.

Fourteen days. November 4th. That was her deadline.

She hung up on John. She broke into a flat-out run to find Wachs.

CHAPTER
SIX

She didn't have to go far to find Wachs: there he was, right outside the Sutter Point Police Department, heading east toward Main Street. It was twelve fifty-three p.m. From here, it would take him seven minutes to walk to Tony's. Wachs was fastidious in keeping his meal appointments, a trait Kate once found charming, if a little compulsive. How could she *not* be charmed by the handsome-ish cop who promised to alleviate her trauma? He dripped with authority, and that was comforting. Call it Stockholm syndrome. Cops were trained to protect exactly her—women grieving the deaths of their children—and she was conditioned to trust them. But that illusion had shattered pretty quickly.

Now Kate intercepted Wachs before he turned onto Main Street by placing her hand lightly on his arm. Wachs looked down at the hand, his dark eyes glittering with a mix of mild amusement and resentment. Kate quickly retracted it. Since when did she think it was okay to touch police officers?

"Can I help you, Kate?" he said.

"Actually," Kate said, "I think I can help you."

He sighed. "Walk with me," he said, continuing on toward his destination. Kate had to race a little to keep up with his long strides.

"I found a note," Kate said. "It was stuffed inside one of Jake's diaries."

"You believe it's a suicide note?"

"I do."

"You know we'll need to see it."

There was a part of her that never wanted to tell Wachs about the note. She hated the thought of handing over any more of Jake's things than she already had, and this piece of him was especially precious, the page itself so suffused with his essence. She thought of Luna's tattoo, how she had branded herself in her father's handwriting. Kate understood the impulse.

But the sooner the police officially ruled Jake's death a suicide and closed the case, the sooner she could get ahold of Jake's phone and laptop and carry on with her own digging.

"I know," Kate said. "That's fine. I just hope you'll return it to me soon."

Wachs must have heard the weariness in Kate's voice. He stopped, turning to face her. He stuffed his hands in his pockets in a show of submission.

"I know you think the investigation is taking too long. You've made that abundantly clear." Wachs let free a small, mirthless laugh. "Trust me, I take no pleasure in knowing that this is causing you more pain. But this is all standard procedure. Cases like this take time. We need to cover all our bases."

"How could it possibly take so long to get into a kid's computer?"

Wachs ran a hand over his five-o'clock shadow. When they'd first met two weeks before (incredible that it had only been two weeks, Kate thought; there was nothing like trauma to warp one's sense of time), Wachs was consistently clean shaven. Once Kate spotted a cluster of razor bumps along his jawline, which made his already youthful-looking face seem downright adolescent. But today, his nascent beard's bluish cast lent his whole demeanor an exhausted quality, more spiritual than physical. It endeared Kate to him in that moment. If a police detective wasn't utterly exhausted all the time, in body and soul, then he wasn't doing his job properly.

Then he moved an inch closer to Kate, dipping his head low in a conspiratorial position. "I'm only telling you this because—well, your persistence paid off," he said. "You know Signal, the encrypted messaging app? Jake was using it for most of his text conversations. With all the ways to keep in touch with people digitally, he almost solely uses the one that locks everything away, completely hidden? We need to follow up on that."

Kate felt a sick sense of validation—Anjali had just told her that Sasha became suddenly obsessed with encrypting her data, shortly before she died. But Kate wasn't about to divulge her theory about Sasha and Jake to Wachs.

Instead, she said: "Is that a cause for concern?"

Wachs picked up his stride again. "A cause for curiosity. And some caution, too. It complicates things, I'll say that."

"But the note must simplify things again."

They walked in silence for the next minute or two until they reached Tony's. Wachs peered inside the café, but Kate lingered on the sidewalk. She'd kept the note with her ever since she found it. Now, it pulsed heavily in her back pocket.

Wachs kneaded the back of his neck. "This has been terrible for the whole community. And I know you think of us as heartless automatons, but we're not. All of us, the whole department, are grieving very deeply. For ourselves, and for you."

"Thank you for saying that, but I'm starting to get sick

of thanking people for their sympathy. I don't need sympathy anymore. I need progress. It's the only way I can even consider moving on with my life."

Wachs nodded. "I want that for you."

He'd allowed a softening of his expression then, an openness in his gaze, and that made Kate, ever vigilant, tug at the reins of her campaign. She had ground Wachs down to render him pliable; not to coax any kindness from him. Typically, Kate's "victims," as her associate Daryl had lovingly dubbed Chalice's more stubborn clients, were compelled to take a knee after a battle of litigation with the duty-bound integrity of an athlete after a vigorous, well-matched game. If those clients harbored even a kernel of kindness within them—which Kate, in one of her many contradictory traits, secretly believed that they did, for the most part—they guarded it jealously. They schmoozed, they shared meals, they revealed certain details about their families and hobbies that cast them in a sympathetic light, but they did not become friends. They did not extend favors, expecting nothing in return.

So Wachs's generosity was mildly alarming. Why was he being so nice to her? What could he possibly want in return?

Well, there was one obvious answer, and so often the right one. If considering it made Kate's thinking reductive, so be it. It wouldn't make it any less true.

"If there's something you want from me," Kate said carefully, "you should tell me exactly what that is."

Wachs looked truly confused, which made her feel a little bad.

"You're being so generous with me," Kate continued. "You're entertaining my theories. You're maybe even hopping on board with them."

"I didn't always."

"No, you didn't always. But now you're offering inside information, and you're doing it with that—look on your face."

Kate watched Wachs rearrange his face to convey sternness. "You can't blame me for my skepticism."

Wachs ran an exasperated hand over his face, understanding Kate's implication. "Have I ever made you feel uncomfortable? Threatened? Manipulated? Unsafe?"

"Not as such." Kate had to admit it.

"Good," Wachs said. "You seem to believe I need an ulterior motive to do my job well."

"And sleeping with me isn't it."

Wachs blanched. "No, Kate," he said. "That is not something I would ever want to do." After a beat, during which Kate fought to quell a pang of offense, Wachs added, "I have a partner whom I love."

"That's almost never stopped anyone."

And then Wachs gave her that *look*—that look she'd shared with so many people, in so many places. Bars, grocery stores, the gym, the street, and once even Jake's nursery school pickup. Kate had suspected the woman was a babysitter; Kate had never seen her before, and she was pretty in a knobby way, alert and spiked, lacking the glossy authority the moms possessed. The rips in her jeans were not intentional. The woman had been probing the wide school doors for sudden movement, preparing for the ensuing rush and search, when her gaze had hooked on Kate's, a patch of heat on the homing device. They glowed; they understood. Nothing had come of it, but that wasn't always the point. There was a sense of rightness about the discovery, like slipping back into your native tongue after a long stint abroad.

Now, Kate returned it to Wachs. *I see you.*

Wachs continued. "When I was around Jake's age, I suffered a . . . trauma. After it happened, I felt like I had only one option. One way out. Someone—a close family member—helped me find a better one." Wachs cleared his throat, brushed imaginary crumbs off his tie. "So that's why I'm interested in Jake's case. Okay?"

Kate handed him the note. That was her answer. She felt immediately lighter, freed of its complicated grip, but the lightness was an absence, not a relief.

Wachs took the note and slid it with care, even tenderness, into his breast pocket. "I'll call you in a few days. Three, tops. We'll finish this up for you, Kate. I promise."

———

The next morning, Kate went downstairs to find Luna waiting on the sidewalk, bearing two cups of coffee in a carrier tray and two waxy pastry bags.

"I don't know how you take your coffee," Luna said, "so I have one black, and one with oat milk." She shook one of the pastry bags. "Creamer and sugar right here."

"I'll take the black one," Kate said.

Luna handed her a cup and led them across the street to her car, a newish, slate-gray Nissan Altima. The carpet bore fresh vacuum marks.

"Nice car," Kate said.

"Looks can be deceiving. It's a salvage title that cost about five thousand dollars. I bought it as a gift for myself when I got into the PhD program."

Kate ran a hand over the dash; her fingers came away spotless. "Jake's father bought him a Lexus when he graduated from high school," she said. "I was so angry with him. Jake had already been saving up to buy a Mazda on his own; then his father swoops in with this flashy luxury car. Jake was mortified. But John did things like that all the time. I worked so hard to make sure Jake never felt entitled to anything—I always made him get jobs in high school, do chores at home—and then John would show up with a new phone or laptop. Once he got him a pair of limited-edition Air Force 1s that cost something like six hundred dollars. Absurd."

Kate felt her chest flush with anger just thinking about it. John had always tried to buy Jake's love. Hers, too: From the moment John began making any real money, soon after they first married, he lavished her with shit she didn't ask for and certainly didn't need. A mink bolero, a three-hundred dollar face cream infused with caviar and rare mushrooms, a sterling-silver ice cream scooper from Tiffany's. He may as well have thrown the cash in her face. As secretive as John could be in his professional life, so often his behavior was disappointingly predictable.

When she reemerged from her thoughts, she realized Luna had fallen silent. Over the next twenty minutes or so, the scene outside gradually evolved from town to country to thick forest. Soon they were fully enclosed in dense foliage, pricked by red-golden light.

Then Luna pulled into a small dirt parking lot. It was occupied by just one other car. The only indication that this swath of woods was hikeable was a simplistic, brown-painted sign—Hiking Trail Here, it read—and if not for the city's seal affixed to the bottom, Kate would've thought the sign had been hastily constructed by some backwoods serial killer to try to lure victims to his dilapidated shack. On top of everything, Kate had been listening to far too many true-crime podcasts, more than was good for her.

They left their empty coffee cups in the car, but Luna slipped the pastry bag into her backpack. They set out onto the trail beyond the sign, and Kate's fears about hidden murderers were quickly assuaged by the woods' exquisite peace. The air out here felt five degrees colder, and Kate reveled in every rich, crisp breath, the viscerally satisfying crunch of the dead leaves beneath her feet. She caught a cadence with her stride, lulling herself into a sense of remote calm. She felt like she was watching herself from a bird's-eye view, and she was overcome with compassion for that tiny, innocent figure. Maybe this was what enlightenment was supposed to be, she mused: the state of being both you and not-you at the same time.

The two remained quiet for a few paces, Kate out of reverence for the scene—even a generally nonoutdoorsy person like Kate had to honor this hushed majesty—but Luna's silence seemed subtly irked.

"Did I say something to offend you earlier?" Kate asked softly.

"Do I seem pissed?" Luna said. "I'm sorry. I think I just felt sad when you mentioned Jake's dad. I would've loved to have my dad around while I was growing up. With or without the free car."

"I didn't even think about that," Kate said. Another of grief's hidden qualities: it made you selfish. "I'm sorry."

"And I doubt Jake was as mortified as you think to get that Lexus. No offense to Mazda."

The trail had been gradually inclining upward, but now the elevation intensified. Kate's breaths shortened, pressure building in her chest.

"This is the hardest part," Luna said, clearly noticing Kate's labored breath, "but I promise it's worth it."

After a few more yards, they emerged into a clearing of trees. To the left of the clearing lay the sparse remains of a large house, an imposing chimney surrounded by freestanding stone walls—the skeleton of the home, stripped of its muscles and tendons. Tree branches snuck through the openings carved for the doors and windows. Ivy crept up the walls, already furred over with moss, and on the ground lay a cushiony carpet of fallen leaves.

Kate gravitated toward the ruins. Luna followed her. They sat on a makeshift bench constructed of a waist-high, L-shaped chunk of the building's stone foundation. Small nests of cigarette butts and shreds of paper punctuated the overgrown flora. A collection of beer cans huddled inside the fireplace.

"Told you it was worth it," Luna said. She stroked the stone bench beneath her, then gave it a little pat. "This was a mansion, once upon a time. Some gold-rush tycoon built it in the late nineteenth or early twentieth century. It burned down in the twenties. According to local legend, the owner locked himself in his room and set the bed curtains on fire while in the throes of syphilitic mania. But the accepted version of events is that it was a gas leak."

"Looks like people have been partying here," Kate said, fishing a crumbled wine cork out of the leaves with her sneaker.

"Wouldn't you, if you were in college? It's an ideal party spot. Remote, open to the elements, a little bit spooky."

That was true, but the beer cans and cigarettes made her sad. Without them, these traces of human greed, the desolation here could have felt peaceful, prelapsarian. But with the trash, it was just pathetic.

"Does it have a name? I didn't see it on Google Maps." Incredible that this place could've gone unnoticed, Kate thought; in here, surrounded by those ominous walls and that endless ceiling of sky, she felt like she'd been plucked from the real world and set down onto another one.

"Not officially," Luna said. "But locals call it the Wayside."

Luna glanced behind her, and Kate followed her gaze. A few yards away, the earth gave way entirely. It took Kate a moment to register the nothingness there, like it was an optical illusion, but a moment later she arrived fully in her consciousness: they were perched at the edge of a cliff.

Kate felt suddenly dizzy. She rubbed at her knees and dug her feet firmly into the forest floor, attempting to ground herself back into her body, but her breath kept snagging in her throat.

A hand fluttered against her back, then came to a rest. For a moment, Kate thought it was a butterfly or a hummingbird, some creature buzzing at a high, trilling frequency.

"Afraid of heights?" Luna asked. Her hand wasn't comforting, exactly, but Kate still liked how it felt.

"Not quite." Kate looked back behind her, toward that sheer drop and the emptiness engulfing it. A mistake. She tipped forward and put her head between her knees. "Jake," she told the ground. "He could've died here. If not here, then somewhere like this."

"Shit. I should've thought about that before I took you here." Kate heard Luna unzipping her backpack, then the crinkle of a pastry bag.

When Kate raised her head again, she found Luna brandishing an oversized cookie studded with chocolate chunks. Kate recognized the cookie from the display cases at Tony's, where she had acknowledged that those heaving stacks of cakes and pies and pastries looked sublime, borderline lascivious, but that, like so much else, was like watching a movie in a language she didn't understand. The experience of desire no longer seemed to apply to her.

But now, face-to-face with that cookie, Kate actually wanted it. Her mouth watered with the wanting.

"Let's split it," Kate said.

Luna broke the cookie in half. They sat quietly together, side by side, eating their treats. It was so puerile, like snack time in grade school, though she did notice the way Luna's tongue, kitty-cat pink, darted into the cookie's deeper crevices and scooped up the melted chocolate with the tip. Luna noticed Kate noticing her.

"Sorry," she said. She smiled apologetically, and at that very moment Kate wondered if Luna had a partner. She hadn't mentioned it during dinner.

Kate laughed. "I don't think you're that sorry."

"I did warn you about my raging sweet tooth."

"That you did," Kate said. "And here I'm seeing it firsthand."

When Kate was done, she licked the chocolate off her fingers, unencumbered by refinement. Then she got up and wandered toward the fireplace, feeling Luna's eyes on her back. She liked how that felt, too. With the flat of her hand, she swept the cigarettes into the chocolate-streaked pastry bag, then tumbled the beer cans straight into her backpack, first tipping them upside down to make sure they were empty. Cleared of its scrim of debris, she noticed that the mantel was mottled with crusted brown spots. Not spots, really—more like a single puddle that had naturally separated when it dried, then been chipped away by the elements into smaller, discrete blotches, Pangaea-like.

Kate didn't need to be any kind of forensic specialist to know that this was blood. She also knew that this blood was old enough to have oxidized completely, its brightness dulled to a walnut brown, but it wasn't so old that it had totally dissolved, fused into the rock itself. The puddle was raised slightly from the surface on which it was spilled; if she had scraped at it, which she did not, tiny clumps of it would have flaked off. Whoever had drunk the beer and smoked the cigarettes had also spilled this blood, she surmised. Probably no one had come up here since each of those events had occurred. Unless that person was oblivious or scared into silence, both of which were possible scenarios.

In any case, Kate wouldn't tell Luna what she had seen. Her theories were too precious to her to share. Sometimes, she felt like her theories were the only thing she really had, perhaps because she had created them, and the other thing she had created no longer existed. (Not *invented* them, she reminded herself. She might be obsessed, but she wasn't crazy.)

Then she rearranged her private face into her public one and walked back over to Luna on the bench, where the other woman reclined back onto her arms, aiming her face at the sun now directly overhead.

"Is it noon already?" Kate said.

"You have somewhere to be?"

"No, actually. I'm quitting my job." As soon as she said it, Kate knew this was true. Of course she wasn't going back to work—not now, maybe not ever. The only delusion she had allowed herself was that she would ever walk into that office again. She would call Tracy this afternoon, when she got home—whenever that was; she was beholden to nothing and no one—and give her the news. Tracy would be unhappy, and probably offended, but Kate truly didn't give a shit.

Luna sighed, then lifted herself off the rock. "I do, unfortunately. A stack of ungraded papers is waiting for me at home."

In the car on the way back, they sat in satisfied, comfortable quiet, the kind that settles over a person after a good meal or a mildly strenuous workout, interrupted occasionally by observations or stray comments. When Luna pulled up to Jake's apartment, Kate didn't want to leave. She didn't want to go back up to that haunted apartment, where she would be left to consider all this blood and death and loss and read some kind of meaning into it—a task that she felt was fated, but which was still hard and sad—but equally, she didn't want to leave Luna's car. She didn't want to leave Luna.

So instead of leaving Luna, she kissed her. Luna kissed her back. It was so easy. Kate's mind went blank. They kissed gently at first, but then Luna eased her mouth open a little bit more, leaving a space for Kate's tongue to go. Kate offered it to her lightly, shallowly, but Luna drew her deeper in, where the fruity tartness of her lips gave way to something mustier but still sweet, like a patch of earth dampened by rain. It was such a cliché to say that women were softer than men, but it was true, and the difference was undeniable. Kate hadn't kissed a woman in a very long time—probably not for five years, when she slept with a woman she had met at a rock-climbing gym, of all places, on and off for a stretch of six months—and now, kissing Luna, she remembered how much she had liked it. She didn't like sleeping with women more than she liked sleeping with men, not necessarily, but she loved women's familiarity, an immediate recognition that made the progression into intimacy so much easier for her, even inevitable.

When they pulled away, Kate thought she should feel embarrassed, but she didn't. She felt no shame at all. Only a small but stubborn sense of regret, bordering on heartbreak, that she hadn't let herself feel this kind of pleasure in so long. And that it had to happen now.

"I'm happy you did that," Luna said. Her hands had been in Kate's hair, but she put them back on the wheel, bringing a golden strand along with her. "I was hoping you would . . . kind of knew you would. I have a sixth sense about these things." If a man had said that to Kate, she would've bolted. But coming from Luna, it wasn't predatory—it was flattering. Kate loved the idea that Luna had secretly been pursuing her. That she desired to pursue her at all. This was a concept she would turn over and over in her mind, she knew, savoring it like a piece of hard candy.

"I just wasn't sure if you were interested," Luna continued. "I know you're in a difficult place, and I would never want to force you into something you weren't ready for."

Kate moved forward, expanding into the light.

"Strangely," she said, taking Luna's chin between her fingers, "this doesn't feel so difficult."

———

The kiss imprinted onto Kate. She felt it on her lips, the pressure and the taste, as she climbed the stairs to Jake's apartment, peeled off her clothes, and stood under the shower. She made the water very hot, hotter than usual, and when she stepped out, the palms of her hands and the soles of her feet were pink like uncooked steak. She felt lightheaded and lay down on the bed, her towel coming undone. When her head hit the pillow, she imagined that it was a rock, her head splitting open upon it. The wetness of her hair seeped in a pool around her.

After lying there awhile—she didn't know how long; she'd taken off her watch this morning, before the hike—she dressed in a slate silk blouse and a pair of tailored, dark-wash jeans, the ones she wore on Fridays in the office in order to exhibit some modicum of casualness. (But not coolness. Kate had accepted that she was not cool.) She confronted her face in the mirror, drained of color. She put red lipstick on it.

Then she sat down at the desk, opened her laptop, and composed an email to the school registrar's office. She requested Jake's username and password for PalomaGate, the platform the students used to manage their classes, send messages internally, receive their assignments and grades, and view each class's roster of enrolled students. Kate had come across mention of PalomaGate in an informational brochure she'd found in Jake's desk, when she'd first begun to rummage through it, and at the time she had not considered it to be a piece of information worth further investigation. Why would she?

But something had happened to Kate on that hike. Now,

valuable information glimmered among the dark heaps of the invaluable, chunks of raw diamonds flaring inside a murky cave. If it wasn't an epiphany per se, it was the openness to the *possibility* of epiphany. Maybe it was the blood that had done it. Maybe it was the hint of progress with Wachs. Or maybe it was the kiss with Luna. All of these elements drifted apart and together, hovering on the brink of cohesion: The question of what happened to Jake. And just beyond that, the answer to his death.

So Kate was not surprised to receive an email from the registrar's office with Jake's requested log-in credentials under an hour later. Nor was she surprised to scan the roster for his Classical Mythology lecture and find Sasha Williams's name on it, right there at the end.

CHAPTER
SEVEN

Whatever fantasy of divine intervention Kate had imagined yesterday punctured almost instantly upon entering Dr. Steve Lowman's office. Somehow, through some evil trick of the light, the window behind the professor's desk did nothing to soften the industrial overheads that cast the room and everything that light caressed—including Kate's own hands, to her minor horror, when she looked down at them—in sepia. Not the romantic sepia of old photographs; the sickly sepia of an old slasher film. The professor himself wore thick plastic-framed glasses, a pointy little beard, and a tweed newsboy cap, a tableau that altogether brought to mind a kind of satyr version of Elvis Costello.

The intervening god has left the building.

"My students don't share with me the intimate details of their personal lives," the professor said, "and I don't encourage them to do so. There is certainly a culture of socializing between students and professors here—a few of my colleagues regularly host potlucks, for instance—but at the undergraduate level, I find it inappropriate. And a distraction, for many students."

"I'm not asking for you to disclose intimate information," Kate said. "I'm only asking if you remember seeing Sasha Williams and my son, Jake Cleary, in your classroom; and, if so, if you remember seeing them interact in any way. Sitting beside each other, maybe, or walking into or out of the classroom together. That's all."

The professor tipped his hands over on his desk, revealing his open palms. On a podcast Kate listened to recently, Brené Brown had said that this open-handed position telegraphed to the listener that one was willingly making oneself vulnerable to criticism. Sometimes people took on this position unconsciously, but Kate supposed that one could also assume the position purposefully, as a means of subtle manipulation.

"Here's the truth, Ms. Cleary. I've been teaching for thirty years, two classes per year, with an average of, let's say, one hundred students per class, taking into account the combination of lectures and seminars I've conducted. That amounts to six thousand students. Some of those students I've had the privilege to know more personally than others; many of them, quite frankly, I wouldn't recognize if they sat down directly across from me, right where you're sitting. All of them are important to me, including your son. But he falls into the latter camp."

Judging by the brief emails they'd exchanged yesterday to set up this visit, Kate should have known that speaking to the professor would be a fruitless exercise. He'd said it himself, in as many words: *I don't believe I will be of any help to you,* he'd written, *but please feel free to stop in during my office hours.* Kate knew that some leads led to nowhere. She also knew that some leads led to worse than nowhere. But she didn't know this guy would be such an asshole.

Kate took a moment to steady herself, before she said something deliciously petty but which she would later likely regret. She heard someone cough dryly in the office next door. She looked to the wall to her right, which bore some evidence of the professor's credentials: a PhD in Classics from a boutique, egregiously overfunded liberal arts university in the Northeast; an MA in Classics from a slightly larger, slightly less well-funded university here in California; a BA in English from a city-sized state university in the Midwest.

When she turned back to Dr. Lowman, having decided what to say to this person and precisely how to say it, her eye caught on a photograph lying on his desk. It showed a younger version of the professor shaking hands with an even-younger-looking man, each considering the other with some indiscernible expression—closer to resignation than celebration, Kate supposed, from her upside-down vantage—and with his other hand, Dr. Lowman laid a crown on the young man's head. Hard to tell, but it seemed that the crown was made of thorns. Not gilded or lacquered, not gently rounded like the verdant laurel wreaths of the ancient Greeks and Romans, but the raw thorns of some vicious-looking plant ripped from the root, its woody stems manipulated into an ovular shape and bound together with twine. Kate had never seen such an object before. She was disturbed by its primitiveness, how it contrasted so starkly with the jeans and T-shirt the young man otherwise wore, both rumpled and a little dirty looking. The date glowed, in neon orange, in the bottom-right corner: *9/9/1992.*

"What's going on here?" she asked, nodding toward the photograph. "A student of yours?"

Dr. Lowman picked it up, like he'd forgotten it was there. "One of my favorites," he said. He tapped a finger gently against the boy's face. "Parker Deily." He said the name quietly, as if to himself.

"I thought you disapproved of professors socializing with their students."

"Well, this was thirty years ago," Dr. Lowman said. "More

than that. My opinions have changed over the past three decades. Haven't yours?"

"Is that a costume?"

"You can see from there? Good eyesight."

"LASIK."

Dr. Lowman let out a little hum. "A costume. I suppose you could say that. It was just a silly ritual." Kate waited for him to say something more, but he'd turned silent, his features slack, subsumed by the hypnosis of a memory.

Kate had once said something similar to Jake. It was the Halloween shortly after he turned seven. He'd always hated Halloween, found everything about it overwhelming—the fevered, sticky-fingered competition for resources, the masks that made it impossible to identify friend or foe, the recklessness, the lawlessness of it all—but he was a child, a baby, and he didn't know that he could say no. So every year he agonized over his costume, as he wanted it to be an accurate physical representation of his inner emotional landscape (a quokka, he offered; a red balloon), and every year he became overwhelmed by his ideas, paralyzed by them, but he refused to set foot in Party City until the very last minute, when he had no choice but to pick something off the rack.

That year, the only costume left in his size was an English butler costume, complete with a serving tray, a white bow tie, white gloves, and a tiny tailcoat made of a shiny, highly flammable polyester fabric. John insisted that Jake didn't have to wear it—*Here*, John had said, emerging from the linen closet, *we can cut holes in this old bedsheet and you'll be a retro ghost*—but Jake was insistent, too. He paired the costume with his squeaky dress shoes, worn once at John's niece's wedding the year prior, and asked Kate to draw a thin mustache in black eyeliner over his top lip. *Curlicues at the ends, please.*

When they gathered in front of the Clearys' house for

trick-or-treating that evening, his friends, clad in capes and wings, weren't cruel; they were merely confused. On the one day a year that you could be anyone or anything you wanted, why a mustachioed old man whose job it was to serve another mustachioed old man?

Jake hated every second of it. *It's just a silly holiday,* Kate said when he and John came home from trick-or-treating, his plastic silver serving tray piled high with candy. He had already removed the bow tie and smeared the mustache off, as best he could, with spit and a tissue.

The next year, and every year after that, everyone in the house—which, by that time, was only Jake and Kate—tacitly agreed that Halloween would go unobserved.

The sound of a metal drawer banging shut snapped Kate back into the room. The photograph was gone.

"Have you considered that drugs might have played a part in your son's death?" the professor said. Any vulnerability he'd just revealed was gone, packed away the second he peeled himself from whatever memory the photograph unearthed.

"Yes, of course I have," Kate said.

Yes, of course she had, and she couldn't quite locate her emotions when the toxicology report came back clean. There was relief, but also some confusion, and even, at the very bottom of the barrel, a splinter of disappointment. After she read the report, she climbed into Jake's bed, swallowed an Ambien, and allowed herself to pick at the splinter. Wouldn't it have made things easier, in some ways, if there *were* drugs in Jake's system? That would have been an answer, albeit an answer that would have spawned a whole new breed of dread and regret. Several new breeds, probably. But what was one more pet, she wondered—here she sank deeper into the mattress, the midday light above her shrinking to a globe, an egg, a pinprick—when she was already tending to a litter of the fuckers? She woke up in complete darkness and apologized to the ceiling. *I'm sorry*, she said to it, to Jake high above.

"But if Jake had been on drugs," she said to Dr. Lowman now, "are you implying that would have excused his death? Or that he would have been guilty in some way? And whether there were or weren't drugs in Jake's body when he died," she continued, losing herself now, "what gives you the right to pass judgment on the way my son—whom you said yourself you wouldn't recognize if he sat right here and slapped you in the face—lived and died?"

The professor sat back in his chair. "I'm sorry if I offended you, Mrs. Cleary. It was truly not my intention to do so."

Kate rose, the chair cushion spewing yellow filling from a gash in the fabric. "I accept your apology," she said, "but you can go fuck yourself."

Her phone dinged as she walked out the door, but she didn't pull it out until she was safely back on the street, tucked away behind the bustle of the quad. She put her hands on her knees to catch her breath, then found herself sinking closer to the ground. A couple was silently approaching her from down the street, their pace quick and precisely in step, a two-person military march. They passed close enough that Kate could see the tendons in the boy's forearm twitch when he squeezed the girl's hand tighter. There was a baby-like smell about them, like laundry detergent and white flowers, undercut with the bite of sweat.

Kate checked her messages. It was from John, sending his daily *are you alive* in a text instead of a call. She supposed John was on the road. She never thought to ask him where he was.

I just told a tenured Classics professor to go fuck himself, Kate texted back. The girl let out a trilling laugh behind her. Kate turned, smoothing back the hairs that had escaped from her ponytail, but they had disappeared around the corner by the time she could see.

It was almost noon, right around the time Jake would be

heading to the Rice dorm's dining hall for lunch before his Brit
Lit lecture. She supposed she should have something to eat, too;
she hadn't had anything since the slice of lemon-chiffon pie she
chose over a real dinner last night. That cookie she and Luna
split on the hike yesterday seemed to unlock something in her;
she was only interested in sugar now.

She hauled herself up from the sidewalk and headed over
to the dining hall, stopping briefly outside to read the text that
buzzed through her phone. It was John.

Did he have it coming?

He asked me if Jake was on drugs when he died, Kate offered.

What's his number?

Why do you need his number?

So I can call him and tell him to go fuck himself.

She let the text lie. John would do it. He often followed
through on his shows of bravado, which could be, in turn, both
noble and idiotic.

*Apartment gone this morning, btw. New tenant moving in
Nov 6. You'll need to be out by the 4th, latest.*

Kate leaned against the cool brick wall of the dorm building. She closed her eyes. She attempted the calming box breath
Daryl had taught her amidst the shitstorm of the merger—in
for four, hold for four, out for four. Apparently, this was the favored breathing technique among Navy SEALs in preparation
for high-pressured military operations.

If we hadn't happened to have been texting right now, Kate texted
furiously, crushing that fragile box underfoot, *would you have even
told me this?*

*Always looking for ways to hate me, huh? Even thousands of
miles away is not enough to escape your wrath.*

No, Kate thought, pocketing that evil phone in her jeans,
we will never escape each other's wrath. Dramatic, but true.

She only had twelve days left.

Now she used Jake's ID card to swipe herself through the dorm's turnstiles. She couldn't believe how easy it was to get into these university buildings. At least this was a thing on her side.

But the security guard stationed in the lobby stopped her before she could get any farther, summoning her to the small desk.

"Are you a student here?" he asked. He motioned for her ID with a backward flick of his fingers.

Kate handed over the card. "Yes," she said. The lie slipped so easily from her mouth.

The guard slipped on a pair of reading glasses and took his time studying the ID. "This isn't you."

"I'm sorry. I have no idea why I just lied to you." The guard gave her a look like she'd just stripped all her clothes off, right there in the cafeteria. "That's my son. This is my son's card. He was a student here." She pulled her driver's license out of her purse and slid it across the desk. The guard compared the two, then handed them back to her.

"I see the resemblance," he said. He waved her through.

The dining hall was busy at this hour, but it was oddly hushed, just a few decibels above the common rooms in the library. The light was dim, the space windowless and partially carpeted. It smelled of antiseptic. She expected everyone to look at her as she walked to the food stations at the back of the hall, but not a single person did. Most were engrossed in their laptops or their phones, their faces subtly lit by the weak lights, like small scaled creatures inside a terrarium.

At the cereal funnels she filled a bowl with chocolate cereal, the sugary glaze crackling beneath a stream of milk, then topped it off with a ladleful of syrupy strawberries. After she paid with Jake's ID card—she'd just re-upped it with cash for his meal

plan—she sat at a round table tucked into the back corner of
the room. It was taken up by one other person, a willowy girl
in a black beret, her lips painted a deep mahogany. Her fingers
skittered quietly over her phone, punctuated occasionally by
the *clack* of her long fingernails, which were tapered to sharp
Vs and adorned in gold filigree.

Kate pulled Jake's journal out of her purse. It was his most
recent journal, its final entry dated just a month ago. Kate hadn't
chosen this journal for any particular reason; she just took one
from the stack on his desk and put it in her purse, the Swiss
Army knife hidden beneath it. Her twin talismans.

She opened the journal and scanned over an entry, even
though by this point she was positive she'd had it all memorized.
*Lunch 9/17 @ Rice: sweet potato fries, mac and cheese, mesclun
salad, iced tea/lemonade mixed.* She looked down at her bowl
of cereal, the milk turned the palest brown. A single shriveled
Cocoa Puff floated in its shallow pool. The sight of it made her
feel sick. The girl in the beret hadn't looked over at her, not a
single time. Could she have passed for a student? she wondered.
There was no way. This morning she noticed a new crop of gray
hairs sprouting along her temples. She got up and dropped her
bowl and spoon in the communal basin. Before she left, she
grabbed a tall paper cup from the drinks station. She filled it
up with iced tea, then topped it off with a glug of lemonade.

At the English building she swiped in seamlessly—her entrance was concealed amidst a school of students entering and
exiting, just one more minnow swimming downstream—and she
cross-referenced Jake's class schedule to make sure she went to the
right lecture hall. She didn't know exactly what she might find by
attending Jake's classes, but it was better than holing herself up
in his apartment. And there was something intimate about following his schedule, stepping into the footsteps he'd left behind.

The space was cavernous but warm, well insulated by maroon carpeting and blond wood desks arranged in arena seating. The threat of drowsiness loomed; one student had already fallen asleep, curled up in his chair, his sneakered feet pressed against the wall. Kate slipped into a seat in the back row, toward the middle, offering a clear, diagonal line of sight to Dr. Chapin, the professor, now shuffling through papers at the lectern. The professor looked to be around Kate's age, wrapped in a complicated jersey ensemble and a tangle of turquoise necklaces.

And there, stage left, at the end of the front row, Kate spotted a sheaf of blond hair, its ends pooling on the desk in front of her: that was Luna. She sat with her chin resting in her palm, gazing intently at the professor. Kate hadn't heard from her since the hike. (The car. The kiss.)

Five minutes later, at exactly twelve thirty-five p.m., the lecture hall filled nearly to capacity. Chapin pointed a small remote behind her and lowered the lights. The oversized projector screen unfurled slowly, accompanied by a low, mechanical hum. On the screen, an image flickered to life. It was a behind-the-scenes photograph of Boris Karloff as Frankenstein. He sat at a small round table in a full face of makeup—his shadowed features were arranged in a collection of carves and juts, craters and protrusions, famously squared off like an Easter Island head—but strangely, he was shirtless. His torso was surprisingly gaunt, the tendons of his neck webbed above his collarbone. Birdlike shoulders, pointed at the ends. He held a cup of tea with his left hand, paled with milk, his pinkie daintily separated from his first three fingers.

"Something to set the mood," Chapin said. The class laughed. "Remember, Boris Karloff's on-screen monster is nothing like Mary Shelley's on-page monster. Not the grunting lunk built like a linebacker. The real monster, the original one—the monster birthed by its actual mother, if you will—is eloquent and deeply feeling. Eventually loquacious, as we know from that climactic scene in chapter ten when the monster confronts Victor on the mountaintop, begging for a companion to accompany him through this horrific, unasked-for existence. He is a creature in desperate pursuit of love, acceptance, and understanding. A creature as human as all of us—maybe even more human even than his creator, who lost his humanity the second he turned his back on his creation. Obsession is a destructive force. But so, too, is neglect."

Kate took Jake's journal out of her bag and ran a hand over its pebbled leather cover. She opened it up; the space behind the front cover was blank. The first page was blank, too, other than the open field where Jake had written his name, quietly declaring himself as the notebook's owner. *Chronic neglect is a destructive force*, she wrote, as small as she could, in the top left-hand corner.

An hour later, Chapin wrapped up the lecture and dismissed the class. Kate stalled, taking her time to pack up her few belongings; on the other side of the lecture hall, she watched Luna slowly make her way up the stairs, teetering between two bulging canvas bags. Kate waited until Luna was nearly at the top of the stairs to leave her seat, intercepting her before she could reach the double doors.

When she saw Kate, Luna pressed a hand to her chest, some haziness behind her eyes sharpening. Kate felt bad for startling her. But it was Luna who apologized first.

"I wasn't expecting to see you here," Luna said.

"I just . . . wanted to feel closer to Jake," Kate said. "I'm glad I came. I actually learned something."

"How did you get in?"

"Jake's ID card."

A smile broke over Luna's face. "Sneaky."

Should Kate say something about yesterday? She supposed

she could. She'd never been particularly fluent in the nuanced language of flirtation—in the battle of communication, she'd sooner wield a hammer than a scalpel—but Luna seemed jumpy today. Fragile, even. She angled her body toward the door, the occasional dart of her eyes following suit. It was just as well, really. How could Kate have felt even the remotest lick of interest? Not even specifically toward Luna, but toward anyone? Lust, romance, even friendship—it would all take up too much time and emotional energy, and she needed both to complete her investigation. Now she physically shook her head, the briefest shiver, like she could shake the delusion off her.

"Are you hungry?" Luna said. "I'm grabbing a bite before I head back to the library."

"I'm actually busy today," Kate said, her voice edged in apology. Maybe this was an avoidance tactic, but it was also true. Suddenly she felt she had so much to do. Thursdays were Jake's heaviest class days. He still had two lectures and a recitation this afternoon, and by this point—Kate confirmed the time on her phone—he only had nine minutes to make it to Econ, all the way in the Sheridan building across campus.

"Okay," Luna said. Whether her tone conveyed relief or disappointment, Kate chose not to identify. "Give me a call, okay? I mean, if you want some company. Anything you want, I'm here."

Her awkwardness was touching. Seemed sincere. But Kate would not be calling her. She might never see this woman again, Kate realized, following Luna out the door before they peeled off in separate directions. Luna had been an indulgence, and Kate couldn't blame herself for having wanted that. But it was an indulgence that took up too much of her time—her most precious commodity. She couldn't afford to sacrifice it.

In Econ she learned about price elasticity. On the whiteboard, in a green marker that skipped, the professor gradually pieced together a demand curve graph against an elegant-looking formula. $Q = a - bP$. Kate copied the formula down in Jake's Moleskine and sketched the graph in miniature, fitted the x- and y-axes precisely along the bottom left-hand corner of the page. Shakespeare II was conducted in a lecture hall much smaller and brighter than Brit Lit and Econ, the students livelier. The professor asked for a volunteer to recite Prospero's monologue on the stuff of dreams; Kate counted eleven upraised hands. The pink-cheeked professor picked a volunteer and requested gusto. *You do look, my son, in a moved sort / As if you were dismayed: be cheerful, sir,* the volunteer recited, in fact with great feeling. Kate clapped along with the rest of the class at the end. She felt invigorated. She felt proud. She copied down the lines that moved her most. *The solemn temples, the great globe itself.* The rhythm of it made gorgeous sense; a second heartbeat, coming from within. Kate recognized three people in her Classical Mythology recitation, held in a close but cheerful basement classroom twenty minutes after Shakespeare let out. Kate took her time walking over, stopping at the Rice dining hall to pick up an iced coffee and a cranberry granola bar. The TA didn't seem bothered by the presence of a stranger in his classroom. *I'm auditing the class,* Kate told him, which the TA accepted with no follow-up questions other than her first name. The class discussed the Pygmalion myth, in which the titular king, a paragon of male arrogance, created an ivory statue depicting his ideal of womanhood and proceeded to fall in love with his creation. The connection between this story and *Frankenstein* was not lost on her. Kate didn't participate in the discussion, but she was tempted to, a couple of times. It was close to six p.m. when the class was finished. *See you in lecture tomorrow,* the TA said cheerfully, on her way out the door. *Yes, see you tomorrow,* Kate said back.

Kate was hungry. She went to Tony's, taking her usual seat in the back—open, as usual, though the rest of the diner was full—and she told Richard so.

"That's wonderful," Richard said. "May I suggest the mac and cheese? It's made with our four-cheese blend, one of which may or may not be Velveeta."

"Okay," Kate said. "That sounds perfect."

After Richard left, Kate opened the journal; the once-empty page was now covered in her notes. *How do we know that life is real and not an illusion? Does it matter either way? What makes a thing human? Gasoline is a vital product, and therefore has pricing power; an apple does not. Remember: the monster kills himself at the end.*

A sense of satisfaction, of completion, filled the sparse parts of her that could still be filled; the parts that Jake's absence had not drilled clean through. Her mind felt properly worked.

"Jake's notes?" Richard delivered the casserole dish of mac and cheese, his hand wrapped in a dish towel. The crust was a perfect golden brown, an overspill of cheese lavishly dripping down the sides. A bubble popped on its molten surface.

"No," Kate said. She picked up her fork, reconsidered, then picked up a spoon. "They're mine."

CHAPTER
EIGHT

The crown haunted her, that grotesque halo. She wondered if the thorns were sharp enough to break the skin when Dr. Lowman placed it on Parker Deily's head. Sharp enough to draw blood from the boy's forehead, leaving behind a diadem stippled in rubies.

Parker Deily. Parker Deily. The professor might have been unhelpful, but at least he left her this.

Kate woke at dawn. The light filtering through the slats was a frail dove gray. Her limbs felt strangely hollow. She should go for a run, she thought, something to get the blood moving. She'd packed her sneakers, but no gym clothes. A weird oversight.

She got up and dug through Jake's dresser drawers. She found a pair of gym shorts and a hunter-green T-shirt that read *Read Me* in a thick yellow font across the front. She had no idea what that meant. She smelled it; he was still there. It was an effort to pull her face away from the fabric, so she stayed there for a while, the bottoms of her feet turning cold on the parquet. Finally she peeled herself away and got dressed, rolling the waistband of the shorts twice for a better fit. She considered bringing her ID with her, as she always did—it was common knowledge that one must never run anonymously, in case one got hit by a car, mauled by an unfenced dog, or otherwise terribly injured in any of the innumerable ways it was possible to do so while out in the wild—but Kate decided against it. If anything happened to her, they would figure out who she was eventually. And anyway, she didn't think she was going to die today. What would the chances be of that happening, so soon after Jake? The universe worked in more mysterious ways than that.

At the last minute she grabbed Jake's ID card and slipped it in the shorts' deep pocket. Maybe she would want to stop at the dining hall to pick up a coffee on her way back.

She didn't have a route in mind, so she just started moving. Her ears ached with the cold. She tried to will her mind to clear like it had on the hike; tried to focus on the steady inhale and exhale of her breath, to self-soothe in its oceanic rhythm. But there was too much to think about, and far too much to do.

The first: get a handle on Parker Deily. She knew, in her gut, that something was there. Why else would Dr. Lowman be so defensive about Jake and Sasha, and then so reticent about the photograph?

By the time she returned to Jake's apartment, the sun was already up. In the bathroom, she slid open the small window above the toilet, letting some cool air nip inside. She took off Jake's shirt and shorts and arranged them neatly over the closed toilet seat while she showered, scrubbing herself clean with Jake's peppermint soap. After, she salvaged two plastic hangers from Jake's closet and hung up the shirt, then the shorts, and hooked them on the shower rail to air out. She didn't need to wash them. She couldn't let the detergent strip away Jake's scent. She didn't even sweat that much, anyway.

She dressed in jeans and a thick cable-knit sweater. In a

matter of weeks the lightweight trench she'd worn here wouldn't be defense enough against the sneaking chill, and she hadn't thought to pack something warmer. She hadn't known she would be living here. She'd have to buy another coat. There was an outdoor sports store on Main Street, independently owned, complete with a full-sized rock-climbing wall in the back and an array of neon five-finger running shoes in the front display. She would get something sensible there, a windproof parka or packable down jacket. In the meantime she slipped on Jake's down parka, relegated to the back of the closet. He wouldn't have worn it since last winter. What was he doing last winter? Kate tried to remember a conversation they'd had from that time. Couldn't do it. But she liked to think of him cocooned in the warmth of this coat, with its thick folds and many secret pockets.

She gathered up her things for the day—laptop, Jake's Moleskine, the blank notebook she'd picked up from the campus bookstore last night—but she couldn't open the door. There were the smudged fingerprints she noticed on the edge of the medicine cabinet mirror, and there was the balled-up tissue she discovered, just now, in Jake's jacket pocket. All of him was here. She sat down on the bed for a few minutes. Willed her mind blank.

—————

She arrived at the library soon after it opened at eight. At the little canteen on the first floor, she picked up a coffee and whatever pastry was closest to hand at the register. On her way down to the basement she unwrapped the crinkly cellophane and quickly ate the thing inside. It was a muffin, bejeweled in tart blueberries, its moist cap smushed against the wrapper.

She claimed her usual carrel and pulled out her laptop. The

basement was mostly deserted. In the far corner of the room, a janitor shook open a blue recycling bag and folded it neatly over the top of the bin. The sound of it, the pop and shimmer, only deepened the silence around her.

Before she got to work, she checked her email. There was the usual spread—the newsletters for which she had never signed up, the promotional emails from stores at which she never shopped, the slowing trickle of condolence letters from the thinnest edges of her social circle—but near the top, she spotted an unfamiliar name with a familiar URL: Sarah Stark at *People* magazine. Kate had received a handful of emails from local journalists since Jake's death, and she had provided some quotes, briefly, but never from a national publication with this kind of reach.

The journalist was working on a story on the recent spate of suicides among college students, she wrote to Kate. Would Kate be open to discussing Jake's passing?

Kate understood why Jake's death was newsworthy at the local level. His youth alone was headline fodder, but beyond that the college was a locus of community pride. The people in this town were inherently tuned in to what happened here, and in her most generous perspective Kate believed the Sutter Point community had the right to know about Jake.

Beyond the community level, though, Kate had a hard time imagining how a stranger in some town across the country knowing about Jake's death held any value other than spectacle.

She hit Reply and expressed a kind but firm decline. Kate didn't owe the journalist a response, but she didn't want to leave the door open for her to return.

She closed out of the email. Opened a new tab. Recentered herself. She googled Parker Deily's name.

The machine spit out duds, a disjointed combination of LinkedIn profiles, obituaries, family trees, and Instagram accounts containing one, or none, of the search phrases *Parker* and *daily*. Kate supposed she should have pursued a more legitimate research tactic, but still she trundled doggedly down to the second page, the subbasement of the search engine.

Paloma College Student Dies in Apparent Suicide. Her heart seized. The link lay halfway down the page. When she clicked on it, it led her to an article deep in the *Sutter Point Courier* digital archives, scanned and uploaded from the original hard copy. It was dated October 19th, 1992.

Kate skimmed the article first, fearful and expectant. Then she studied it a second time, handling each word like a precious stone.

In the early morning hours of October 18th, the article read, Parker Deily's body was found by a school groundskeeper at the foot of the bell tower on the quad. Authorities believed Deily jumped from the sixty-foot structure. Later that day, his parents, Ted and Martha Deily of Monterey, California, received their son's suicide note in the mail, confirming that Deily had taken his own life.

Before Cleary, there had been no student deaths on or around the Paloma campus in over thirty years. Kate remembered the line from the *Sutter Point Courier* article announcing Sasha Williams's death. Like Jake and Sasha, Parker was a twenty-year-old junior.

Ted and Martha Deily of Monterey, California. Kate imagined the couple, older but sprightly, clad in climbing shoes and moisture-wicking fabrics—Ted an avid rafter, Martha the hiker—sitting beside each other, in twin rockers, on the porch of their craftsman home. Nearly identical with their soft cotton hair, their redwood-bark skin, their unnameable grief. How could a person endure thirty years of hell? With a partner, Kate supposed. She watched the breeze rustle the leaves above them, lift the fine hair from their necks. Would they imagine this was Parker's touch, this reassuring hand?

Kate closed her eyes against the vision. She could feel the cool damp, smell the sycamores' dull tang. She felt a strange yearning to be there. She wanted to be held by them, this sad, serene couple in the woods. Wanted them to imbue her with their veterans' wisdom.

Over the past few weeks, several of Kate's friends and colleagues had gently suggested that she join a bereavement support group. Carson, Kate's closest friend from her Abrams & Frank days, who'd flown out from New York to attend Jake's funeral, had even told Kate, in confidence, that the support group she'd joined after the sudden death of her first husband had saved her life.

"What I mean is," Carson said to Kate after the funeral, when everyone had gathered in Kate's apartment to drain her reserves of white wine and not eat the leaning towers of meal-laden Tupperware, "the people in that group encouraged me not to kill myself."

Kate had never known this about Carson. Kate knew Carson as the hungry junior partner who'd returned to work three days after her thirty-eight-year-old husband's funeral, and who every day thereafter was already in the office before Kate arrived at seven in the morning, and who stuck around after Kate left, which was often well past ten. Now, with unrelenting hindsight, Kate understood that this was not an indication of how Carson had nobly and seamlessly processed her loss. It was precisely the opposite.

Still, Kate bristled against the notion of a support group. She knew that she and John were not the only people on earth who had lost a child. But no one else's child was Jake.

Ted and Martha Deily, though—they had Parker. And Parker and Jake had something in common.

She opened a fresh tab, tucked beside the one that held their son's obituary, and googled their names.

Martha was on Facebook. From her picture, taken at the summit of a dusty red mountain, the woman looked exactly as Kate had imagined her. The long white braid, the majestic natural setting. Kate hoped that it was Ted behind the camera.

She clicked the Message button beneath Martha's name.

———

Jake only had two classes today: Dr. Lowman's Classical Mythology lecture and Luna's Brit Lit recitation. It would be a stupid choice to go to either—first to confront Dr. Lowman again, and then to confront Luna—but still Kate found herself packing up her things at ten thirty, twenty minutes before lecture began, then taking a left out of the library and straight toward the Nolan building. If she had the bad luck of being spotted in lecture, she doubted Dr. Lowman would let her sit in on the class as freely as the other professors and TAs had thus far. And she couldn't use the auditing excuse. He'd never buy it. Her best bet was to catch him early, before class, and make amends. Ask nicely if she could sit in on the class, just for today.

And the awkwardness with Luna—well, she would deal with it. She was forty-eight years old. It wasn't like she lacked experience navigating awkward romantic situations.

But her ringing phone intercepted her entrance to Nolan.

She veered into a quiet spot beneath the concrete overhang of the neighboring building. She took a breath to steady herself and picked up the call.

"Hello, Kate." Wachs didn't need to introduce himself. She'd know his voice anywhere. "Will you come down to the station? We believe we found something."

———

Twenty minutes later, Kate sat in Wachs's office at the Sutter Point Police Station. A paper cup of water sat on the desk in front of her, slowly disintegrating. Felix, the station's secretary, had handed it to her wordlessly when she walked in—she'd high-tailed it here from campus, and she entered breathless, close to panting. Now, she took a sip. The water was so cold her front teeth ached, right down to the core.

"So," Kate said. "Tell me what you found."

"Okay, then," Wachs said. He didn't question her impatience for pleasantries. "We were able to get through the passcodes locking Jake's phone and laptop."

"How? I thought that was impossible."

"You heard of Code Gray, this digital cracking tool? It's not well known to the public, I don't think. I only ask because you're in the business."

"Business adjacent, maybe. I don't think blockchain has anything to do with this."

"Clearly, I'm no technology expert. But I can say that this tool has been instrumental for law enforcement agencies, so long as they have access to it, which this department is privileged to. Anyway, the upshot is that we got in."

"That's good news."

"The caveat is that we can't uncover content from the encrypted messaging apps that Jake used for so many of his exchanges. It's impossible, even with the search warrant. All we can get is the date and time that Jake registered for the app, and then the date and time he was most recently active on it."

"That's not so bad," Kate said. "Any information is useful."

"Well, I'm glad we didn't dash your hopes." Wachs shook his desktop awake and clicked a few times. He squinted at the screen. "Here's what we got: Jake registered for the app at eleven seventeen p.m. on September eighth, 2023. He last used the service at seven p.m. on October tenth."

"That would have been just a few hours before he died," Kate said. "Do you think it's strange that Jake only started using the app a few weeks before that?"

"I won't presume to comment on that. You would know better than I." Then he picked up his desk phone and hit a single button. "Felix, hi. Can we get the Cleary materials in here? Thanks."

Felix arrived seconds later, carrying a bundle wrapped in plastic against his chest. He set it down on the desk between Kate and Wachs. He gave Kate a cheerless smile before he left, closing the door behind him.

"They're yours now," Wachs said. "Unlocked, of course."

Kate pulled Jake's phone and laptop onto her lap and laid a hand over them. She sat there quietly for a moment, then put Jake's things carefully into her tote bag.

When she rose from her chair a few minutes later, Wachs mirrored her on the other side of the desk. Neither gave any indication of moving.

Finally, Kate said, "What about his search history? Or his unencrypted messages, whatever was in the cloud? Did you find anything there?"

She swore she saw Wachs's neck flush. "Not particularly," he said. "Not in the way you think. Though we did notice that he used a specific sign-off with a few of his friends. S&S. Does that mean anything to you?"

"No," Kate said.

"This was the best we could come up with. I'm sorry we couldn't help you more."

It was almost noon when she left the station. She'd missed the Classical Mythology lecture, and the English Lit recitation began in five minutes. She couldn't get there in time. This was probably a blessing in disguise, but still she felt anxious about it. She'd never missed a class in her life.

She considered going back to the library, but soon veered off her usual course and instead headed toward Toller. She'd seen the old library on a map of campus and occasionally overheard students mention it with a sort of abstract reverence. Toller wasn't used as much as Baskin, the newer library that had initially been built in the late 1950s but was renovated and rechristened in 2002 in honor of its thirty-nine-year-old tech billionaire sponsor. In contrast, the quainter Toller, which had stood seemingly untouched since it was first erected as the college's inaugural building, was favored by graduate students or those seeking intensely focused work, without the distraction of Bluetooth-enabled printers. Plus, Baskin had been dropped right in the middle of campus, a hulking cube that forced traffic inside itself. Toller was tucked into the campus's sleepier edges—which, in part, explained why Kate had yet to visit it.

Inside, Kate found Toller to be a cozy, ornate reprieve from Baskin's efficient sterility. The floors were covered in high-pile maroon carpets, and the entranceway was flanked by twin posts made of carved, glossy oak. They gave way to a pair of matching staircases, elegantly flared, that curved up through the library's four floors. From the ceiling hung three tiered pendulum chandeliers, and this absence of fluorescent overheads in an academic building seemed, to Kate, an absurd luxury.

On the way over to Toller Kate had read about the history of the building on the Paloma website. She learned that it housed the book collection of John Willets Rollinson, who matriculated in the university's first graduating class in 1903 and went on to become one of the school's most generous benefactors. Though Rollinson earned his fortune in the oil industry, his personal book collection was focused on less terrestrial matters—by the end of his life, he had become one of the nation's foremost collectors of occult literature. His esoteric interests were apparently indiscriminate, the texts he amassed hopscotching cultures and centuries with the frenzied abandon of a magpie.

Kate hiked up the staircase to the library's uppermost floor, where the Rollinson room was behind a door—a heavy, dark wood, its name etched in gold lettering to match the chilled golden knob—that was hidden inside the stacks. A librarian manned a single desk near the entrance, slowly picking away at a Bush-era keyboard.

In the center of the room stood a waist-high, illuminated display case showing a selection of the collector's treasures. There were eighteenth-century editions of both the *Malleus Maleficarum* and the *Splendor Solis*, a grimoire once owned by a Bavarian healer and midwife who practiced her craft in the late 1600s, and a compendium of demonology dated 1711 and authored by a Breton nun. And then, at the end of the line, sat an illustrated early edition of William Blake's *Songs of Experience*. The pocket-sized book was opened to "The Tyger."

Kate lingered there, studying the watercolor illustration. It showed a surprisingly juvenile rendering of a tiger, prowling beneath the bright-orange text with a look of bland contentment on its half-smiling face. Why had this poem been so important to Jake and Sasha? What keys had it held to their understanding of themselves—and how had that discovery turned so catastrophic? Kate had read the poem many times over—and she read it over again now, straight from the original source—and still found little more significant in it than its stated meaning. Though, admittedly, she never was one for poetry.

"This was one of Rollinson's favorites."

Kate looked up to find the librarian standing beside her. He clasped his hands behind his back and leaned over the display case, squinting over his wire-frame glasses. The man was much younger than Kate had expected of a university librarian—Kate placed him somewhere in his late thirties—but in his well-worn burgundy sweater he still had a wise-old-owlish look to him that Kate found comforting.

"The Tyger?" Kate asked.

"*Malleus Maleficarum*," the librarian corrected.

Kate shuffled nearer to the text the librarian studied. This one was also splayed open. Each page held two columns of narrow, densely packed text, the print a remarkably rich black, considering its age; according to the title card beneath it, this edition was dated 1506.

"You can practically feel the hatred simmering off the page, can't you?" the librarian said. His voice remained just above a whisper.

Kate made a soft sound of agreement. She, too, felt compelled to keep her voice tamped to a low register. Even without comprehending the meaning of the words—it was written in Latin, as far as Kate could tell—Kate was filled with a sense of deep dread just looking at it. The text seemed to suffocate itself, as if the writer had intended to hold each individual character hostage within the prison of his own resentment.

"What's the story here?" Kate asked.

"*The Hammer of Witches*, originally published in 1487. It's considered to be the first document that codifies the process of sniffing out and punishing witches. This, in part, triggered the mass witch-hunting hysteria that followed over the next couple of centuries. Not only did it prove—quote, unquote—that witches existed, but it empowered the public to actively hunt them down in the most unthinkable, the most brutal ways. It was written by Heinrich Kramer, a German-Catholic inquisitor whose life's sole purpose was to exterminate those he was convinced were in league with the devil. The year before he'd brought a witchcraft trial to the court at Innsbruck and was promptly dismissed by the bishop. Clearly, he wrote this in a rage. And humiliation. He was already deranged, but rejection seemed to unlock a whole despicable new dimension in him."

"Hm. That reminds me of a certain Austrian art school reject."

The librarian clucked his tongue in agreement. "You're not the first person to draw parallels between this guy and Hitler. What it says about Rollinson that he considered this to be the crown jewel of his collection . . . well. I'll try not to speak ill of the dead in the room he paid for. That said, we now understand that the man was a raging misogynist."

"But of course. I would expect nothing less." Kate gestured toward "The Tyger." "And what about this one? What did Rollinson think of this?"

"I can't say for sure. We don't have any of Rollinson's personal notes on *The Songs of Experience* on record. In my estimation, though, this is a wonderful addition to the collection. Blake is fundamental to early English Lit syllabi, so it's nice that the kids have the original source at their disposal while they're studying him."

"Do English students typically come here? To see it?"

"I know some professors make it a requirement to do so. If nothing else, I think it gives the students a greater appreciation for the lost art of bookmaking."

Would Jake have made a pilgrimage here, to pay a visit to his foundational text? He hadn't written about doing so in his journals, but Kate couldn't imagine why he wouldn't have. Plus,

Jake had worked in the library over the summer. His employment was limited to Baskin, as far as Kate knew, but perhaps he could have been sent over to Toller for some sort of book-retrieval mission.

Admittedly, Kate couldn't remember many details of Jake's most recent job. She couldn't even remember if she'd asked him for them.

"This is a long shot," Kate said now, "but do you recall meeting a student named Jake Cleary in this room? He would've come to see 'The Tyger.'"

"Jake Cleary?" It wasn't a question—it was a confirmation. Kate nodded. *Yes, that Jake Cleary.* "I'm sorry. Off the top of my head, I can't remember. Most students aren't interested in chatting it up with the nerdy librarian." Before Kate could elicit any kind of pity, the librarian smiled. "A standard occupational hazard. You don't think I went into library science because I'm an insatiable extrovert, did you?"

Kate offered him a sympathetic smirk: fellow easily satiated introvert here. Then she pulled Jake's ID card from her pocket and handed it over to the librarian, giving him a visual. The librarian studied it for a moment, then two—long enough to stoke an ember of hope.

"You know," he said then, "I actually think he did come in once over the summer, about a week before the semester began."

"Really? Did he say anything to you? Or do you remember anything of note from that visit?"

"Well, it was noteworthy that he came in at all. Usually, very few undergraduates set foot in Toller until well into the school year. But yes, I do remember him looking at 'The Tyger.' He spent maybe five, ten minutes here. I asked if he needed help with anything, but he didn't take me up on it. It seemed that he just wanted to be in the book's presence." Then the librarian gave her a look of such kindness she couldn't bear to hold his gaze. "He seemed peaceful. Like he was happy to be here."

"And he was here alone, right?"

"He was alone," the librarian confirmed. Then he added, "Though someone was waiting for him outside the door."

"Did you see who it was?"

"I only caught a glimpse when he left, but I do think I saw a young woman with blond hair."

It couldn't have been Sasha, then—not if the woman had light hair. Still, Kate figured, this meant at least one more person knew that Jake had paid a visit to Toller over the summer— which likely meant they also knew how unusual his devotion to this book was.

Leaving the library a few minutes later, after thanking the librarian for his graciousness, Kate allowed herself to feel comforted by the image of Jake at peace. But by the time she reached Jake's apartment, that comfort splintered into resentment.

Inside, she set down her bag and carefully unwrapped the phone and laptop from their plastic sleeve. She laid them on the desk. His phone bore the evidence of a hard-worn tool—the plastic tie-dye case was chipped at the edges, and a long, single crack bifurcated the screen diagonally. She slid that aside and turned to the closed laptop, placing her thumb in the groove between the screen and the base, preparing to crack it open.

But her phone buzzed inside the bag at her feet. She took it out and glanced briefly at the screen. Martha Deily had sent her a message on Facebook.

CHAPTER NINE

12:22 p.m.: Thank you for your message, Kate. I am on the Paloma College newsletter email list, which is open to both current and alumni students and parents. This is where I heard about your son, Jake. I am terribly sorry, and I understand what you are going through. I will try to help in any way that I can.

12:30 p.m.: Martha, hello. I'm so glad to hear from you. Thank you for your condolences. As you can imagine, I am doing everything within my power to understand the circumstances surrounding Jake's death, but I am coming up short. We now know that Jake took his own life, but I can't make sense of it.

12:51 p.m.: I am sorry to be the bearer of difficult news, but you may never make sense of it. My husband Ted and I never did. But we have come to accept it, and this has been something of a balm to our suffering. Talking about Parker also helps. We talk about him constantly. He continues to be the light of our lives and the center of our world.

12:56 p.m.: I've been staying in Jake's apartment for the past few weeks while I tie up some loose ends on campus. I feel his presence everywhere. I can still smell him on his clothes. I don't know if this is helping me or hurting me, but I can't imagine leaving.

12:59 p.m.: That's okay. You take all the time you need.

1:13 p.m.: I have to tell you, Martha, that I saw a picture of Parker in Dr. Steve Lowman's office the other day. Something struck me about that photograph, I don't know quite what. I think Parker reminded me of Jake.

1:45 p.m.: Oh. That's a wow moment. Parker was in Dr. Lowman's Classical Mythology lecture. He was a Classics major. He admired the professor very much. Dr. Lowman also attended Parker's funeral up here in Monterey. He spoke very highly of Parker. He had so much promise. I believe the prof had a hand in a club that Parker had joined so he knew Parker better than some of his other students.

1:45 p.m.: What kind of club was that?

1:59 p.m.: I am not entirely sure. In those days we couldn't text and email. We spoke to Parker once or twice a week. It was much harder to keep in touch. I envy parents these days. But Parker was very happy about joining the club. I believe it was a "literary society." More social than academic.

2:01 p.m.: Don't societies tend to be student-run? I wonder what Dr. Lowman's involvement would have been.

2:11 p.m.: I am sorry, but I wouldn't know that. Parker wasn't big on the details. He had a lot going on besides. He wrote theater reviews for the school newspaper and he volunteered at the retirement home down on Spring Avenue. He read to the residents there in the evenings. He loved hearing their stories. He once said to me that he found it easier to connect with the elderly than with people his age. He had some good friends though. He struggled in high school socially but at Paloma he found his fellow nerds, LOL. We thought he started to find his "groove." I never knew that Parker was in such distress. That will haunt me until my final days.

2:12 p.m.: I'd thought that about Jake, too. And I feel the same way you do.

2:37 p.m.: I'm curious—do you remember what the club was called?

3:41 p.m.: Yes. I will not forget that. It was called Stars & Spears. But sometimes he referred to it as "S&S."

Kate stared down at her Greek salad. Triangular wedges of feta were fanned around the lip of the wide bowl. Arranged inside the deep well were thick purple curves of onion, shiny shriveled olives, and long ribbons of olive oil, tinted the palest yellow.

She wanted to throw it at the wall. She could see it there, the bright mess it would make. Then the look of horror on Richard's face, and the shame that would follow.

S&S. Stars & Spears. After she received Martha's message, Kate googled the term, then the term plus *Paloma College*, but she came up with nothing.

Jake's phone and laptop sat beside her, replete with life. She only needed to tap them awake, then to set free whatever answers hummed within them, but when she hovered a hand over the devices, she was overcome with vertigo. She removed her hand; the breath returned.

Wasn't that always how it went, when she got the thing she'd wanted so badly? When the fantasy of the future slammed into the solidity of the present? There was always a moment of paralysis, of staring down at the thing in your hands and wondering what to do with it, now that it was real.

So she'd gone down to Tony's, because she couldn't handle being alone. When Richard approached her, notepad in hand, she'd first ordered the salad, and then very nearly added that she believed her son and Sasha Williams and Parker Deily were attempting to move her hand toward a sinister conclusion spelling out the unjustness and complexity of their deaths. Instead she also asked for an iced tea and lemonade in the tallest glass Richard had, with a lot of ice.

She was startled when her phone buzzed on the laminate table. It was John.

Sorry I didn't text this morning. Was in a dead zone.

Just got to the Kota Kinabalu airport. Wi-Fi surprisingly solid.

Kate typed, then deleted: *Where the hell is Kota Kinabalu?*

She put her phone on silent and tucked it into her bag. She felt more alone now than she ever had since coming to Sutter Point, and suddenly desperate for connection. Again she considered talking to Richard, but he was so good humored and, as far as Kate knew, fundamentally levelheaded. He would think she was crazy, he would express that opinion in a gentle and compassionate manner, and his kindness would be agonizing.

There was only one other person Kate knew in town.

Sheepishly, she pulled her phone back out of her bag and opened a fresh text message.

The response arrived five minutes later, during which time she forced a cucumber coin into her mouth.

I have some work to do this afternoon. Maybe a drink tonight? 7ish?

It's good to hear from you, by the way.

Luna picked the spot last time, so tonight she let Kate choose. Kate hadn't eaten anywhere in town, apart from Tony's, the Paloma dining halls, and the restaurant Luna had already taken her to, so she chose the first place she could think of—an Edison bulb–spangled nouveau American place she'd passed a couple of times on Main Street, and which she'd thought, in an abstract way, could be a nice place to get a glass of wine.

"I wouldn't have thought Parker's mom would want to dig everything back up again," Luna said, perched beside Kate on a reclaimed-wood barstool. "Especially not for a stranger. No offense."

"I agree. It was a shot in the dark." The bartender refilled Kate's wine glass with a heavy cabernet. The liquid was so thick it hardly moved when he slid it across the zinc bar top.

Kate hadn't necessarily planned on telling Luna everything—she hadn't planned on seeing Luna ever again, up until
a few hours ago—but then Luna appeared next to her, ordered
a whiskey sour, and sustained a hug just long enough for that
sun-and-leather scent to emerge. The familiarity was enchant-
ing. Luna asked how she was, and Kate found herself saying she
thought she was either the most or the least sane person in this
town. Possibly on this particular plane of existence.

"So, okay," Luna said now, one hour and two drinks each
into their meeting. "You think the connection between Parker
and Jake, and possibly Sasha too, is Stars & Spears. Whatever
Stars & Spears is."

"Correct."

"Why don't you push Dr. Lowman about it? He's the only
person you know for sure has a direct connection to all of this."

"I'd like to do some independent research first," Kate said. "I
don't want to spook him. But it's likely that I *will* need to circle
back with him, in which case it's also likely that he'll only give
me a single meeting before he blacklists me. I'd like to come to
that meeting having done my due diligence."

"That makes sense," Luna said. She pulled the short red
straw from her drink and worked it between her front teeth
like a rope of cherry candy. She made a humming sound. "But
how can you account for the thirty years between their deaths?
I'm not trying to poke holes in your theory, but I think a time
gap like that kind of invalidates the pattern."

"Which would mean it's all a coincidence. And I'm back
to where I started."

Luna cocked an eyebrow. "Or where everyone *wants* you to be."

"Have I made a conspiracy theorist of you?"

"What makes you think you made me this way?" Luna
flagged down the bartender and ordered her third whiskey sour.

To Kate, she said, "You said the cops gave you back Jake's phone and laptop, right? You can probably have most of these questions answered by looking there. Even if they couldn't uncover the encrypted stuff, there must still be something there."

"I know that. I just haven't worked up the nerve to do it."

"Are you afraid of what you'll find?"

Kate thought about this for a moment. Luna sat in the silence with an apparent lack of discomfort, mildly observing Kate. Below the bar, Luna's legs—bare between a short pleated skirt and a pair of brown cowboy boots—crossed over and around themselves twice, first at the knees, then at the ankles.

On the barstool behind her, Kate heard a man talking loudly about a low-pressure, magnet-powered travel tube that would span the length of the continent. *It's gonna happen, babe, I'm telling you. It'd get us to New York in forty-five flat.*

Eventually, Kate said, "That's part of it. But I'm also afraid that I won't find anything. That this is all exactly as simple as it seems to be on the surface, which would mean I would have to start moving on. Or at least begin accepting this new reality."

"Who told you that you have to do either?"

"Martha did. John, too. And they're right. If this *is* all a fantasy—some elaborate scheme I've unconsciously created to stay stuck in the denial phase—then I'm going to need to be disabused of it eventually. Sooner is probably better."

"Well, Martha could be wrong. And also, John isn't here. He doesn't exactly know what you're going through." Luna accepted her fresh drink with a distracted smile pointed in the bartender's general direction. "I don't doubt that John loves your son. I just have a hard time finding compassion for absent fathers. At the end of his life, I know my dad would have given anything to have just an hour longer with me."

Kate should have been offended by Luna's outburst, but

when Luna quieted herself with her drink, any surprise at
Luna's quick turn to temper morphed into righteous validation. Luna was right about John, and she was only reflecting
back to Kate what she already knew. And wasn't this precisely what she'd sought in reaching back out to her? Kate was
overcome with gratitude, followed by a wave of general goodwill. Even the man behind her, whose neon-fleeced arm kept
bumping up against hers, ceased to annoy her to the point of
attempted homicide.

"No, you're right," Kate said now. "John and I are closer
now—sometimes it even feels like we're becoming friends—but
I'm so angry with him. Honestly, I've been angry with him since
Jake was born. He was never cut out to be a father. He values
his freedom too much. I don't know if he did the *best* he could
with Jake, but he did what he was capable of. And now that Jake
is gone, I think John feels license to indulge in the anonymity
he always wanted for himself."

"I can understand valuing freedom," Luna said, "but there's
a fine line between freedom and selfishness." She shook her head,
signaling the end of the subject. Kate was happy to move on.
"Where are you in that due diligence?"

"Nowhere past the initial Google phase," Kate said, "which
was a dead end."

"I could've told you Google wouldn't help you. When I
want real information, I go to Reddit."

"No," Kate said, putting up a hand. "I don't want to know
what domestic terrorists and incels are talking about."

"Don't worry about that. That shit is on 8chan, and other
fucked-up message boards I definitely don't know about. I guess
people can be twisted on Reddit, because people in general are
twisted, but it's mostly benign. Sometimes I go on there for rec-
ommendations about Japanese skincare products." Absently, she

stroked the side of her finger up and down against her cheek, as if to convey its smoothness.

One more drink for Luna, two more drinks for Kate, plus a shared bowl of almonds rolled in warm, powdery spices. By the time they got the check, it was already close to ten. Kate slid from her stool. The room swirled around her. Her mouth tasted like Christmas.

She followed Luna outside. They lingered on the sidewalk, chatting about nothing, the words coming quick and easy. When they hugged goodbye, they held on for one beat, then two.

"Thanks for texting me," Luna said when they pulled apart. "I'm happy you want to be friends."

Friends. Nothing more. Over the past few minutes, as the end of the night drew threateningly near, Kate had been mildly agonizing over whether she should bring up the kiss. To clarify to Luna that it was a hard stop, a onetime event, not an invitation for something more. But apparently Luna had felt the same way, or sensed that Kate wasn't interested, and she was brave enough to be the one to mention it.

"I do think I need those right now," Kate responded.

Luna ran her thumb over her bag's canvas strap. Her metallic silver nail polish glowed faintly under the restaurant's outdoor lights. "We all do sometimes," she said.

Her gentleness evoked in Kate a sense of mortal relief. With men, there always existed the potential for violent retaliation after a rejection, no matter how seemingly kind the man or considerate the rejection.

Then Luna went one way and Kate the other, across the street and up the narrow staircase to her apartment. The key clacked against the lock three times before it gained purchase. Shoes kicked to the side of the bed, and the parka hung up with care and stuffed into the front of the closet. Kate sat at the desk and opened the laptop. The screen flickered from black to bright; she squinted into the artificial sun. His wallpaper was unremarkable, one of the software's native templates depicting a mountain range gilded in burgeoning amber light. She clicked on the web browser. Into the open field, she typed: *feddut.com.* Backspace backspace backspace. She tried again: *reddit.com.* A fresh page appeared, busy with text and images against an unstylized gray background. A person glyph hovered in the top right corner. *Welcome, Jake.* Below the welcome banner, in the right sidebar, there was a white box with a cobalt band at the top—a message board. Kate scanned the information inside the box.

r/S&S23. 7 Members. 0 Online. August 27th, 2023. Private.

CHAPTER
TEN

The first year of college was hard. This was true. Also true: the seed of sadness had always been inside of Jake. He'd been aware of that seed, which was lodged deep in his belly, from the time he was very young. Young enough to remember, really; he was constantly plagued with a sense of homesickness, even smushed between his parents' sleeping bodies, where, for a time, he often ended up at night, until his dad deemed him too old to be behaving in such a way. Later he thought the isolation of that first year of school simply provided that seed the ideal environment to fully flourish. The loneliness was its soil; the uncertainty its water.

By the end of his freshman year, he had wrested some familiarity with this new life, and then some control over it, and finally he emerged from the greenhouse—tentatively, and only when faced with the probability of failing out of his classes—but it was already too late. The seed had erupted, and the creature it bore grew quick and greedy. Its dense leaves shaded his vision; its ropy, many-pronged stalks coiled around his heart. And by the time he joined up with the others, Jake was no longer himself; he was a thing possessed by another thing.

He wanted to say that he was not responsible for his actions, incapacitated in this way, but he couldn't. The creature, perversely, had left a sliver of space between those dark leaves. This was where the light came in, a peephole through which he could peer out into the world. And then he would retreat, reflect back on what that world did to him.

This, he found, was an exercise in torture. Oblivion would have been easier.

Because he knew exactly what happened that night. He knew what he did, and he knew what he didn't do, and he knew that both were very, very bad.

If you can't help yourself, then I can't help you.

She was right about everything, and she was right about this. Jake was guilty, and the world would not deliver punishment, because the world could not be trusted to do anything good or right or just, and so he would have to punish himself on its behalf.

She agreed with him on that.

CHAPTER ELEVEN

It wasn't hard for Kate to decode the Reddit page. This was Stars & Spears' private message board, created on August 27th, 2023. Every message was scrubbed, every member's handle pseudonymous. Jake's was *batboy1011*.

Kate was starting to feel like she was pounding on a locked box.

Of course, there was Jake's phone. The key, or the hammer. The screen sprang to life with the touch of her finger. His phone background was less anodyne than his laptop setting, showing a series of hanging spiral sculptures that Kate recognized as the artist Ruth Asawa's. Jake had seen an exhibit of her work at a David Zwirner gallery in New York six years ago, when he'd gone to stay with John for a couple of weeks over the summer. He'd spent two hours at the exhibit, he'd told Kate on the phone later that evening, and then he'd gone over to the other Zwirner gallery, the one on Nineteenth Street, and he'd spent another hour there. By the time he'd emerged from the gallery, perched at the westernmost edge of the island, the sun had already begun its descent over New Jersey—a landscape he'd described as "uncommonly beautiful," and which equally brought to mind

Turner's bluster of pastels as the rich desolation of Hopper's oil paintings.

On the phone, Kate had laughed.

That's wonderful, sweetie, she'd said. *You'll do just fine on your PSATs.*

Then she'd asked him if John had let Jake have some wine at dinner. *No*, Jake had said. *I'm all hopped up on art.*

Now Kate navigated to the Messages app on Jake's phone. It showed only a handful of conversations—one with her, one with John, some spam messages, and what looked to be cursory exchanges with study partners and acquaintances. Wachs was right: Jake must have used the encrypted messaging app for most of his conversations.

Other than John and her, there was only one person with whom Jake texted in any substantial way. His name was Rex Orbach. Their final text exchange was on October 1st.

Rex, 4:13 p.m.: gonna come over tn. i think we need to talk

Rex, 8:20 p.m.: u ok?

Rex, 9:01 p.m.: dude honestly starting to get worried

Jake, 9:05 p.m.: yea come over whener. leaving door open

Finally, something she could work with.

Kate saved Rex's number to her own phone, then typed out a message. It would be cruel to text him through a dead person's number.

Kate, 10:43 p.m.: Rex, hi. This is Kate Cleary, Jake's

mom. Would you be open to meeting with me this week? Tomorrow, maybe? I'd like to talk to you about Jake.

Rex, 12:01 a.m.: hi mrs. cleary. not sure how you got my number but thank you for reaching out. sure i can meet you tm. i have soccer practice til 1p so can meet after.

———

John, 2:00 a.m.: Kate, you never texted me back yesterday. You okay?

John, 2:01 a.m.: You want me to come out there?

John, 2:07 a.m.: Will be back in NY tomorrow evening. Looking into flights to Santa Rosa.

John, 2:15 a.m.: Can be there Mon pm or Tues am. Let me know what you want me to do.

———

"I think I recognize you from the funeral," Kate said.

The midday sun ricocheted off the athletic center's sheer white walls. Rex squinted against it. A line of perspiration still beaded his forehead, but his dark-red curls were wet and pine scented, freshly washed.

"Yeah, I was there," he said. He heaved his duffel bag higher onto his shoulder. "Sorry if I was shy. I'm not good at that kind of thing."

Wordlessly, he started down the path that ran parallel to the soccer fields below. Kate followed him.

"No one should be good at these kinds of things," Kate said.

"Good point," Rex said. He sounded tired. Kate felt somehow responsible for that.

"Can I get you something to drink? Or eat?" she asked.

"No, thanks. It takes me a while to get hungry after practice." Rex sat down on a bench overlooking the baseball diamond. Kate sat on the other side of his bag, which he'd stacked on the bench beside him. The bulk of it threatened to slip off the narrow seat.

For a minute or two they stared straight ahead, watching a handful of figures in bright shirts on the field, the occasional *thwack* of the ball and their distant voices floating up toward them.

Finally, Kate said, "Is it okay if I ask you about Jake?"

"Sure." Rex's gaze remained fixed on the field below.

"Do you remember the last time you saw him?" Kate softened the tenor of the question; she didn't want to sound like she was launching an interrogation, even if she technically was.

"Of course I do, yeah. It was only a couple weeks ago. I went over to his place and we talked for a little."

"How did he seem?"

"He was being weird before that. We were close over the summer when we worked in the library together. But earlier this year he kind of ghosted me. I wanted to go over there and clear the air."

"Did you?"

Rex shrugged. "When I got there, Jake was acting normal, like nothing had happened between us. When I asked him why he was ignoring me, he said he was sorry, he didn't mean to ignore me, but he was just busy with this group he'd joined. But then he rushed me out. He said he was meeting someone else that night. I didn't hear from him again after that. I really wanted us to be friends again, but I took the hint."

"Hang on," Kate said. "He said he joined a group?"

"Yeah. He didn't tell me any details, but I'm assuming it was one of the campus societies. Stars & Spears, I think it was called."

Kate felt a flicker of alarm. "He didn't tell you anything about it?"

"No, not really. Some of the members were trying to poach him late last year, but after he joined, he never talked about it."

"So secret societies are actually secret here."

"Kind of. Paloma has a few of them, but I don't think they're as popular as they used to be. It's kind of uncool, actually. Especially now, after Covid, people just don't have the patience for that kind of elitist bullshit. We all just want to get back to normal." Then Rex turned to her. Two bright-pink spots appeared on his cheeks. "I didn't mean to suggest that Jake was uncool. He was actually one of the coolest people I'd ever met. Did you know he was pretty good at photography?"

"I didn't know he was interested in photography," Kate admitted. Her heart sank directly to her feet. "He never told me that."

"He didn't technically tell me, either. Last summer he bought some of those old-school disposable cameras at the drugstore and started taking pictures of everything. One day he just took a picture of me when we were in the stacks. The librarians gave him shit for it, but he didn't care. He just kept doing it."

"That sounds like him," Kate said. Jake had always been quietly defiant—if that was even the right term for it. In reality, Kate reflected now, Jake simply had a hard time doing things he didn't want to do, and that resistance occasionally exhibited itself as rebelliousness. *The kid can't get out of his own way,* John had said to her once.

"I told him he should post some of his stuff, but he was basically allergic to social media. He didn't want the attention," Rex said.

Now *that* sounded like Jake.

"I wonder where all his photographs are," Kate said. "I haven't found any of them in his apartment."

"I remember him putting them into his desk drawer after he showed them to me. I don't know where else he would've put them."

Kate told herself to look through his desk drawers again, though she was fairly confident she could catalog every last item in his apartment.

The baseball players had begun to pack up their equipment and hike up the hill, their faces bright with wind and exertion. Rex began fussing with the strap on his bag. He slung it over his shoulder, waiting for her dismissal.

"Well, I'm sure you have lots going on today," Kate offered. "Thank you for meeting with me."

"That's okay," Rex said. He stood to leave. Then he added, "I'm sorry I couldn't do more for Jake. When I think about it now, it was so obvious he was in a bad place. I should've known he needed help." He paused, his throat working. "I'll never forgive myself for not seeing it earlier."

"We're all telling ourselves the same thing," Kate said. "But we have to believe that there's nothing we could have done. It's the only way to move forward."

She didn't fully believe the words herself, but they were what this boy needed to hear. She wanted him to keep going, to do everything Jake didn't have the opportunity to do, and everything she couldn't seem to do now, either.

After Rex left, she remained on the bench and let the sun beat down on her face. She pulled her phone out of Jake's coat pocket.

Do whatever you feel is right for you, she texted John. It was passive aggressive, and a little bit petty, but that was the truth. Come; don't come. As long as he didn't get in the way of her investigation, she didn't really care what he did.

For now, Kate sensed her next step beginning to take shape.

She swiped to her messages with Luna. From their conversation at the bar last night, the woman had not only proved to be interested in Kate's investigation but seemed to believe in its validity, too—even become invested in it.

It wasn't until that conversation that Kate had realized how alone she was in all of this. And that it felt so much better not to be. So she sent Luna a text.

Kate, 1:27 p.m.: I think I need to follow up with Lowman.

Luna, 1:34 p.m.: Good idea

Kate, 1:35 p.m.: Emailing him now.

Luna, 1:35 p.m.: Eh, that gives him the option of ignoring you.

Kate, 1:36 p.m.: What else can I do? Knock on his door?

Luna, 1:36 p.m.: That's exactly what you do

Luna, 1:36 p.m.: One sec. Checking staff directory

Luna, 1:39 p.m.: 67 Willow Ave

Luna, 1:39 p.m.: Get to work

People didn't really knock on doors anymore, but Luna was right: it was the only way to catch him off guard. And she needed him that way—back in that vulnerable position she'd seen him sink into when he'd looked at Parker Deily's photograph.

She clung to this line of reasoning on her way back to Jake's apartment, where she opened the half fridge in Jake's tiny kitchen, in search of lunch. The leftover mac and cheese had congealed into a wedge inside its recycled cardboard box. It was solid enough to pick up with her hands. She ate it that way, standing in front of the open refrigerator. There was also half a bottle of white wine, sloppily corked. Less than half. She'd opened it two days ago; if she didn't finish it now, she'd have to spill it, and dumping perfectly good wine was one of her cardinal sins.

Fortified, she grabbed her phone and plugged Dr. Lowman's address into the Maps app. It was within walking distance. The phone felt funny in her hand, and it was cracked and encased in rainbow plastic.

This wasn't her phone. It was Jake's.

She supposed it didn't matter either way. It'd get her where she needed to go.

She turned on the app's directions, turned up the volume, and followed its voice—a capable yet insistent female whom, after a few paces together, Kate dubbed Diane—out the door and into the street.

Tethered to Diane's lead, she watched Main Street give way to the quiet main road and then, after a few turns, to a charming residential area made up of tiny bungalows on stamp-sized lots. Most were done up in Halloween decorations. She counted four mailboxes veiled in cottony spiderwebs and stuck with black plastic spiders. Across the street, two skeletons clad in floral sundresses languished on a porch swing; the front yard beside it was transformed into a disconcertingly realistic-looking graveyard.

59, 61, 63. She slowed as she approached number 67, grappling to maintain her nerve. Before it slipped from her grasp entirely, she walked down the pumpkin-lined path to the front door. She pressed the doorbell. Its echo ricocheted through the house.

She pressed it again, more insistently this time, as if the force of her finger made any difference to the intensity of the sound.

And maybe it did.

She heard footsteps approaching the door. The doorknob

turned, seemingly in slow motion, and she really thought she might throw up.

The door opened, revealing a woman who looked to be around Kate's age, maybe a little younger. Not a goateed man in a fedora, then. She wore her hair in two long, dark braids, the ends dangling near her waist. She held a silver soup spoon in one hand, and the other was encrusted in brightly colored rings, each stone the size of a mini jawbreaker. The woman considered Kate with the normal amount of suspicion, though she didn't seem particularly hostile.

Kate took a moment to reorient herself. Then she said: "Hi. I'm looking for Dr. Lowman?"

The woman shifted on her bare feet. "Sorry—who are you?"

"I'm Kate Cleary. I'm the mother of one of his students."

"Is this about a grade?"

"I'm sorry?"

"A grade," the woman repeated. "If your kid is unhappy with their grade, tell them to speak to Steve directly. You won't be able to argue on their behalf. I'm sorry, but it just won't work."

Kate felt her anger rising, her tongue slipping loose of her control. "My kid is dead."

The woman's mouth worked soundlessly as she reached for a response. There was something delicious in the pantomime, in knowing that Kate had reduced this woman to a puppet with four simple, terrible words.

"I'm sorry," the woman said. *I'm becoming a monster*, Kate thought. "But I still don't understand why you're here."

"I believe Dr. Lowman knew my son." Kate took a step closer, edging toward the step that led up to the door. "Is he here?"

The woman looked behind her. Kate followed her gaze into the house. In the foyer, there was an antique console table and a round mirror affixed to the wall above it. The table held a book, a set of keys, and an irregularly shaped orange dish.

A cream-colored crocheted sweater had been tossed carelessly over the end. The smell of onions and garlic wafted toward her.

Turning back to Kate, the woman said, "He's working right now. I don't want to disturb him."

"Are you his partner?"

"Yes, I'm his wife."

"Has he told you about Stars & Spears?"

"Excuse me?"

"Stars & Spears. It's a secret society at Paloma. I have reason to believe that my son was involved in it, as was Sasha Williams, as was Parker Deily before them. I also have reason to believe that all three students died because of that society, and that your husband knows more about it than he initially led me to believe. So that's what I'm here to ask him about. Okay? Will you let me in now?"

The woman's eyes glittered with anger. "I'm very sorry for your loss, and it's clear that you're grieving, but I can't stand here and listen to you accuse my husband of . . . whatever it is that you're accusing him of. This is just ludicrous."

She began to close the door, and at that moment some wildness sprang free inside of Kate; she lunged up the step and caught the door, forcing it open just as the woman attempted to shut it. The woman went still, her face cracked into terror. Time suspended as the two stared at one another, one in shock and the other in purest anger, washed clean of all thought, all intention funneled into the smooth block of wood beneath her hands. She would not budge.

It was the other woman who shattered the stalemate—she screamed her husband's name, turning behind her, and as she did, the door slipped from her grip.

Kate moved. She edged herself through the door, brushing past the professor's wife. She was vaguely aware of the house around her—the walls were painted maroon, and a tiny cotton bud of a dog yelped underfoot—but she followed her instincts, the natural flow of the home, until she reached a closed door down the narrow hallway connecting the kitchen to the living room. The woman's scream for her husband echoed behind her.

The door opened. Dr. Lowman's face was contorted with fear, but it smoothed into recognition when his gaze fixed on her.

"What the hell are you doing here?"

Dr. Lowman's wife appeared then, her soup spoon held aloft like a weapon. Kate stifled a laugh—the comedy was undeniable, even amidst the drama—but then she remembered that anything could be used as a weapon, so long as the person wielding it worked up the right amount of adrenaline. A spoon: you could scoop someone's eyes out with that.

"This woman!" the wife screamed. "Steve, she barged right in! She pushed me! I couldn't stop her!"

The professor laid a hand on his wife's arm. Kate watched the woman's frenzy melting, ever so slightly, beneath his touch.

"Mariah," he said gently, "please, don't worry. She's harmless." He turned his gaze back to Kate. It was strangely empty. "Kate, I told you in my office that I can't help you."

But she was not his wife; she would not be placated.

"That's not true, though, is it?" she started. Technically she could hear herself, but the words took on a telescopic effect, like she was listening to herself from a great distance. "You had something to do with Stars & Spears. You practically told me that yourself. And I know that Jake was in Stars & Spears, and I know Sasha Williams was, too, and don't think I don't know about Parker Deily—I *know* he killed himself. Don't you think that's strange? Too strange to be a coincidence? That's because it's *not* a coincidence—it's a pattern. And the pattern leads back to you. So you need to tell me, right now, what you did to those kids."

Somewhere near the end of the last sentence, she found herself sinking to the floor, and though she knew that she shouldn't do such a thing, that the act would undermine her authority, completely destroy the veracity of her case, she was helpless against gravity and her legs simply wouldn't work.

Dr. Lowman and Mariah murmured to each other above her, but that sense, too, had broken down; their words were strangely muffled and echoing at once, like they were conversing from the inside of a seashell. She also couldn't feel her tongue anymore. She was struck by a memory of herself at a very young age, having just thrown a tantrum and then collapsing to the floor, just like this, and lying fully prostrate at her parents' feet. She couldn't remember what the trigger was, and that detail didn't matter. What mattered was the memory of them humming inaudibly above her, their tone unreadable, likely deciding between themselves whether to mete out punishment or comfort. She remembered an inability to feel her limbs. She remembered the sensation as blissful, a balloon sliced free of its ribbon. She remembered her father's big, warm hand cupping the entirety of her soft head. She remembered his low honey voice coaxing her off the ground. She remembered the smell of garlic and onions, being led to another room, and then being gently pushed into a deep velvety couch, followed by the feeling of something hot and smooth placed between her hands and a question dangled in front of her: "Who can we call for you?"

"What?"

Dr. Lowman—Steve—appeared beside her on the couch. "Can we call someone to pick you up? It looks like you walked here. I don't see a car in the driveway."

All at once, Kate's senses slammed back into her body. Her ears rang with the impact; her vision cleared.

"Oh," she said. "No, don't call anyone. I can walk back."

"I'm sorry, I can't let you do that. Surely there must be someone we can call."

Mariah fluttered into the armchair to Kate's left. "We would drive you back," she offered, "but we're very busy here."

"Making soup?"

Mariah bristled. "We're hosting a dinner party this evening. And it's a very complicated recipe."

"We can call you a car," Steve said, "but I would feel much more comfortable knowing you weren't alone."

Why were these people being so nice to her? Was it possible that these were good people? Was it possible she had been wrong about the professor? She peered down at the tea that one of them had given her. The water turned a muddy citrine color. She hadn't tasted it, and she probably shouldn't, just to be safe. She didn't like tea, anyway.

She set the mug down on the coffee table and stood from the couch. It was an effort to release herself from its deep cushions.

"I don't have my phone with me," she said, somewhat robotically, "and I don't have anyone's number memorized. Except for my son's, and my ex-husband's, but they're not here."

She made for the door. Dr. Lowman followed her, leaving Mariah anxiously waiting in the living room.

"Let me call you a car. It's really no bother."

"No," she said, with finality. "Enjoy your dinner party."

Then she left, and though she was confident she could find her way back from memory, she still summoned Diane to life through Jake's phone. She couldn't shake the feeling that she had just been made to feel crazy. She followed each step of Diane's instructions vengefully, as if to prove to the world that her faculties still obeyed her control.

But when she returned to the apartment, she stood dumbly inside the door. What else was there to do? Today was Friday; Jake had no classes. It was just past four in the afternoon, but the light had already begun to fade. Taking an Ambien and disappearing for the next few hours was tempting, but she was down to her last two pills, and she had to ration them wisely; she hadn't gotten around to refilling her prescription. There was another bottle of wine in the fridge, a pretty nice sauvignon blanc, but the fridge was so far away. Kate took off her shoes and her pants and tucked herself under the covers.

Before she got around to closing her eyes, she heard a phone buzz. She reached for her phone, which she'd left on Jake's bedside table before she left this morning.

There were no messages. She waited for another moment; the phone buzzed again.

It wasn't coming from her phone—it was coming from Jake's.

She pulled it out of the back pocket of her jeans, which lay crumpled on the floor beside the bed.

Kate squinted at the screen. There were texts from an unfamiliar number. Jake hadn't saved the person's contact information in his phone, and Kate didn't recognize the area code.

4:05 p.m.: kate, i know you're reading this

4:05 p.m.: you need to stop whatever you're doing

4:12 p.m.: i honestly don't mean to scare you or anything but i'm actually dead fucking serious. you need to stop

4:13 p.m.: it's for your own good

4:13 p.m.: actually, its for jake's own good

CHAPTER TWELVE

Kate, 4:14 p.m.: Who is this?

Kate, 4:14 p.m.: I know you're there.

Kate, 4:15 p.m.: I'm not going to threaten you. I just want to know who you are.

Kate, 4:17 p.m.: What are you so afraid of?

Kate tried to do a reverse Google search on the number, but other than identifying a Los Angeles County area code, the results came up empty. Still, Kate knew this had to be someone Dr. Lowman had tipped off to Kate's visit that afternoon. Perhaps another member of Stars & Spears, someone with just as much to lose as he did if she blew up whatever secret they were sitting on.

Kate knew it wasn't Dr. Lowman himself—she couldn't imagine the professor using the phrase *dead fucking serious* or typing in all lowercase. That was something Jake and his friends did. No, this had to be a student.

Either way, why play chicken? She wouldn't be scared off so easily, especially not with some meek text messages. A bloody finger in the mailbox, maybe. But this was amateur.

As she typed out her next text, the screen suddenly cut out. A call from John was coming in.

"I don't have time to talk," she said in greeting.

"Hello, Kate. How are you?"

"Busy," she responded. "What's up?"

"Busy with what?"

"I relieved you of the right to ask that question thirteen years ago."

"As you're the mother of my son, I have the right to ask you whatever the hell I want."

"Okay, John. Let's be civil."

"That's what I'm trying to do," John said. "You're the one putting up defenses."

Kate didn't mean to pick a fight with John; she almost never *meant* to pick a fight with him, but 90 percent of their conversations somehow diverted onto that track. It had never not been like this, even in the early days, but in the early days they'd romanticized their oil-and-water dynamic, fancied themselves ironic proof of the "opposites attract" cliché. Plus, they both really liked fighting; it was a sport for them, and usually erotic. But sports were exhausting without breaks. And the eroticism wore off well before they'd benched themselves.

"You know," John said now, "I don't care if you're working the register at some granola bar alfalfa sprout grocery store in the Haight. I just want you to engage in something. Anything."

Well, Kate *was* engaged in something, and it was definitely more meaningful than whatever John had been distracting himself with in Bali these past two weeks.

But she couldn't tell John about any of it. Her investigation was too new to share with him, and he had just as much to gain as she did if she cracked it. She didn't want to make him any promises yet.

And John thought she was crazy enough as it was.

"I'm getting out of bed every morning," Kate offered. Not a lie, but not the truth. "I'm exercising; I'm feeding myself. I'm putting pants on. Sometimes I'm even reading the newspaper. That's more than enough."

"Would you consider moving out of Jake's apartment?"

"I, for one, cannot fathom jetting off to Indonesia directly after burying my son."

John sighed into the phone. Kate had never seen his apartment in New York, but she could imagine him swiveling around in his Eames executive chair to face the outsized window behind him, assuaging his pseudofrustration with the sight of that glittering Midtown skyline unfurling at his feet.

"I didn't 'jet off,'" he said. "I had to meet an important client who may or may not have found himself in possession of a Camille Pissarro, which may or may not have been looted in a certain world war. To his ignorance, I'll add, and through the machinations of a particularly morally corrupt antiques dealer."

Kate physically waved her hand in front of her face. "Please, stop explaining yourself. I don't need to hear about your Nazi-sympathizer clients."

"That's not even remotely funny—"

"But I truly am busy right now. Tell me what you decided to do about flying out here, and I'll put it in my calendar."

"I'm on the six p.m. flight tonight. I get into Santa Rosa at around nine p.m., which gets me to Sutter Point at ten, ten thirty. I'll stay at the hotel downtown. You're welcome to join me for a nightcap at the bar. Good martinis, as I remember. Otherwise I'll see you tomorrow."

"See you tomorrow."

When she hung up, she immediately checked her messages: still no answer from the anonymous number, but that didn't matter. She had no problem asking Wachs for help. She popped in her earbuds, dialed the station, and headed over to the kitchenette. Felix picked up on the third ring.

"Felix, hi, this is Kate Cleary." The same spread from this morning greeted her inside the fridge, sans congealed mac and cheese. "Is Detective Wachs available? I need to speak with him."

"I'm sorry, Kate, but he's not at his desk right now. Are you okay?"

"I'm not in immediate danger, but this is somewhat urgent."

"I can take a message for you. He'll be back in the office within the hour."

A written message would give Wachs the opportunity to ignore her. Better to show up in person, force him to answer her questions.

"No need," she said, "I'll just come down there myself." Felix's dissatisfaction was virtually audible. She hung up, unscrewed the sauv blanc, and poured a third of it into one of Jake's little Mason jam jars. Pants, shoes, coat back on.

By the time she left the apartment, it was dusk, the kind of dusty, concealing light that Kate had to squint in to see.

When she arrived a few minutes later, the station was quiet, almost sleepy. Behind the desk, Felix looked resigned to see her. He had the watery brown eyes and placid, long-suffering demeanor of a hound. His long hair was glossy and thick and pulled back into a slick ponytail, secured with something that looked like twine. That detail broke Kate's heart a little bit. Did he not know that he could just buy a pack of fifty Goody hair elastics for, like, three dollars at the drugstore? Or did he in fact know this but choose to create his own hair tie in a show of self-expression, or self-reliance? Was he one of those survivalist types? That all seemed at odds with the values of law enforcement. Maybe they provided good healthcare, she thought.

"Hi, Felix," she said. "Any chance Wachs is back yet?"

"He just got back a couple of minutes ago," Felix said, "but he's in a debrief right now."

"How long will that be?"

"As long as it takes."

Kate glanced at the waiting area behind her. It was populated by one beleaguered-looking woman in a shag coat dyed the radioactive orange of a Sunkist bottle. Across from her, a white woman with dreadlocks stole bites from a granola bar from beneath her KN95 mask. Otherwise it was empty.

"No problem," Kate said. "I can wait here."

Felix gave her a kind of quavering smile. "Your call."

Kate found a chair as far away from the two other women as possible. There were small plastic tables between the rows of chairs, like in a doctor's office, but without the courtesy of reading material. She reached into her coat's right pocket for Jake's phone.

She gained purchase on nothing. Nothing was in her pocket. A wave of panic washed over her; how could she have forgotten the phone? The very thing she had come here to show Wachs? She searched the other pocket. It was also empty. Scrambling now, she felt around inside the coat, dipped a finger into the hidden chest pocket and another into the other one—both empty, except for Jake's ancient crumpled tissue. She held the tissue in her fist. Then, as she ran an exploratory hand over the smooth nylon lining, she felt something hard, plasticky, zigzaggy: a zipper. Something rectangular lay underneath the fabric.

She unzipped the secret pocket and pulled out the object. It was a sheaf of photographs.

Her hands were shaking. A tang pinged around inside her nose. She glanced over at the orange woman—her eyes were still closed; a little concerning—then over to Felix, who was busy on the phone.

Discreetly, she turned her attention to the slim stack of photographs. There were five in all. She sifted through them, one by one, and then studied each more closely.

The first: Eight people standing in a line, clad in black togas and arranged in height order. Black kerchiefs covered their mouths. The background was swallowed in darkness, but the flash had picked up the outlines of leafy branches behind them and a cleared patch of dirt beneath their feet.

The second: An off-the-cuff portrait, taken from less than a foot away. Three people held up their books of Blake poetry—the same one Jake had—so that they concealed their mouths. The flash had turned their pupils bright red. (It struck Kate as uncharacteristically cruel of Jake to have set off the flash so close to their faces.) The person on the left had long black hair. This was Sasha Williams. Kate didn't recognize the other two girls, one with tight bleached curls and a ring through her right eyebrow, the other strawberry blond, her hazel eyes offset with a slick of lime-green eyeliner, a chunky silver ring encircling each finger. She remembered what the librarian in Toller had told her—that a young woman with blond hair had been waiting for Jake outside the Rollinson room. Could that person have been one of the girls in this picture?

Then the third: The remnants of a party scene, taken in the same wooded area as the first photograph. A girl in a dirt-streaked white dress leaned partly out of the frame. She looked like she was reaching for something on the ground, out of the camera's line of sight. A whitish blur stalked at her back—it was a person, running toward her.

The fourth: the edge of a gilded mirror.

The fifth: Jake's white sneakers, streaked with blood.

"Kate?"

Felix was beckoning her over to the desk. Her nose was running. She used Jake's tissue to dab at it.

"Wachs can see you now," he said as she approached the desk. "Follow me."

Felix led her to the detective's office. The door was open, but he knocked anyway. Wachs summoned her in. It felt like a month ago, a year, that Kate was last here. During that interminable time Wachs had cleaned up his five-o'clock shadow, which was probably regulation, but nevertheless unfortunate; he'd benefited from that concealing dusting of hair, like so many men did. With his newly naked face, Kate saw that his chin was ever so slightly recessed, rendering his long nose—which, in certain lights, could pass for aquiline, or Roman—somewhat timid and birdlike. She hadn't noticed that the first time they'd met.

"What can I do for you, Kate?" he asked. "Felix tells me something urgent came up?"

Was that condescension in his tone? Coddling in his softened gaze? Kate brushed it off. What mattered was that she was here, in front of him, and she would make him see what she saw.

"Originally, I came to tell you that an anonymous number texted me a threatening message," she said.

"Can I see the texts?"

"I forgot the phone."

"Well, then."

"But now I have something else to show you."

She pushed the photographs across the desk. For the next few seconds, she studied Wachs studying the images. The room was silent, intercepted by the occasional click of the photos on the table.

Finally, he said, "What am I looking at, Kate?"

"I found them in Jake's coat pocket. I think they have something to do with how he died. Don't they look suspicious to you?"

"I have to be honest, Kate—no, they don't." He tapped the photographs into a neat pile, then handed them back over the desk. Kate brought them to her lap, careful not to smudge them. "Looks to me like a bunch of college kids doing whatever college kids do. And some creative observations."

"But what about these bloody shoes? And this one, the second one—that's Sasha Williams."

Wachs's voice lowered. "Sasha and Jake died by suicide, Kate. You know this. You brought me his note yourself."

"It's not as simple as that," she said.

"Occam's razor. The simplest explanation is often the truth."

"That theory doesn't always apply. Hence why it's a *theory*, not a rule."

Wachs moved a mug off to the side of his desk. It was chipped at the lip, a gleaming navy blue, and read *My Favorite Niece Gave Me This Mug* in Papyrus font. "I'm going to ask you a serious question right now, and I hope you don't get offended," he said.

"Here we go."

"Have you sought professional help? To process your grief?"

"Oh, please."

"I've seen cases like this so many times before," Wachs continued, unfazed by her pettiness. "People drown in their grief. They lose sight of reality. They sacrifice their wellness, their livelihood, in service of that grief. It can happen suddenly, or it can happen gradually, and I fear that this is happening to you, but it's possible that you don't see it yet yourself. I hope you can get a handle on it."

Kate zipped the photographs back into their secret pocket and stood from her chair. "Look, I appreciate your concern. But

my son needs help—I don't. It's clear that you're unwilling to
provide that for him, so I'm going to find someone who can."

Wachs nodded. "That's your prerogative. But think about
what I said." He held up a finger, signaling for her to wait, then
dug inside his desk drawer. He produced a small white business
card and slid it toward Kate. She squinted to read it: *Dr. Terri
Conover, LCSW, MSW. Clinical psychologist.*

"She specializes in suicide cases," Wachs said.

"Her name ends in an *i*," Kate said.

"It sure does."

"Does she dot the *i* or put a little bubble over it? Or a heart?"

"Be reasonable."

"It's a joke," Kate said, pocketing the business card. "See? I
still have a sense of humor."

The thing was, she didn't know who could help her. She
needed someone tech savvy to trace the number properly, or else
someone who could identify the other girl in the picture, the
one with the eyebrow ring. The office of the registrar, maybe,
though it was already five p.m.; most university buildings were
closed by now. But she couldn't bear the thought of waiting another two days with this information. What would she possibly
do with herself? How would she survive the not-knowing? So she
speed-walked back to campus, her gait hitching to a run when
a ripple of panic overtook her. When she reached the registrar's
office, she hurled herself at the double doors and wrenched them
open. She nearly flung herself backward—they were unlocked.

The building was still, the lights dimmed in preparation to
close. In the far corner of the lobby, a janitor mopped the floor
in successive infinity signs. The receptionist stood behind the
desk, packing folders and a shimmery pink thermos into her
bag. Kate rushed over and brandished the photograph in front
of the young woman.

"This one," she said, pointing at the curly-haired girl in the photograph. "Can you help me identify this person?"

The receptionist froze. A clump of turquoise mascara clung to her inner lashes. "I'm sorry," she said, in a slow, patient voice. "I don't think that's something we can do for you."

"You don't think? Or you know?"

"I know we can't, ma'am," she said, "and we're closing in five minutes."

At that moment, a dumpling-shaped woman in a floral caftan emerged from the office behind the front desk, borne on a cloud of Shalimar perfume. She dropped a bundle of papers onto the receptionist's desk.

"Can you make me three copies of these, hon?" she said. The younger woman eyed the stack like it was a pile of fresh shit.

Then the floral woman noticed Kate, still standing there, still dumbly holding up the photograph like it was fucking show-and-tell. She lowered her glasses onto her nose and squinted at the image.

"How did you get that picture?" she said.

"It's my son's."

The woman pointed to the girl with the curls. "You know her?"

Kate's heart lurched. "No. Do you?"

The woman sighed, then pushed her glasses back up her nose, signaling the end of the conversation. "Not personally, no," she said. "But I hope she's getting the help she needs, poor girl. Tragic. Just tragic."

CHAPTER THIRTEEN

They met a few days before the second semester of his sophomore year. It happened in the bookstore.

Jake was there for books, obviously, but he was also there for a hoodie, or a shirt, or maybe even a jersey. (Actually, no. He could never wear a jersey.) Back in high school, he'd adopted a firm anti-merch stance. Refused his mom when she'd insisted on buying him a token of his success after he'd gotten into Paloma—just a pen, she'd urged, or even a fridge magnet!—and he maintained this stance well into his freshman year. He'd thought it was poser-y to wear a garment bearing a college logo to the actual college. It was like wearing a band's T-shirt to the band's own concert. Or worse: the opener's T-shirt.

But it turned out that everyone at school wore shirts and hoodies and caps and athletic shorts, and even backpacks and messenger bags, even everything all at once. The whole campus was awash in yellow and maroon. And then there was Jake, in his plain white T-shirts yellowed at the armpits and his retro black JanSport, the kind with the camel leather trimming the bottom, nary a patch or key chain adorning the canvas. Not an ounce of school pride to be found, but more importantly no discernible personality. He was the one who felt like the poser. How could anyone think that he belonged here if he didn't have the shirt to prove it?

First day back on campus after Christmas break and Jake headed straight to the bookstore.

He was flipping through an assortment of gray long-sleeved T-shirts at one end of the rack. She was at the other end. They met in the middle. Talk about a meet-cute.

Their knuckles grazed. Jake felt his face go red. The last time he'd touched someone was over two months ago, right before Thanksgiving break. He'd hooked up with a townie girl at the Levee, a dive bar a couple of towns over that famously never carded and which Rex had dragged Jake to, baiting him with the promise that he would buy all their drinks that night, plus optional bar snacks.

There was a girl at that bar. She was cute, he guessed. He liked her drawn-on freckles and the wash of blue-red blush across her nose. Her hair was blond, unbrushed, shot through with black highlights, and shaped into a complicated arrangement that resembled a bird's nest perched on a high, thin bough. So Jake liked how she looked, okay, but mostly he liked that she approached him and then proceeded to talk for almost an hour, virtually uninterrupted, about things that weren't not interesting. Like: Her cousin had special-ordered a dildo in the shape and color of a dragon penis. Or what the manufacturer *imagined* a dragon penis might look like. Also, Baba Yaga, of Slavic folklore fame, lived in a house deep in the forest that stood on chicken legs. Also, did Jake know that Marie Antoinette was only fourteen years old when she was married off to Louis XVI, and that among the public she was called "the bitch," but in French?

This ability to conjure things to say, without hesitation, was a trait Jake admired in people. It must've been like channeling from the beyond. Jake was wondering whether they should exchange numbers or Instagram handles, like maybe he should see if this could turn into something, but then she went down on him behind the dumpster out back and she didn't seem like she wanted anything else. He lost his nerve as soon as he zipped up his pants.

"Sorry," Jake said now, to the girl at the rack whose hand he'd just touched, then instantly jerked back from, inelegantly, like her flesh was a hot stove.

"That's okay," she said. He risked a glance at her, and then he stole another, closer look. Something was missing from her face. A barbell skewered her eyebrow.

"Did that hurt?" he said, gesturing to his own eyebrow.

"What," she said. "The piercing or the bleach?"

So that was what it was, the thing that was off about her face: her brows were bleached to nothing to match her curly wolf cut, which tumbled down her back and narrowed into a V.

"Or when I fell from the sky?" she said next.

"What?" he said.

She turned herself cross-eyed. An imitation of an idiot. "'Did it hurt? When you fell from the sky? Because you're an angel.'" Eyes uncrossed. "You've never heard that before?"

"Oh," Jake said. "You're talking about pickup lines."

The girl arched a nonexistent eyebrow. "For some reason, I believe your ignorance."

They both settled on a shirt—the same one, in the same size—and then they walked over to the actual bookstore portion of the bookstore, picked out what they needed for the semester ahead, and talked lightly about themselves. Her name was Tanya, and she was a junior. She lived in an apartment off campus with two other girls, which struck Jake as enviously advanced; people typically didn't move off campus until senior year. She was a Poli Sci major. He admitted that he was undeclared but leaning toward English. Reading was the only form of escapism he had yet to find that was not only accepted in every way that mattered—socially, intellectually, academically—but rewarded. It was like burying a sleeping pill in peanut butter. *That's a thoughtful response*, Tanya said. It was clear that she was smarter than him, and also more ambitious. He didn't even know what Poli Sci was, technically, or what you did with it after graduation. She said a Poli Sci degree was famously versatile but more functional than an English degree. No offense. (None taken.) She planned to go to law school and ultimately become a human rights attorney. He planned nothing. To clarify: He didn't plan *on* nothing, but he couldn't fathom what lay beyond graduation. It was still two and a half years away. He couldn't even think about next week. Considering either conjured a sensation that felt eerily like vertigo.

In retrospect, Jake didn't know why Tanya had ever responded to his anemic attempt at conversation, nor was he entirely sure why he struck it up with her in the first place. That was very unlike him. Usually, initiating conversation felt to Jake like hard labor, and after weathering the one-two punch of quarantine and the trash fire that was freshman year, his muscles had shriveled into candy floss. He literally had one friend, and sometimes that felt like one friend too many.

But Tanya was easy with herself, and that made Jake feel safe, if not entirely at ease himself. Her voice was loud and steady and had a natural rasp to it, which evoked the glamorous world-weariness of an Old Hollywood film star, and she possessed the stunning competence found more often in people much older than she. For instance, Jake would soon watch, internally slack jawed, as she solved the following problems without hesitation: how to clean the wire rack in a toaster oven; how to negotiate an A-minus to an A; how to remove a splinter from the bottom of a foot; how to effortlessly decline an invitation to a party while maintaining that one was generally a cool and fun person and would be an asset to a future party to which one would, naturally, be invited.

Whatever Tanya's reasons for wanting to be friends with him, he was . . . grateful? No, that wasn't the right emotion. Being with other people was burdensome. But Jake knew that being by himself was "wrong," according to the culture.

Beyond that, a lot of silence and loneliness always enabled that twisted, poisonous creature that'd taken root within himself over a year ago to flourish. That was unacceptable, because that creature no longer made him feel defeated. It made him unbearably angry. And that was much scarier.

And there was nothing wrong with Tanya, as far as he could see, nor was there anything discernibly wrong with the friends she introduced him to a few days after they first met. Being with her, and her coterie of friends, made Jake feel like he was normal. Or at least not-wrong.

Jake met them on a Thursday night, when Tanya hosted them all at her apartment above the health food store on Willow Street, as she purportedly did every single Thursday night. Everyone tossed their phones into a fishbowl, which then went into the coat closet, and then Tanya introduced them all to Jake.

There were her roommates, Taylor and Jess, a pair of milk-fed redheads with sailor's mouths who turned out to be twins, visually distinguishable only by the density of their freckles (Taylor: a scattering; Jess: drowning in them) and the color of their nail polish (iridescent blue for Taylor, black for Jess). There was Jordan, a physics major in a lace bra and a men's leather blazer who volunteered to Jake, much later and many drinks into the night, that she made upward of $1,800 a month selling feet pics. Jake told her he admired her hustle; he wouldn't be brave enough to do something like that. *What people still don't seem to get,* Jordan said, *is that sex work is work like any other.* There was Sasha, who majored in Biochem and minored in Molecular & Cellular Biology—a track even more mystifying than Poli Sci—and who Tanya had told Jake, in the few minutes before everyone else arrived, was the smartest person she had ever met. From this first meeting, Jake couldn't in confidence draw that same conclusion. After saying hello to him, Sasha had sat on the floor before the twins, who held court on the remarkably pristine white couch, and she stayed there for the entire night, save a trip to the bathroom or to top off the twins' drinks. Once, when Jake got near enough, he heard her reciting what sounded like a few stanzas of poetry, which the three of them then heatedly discussed.

Finally there were the boys—gangly Ariel, whose Adam's apple protruded from his neck practically at a right angle; Ryan, louche in a slouchy vintage suit and a silk shirt; and Nic, the only senior of the group—the latter of whom cornered Jake in the kitchen soon after he arrived and asked Jake, point blank, where he'd come from.

"San Francisco?" Jake had offered.

"No," Nic had said. "I mean, like, how did you end up here? Tonight?"

He had at least five inches on Jake and a jaw like a hatchet. He exuded the kind of uncomplicated maleness that felt like an affront, despite the delicate wire-framed glasses and floral button-down shirt he wore in a probable attempt to soften it.

When Jake failed to answer, Nic shook his head and smiled. *Never mind.*

Jake wasn't confident that he had made a good impression

that night. After the party, back in his bed, he tortured himself with a play-by-play of the entire evening, which promptly devolved into a highlight reel of every awkward thing he'd said and every misstep he'd taken, and set it on a loop till morning.

But apparently, things weren't as bad as he'd thought. Tanya texted him the next day to say that she, Jordan, and Ryan were heading over to the library in an hour, and did he wanna come?

Jake had no idea how this was possible. Part of him mistrusted Tanya's intentions. Part of him wondered if the group had snagged him into some complex ruse to mortify him for their own perverted entertainment—targeted him, from afar, for his obvious vulnerability; used Tanya's gregariousness as bait; were currently in the process of obtaining a few gallons of pig's blood to ultimately pour over his head in a public forum.

Soon, though, those parts of him quieted, even if they never completely disappeared. These people were pretty good people, and there were moments with them when Jake had so much fun that he was almost elated. Even Nic cooled it with the aggressive act, and in some moments, he revealed himself to be much more earnest than he'd let on. For instance, he was hopelessly in love with Taylor, and that love went unrequited—she was hooking up with someone else, a different, unaffiliated senior named Rudy, with whom she would disappear for days at a time. That didn't lead him to spin a vengeful smear campaign against her, incel-style, as Jake would have expected. Instead, the more Taylor gravitated toward the other guy, the more Nic retreated from her, with surprising gentleness.

The rest of the semester was spent in a haze of as much socializing as Jake could physically handle. There were hangs all the time. No one in the group seemed capable of or interested in carrying out any task without at least one other representative present. Not eat, or drink, or study, or shop, or pick up groceries, or get dressed, or go for a drive, or go for a run, or go for a hike up to the creepy burnt-out mansion ruins and hang out there for a while, drinking bad wine and speculating about the ghost of its long-dead inhabitant, a syphilitic nutcase who died without a nose.

But Jake couldn't afford to turn down the group's invitations. The further away from himself he got, the less likely he was to give into that thing inside of him that he didn't understand.

He recognized that he was maybe using these people for his own gain. But then again, maybe everyone else was, too.

─────

The final week of the semester arrived, and with it the group's final Thursday gathering. Soon everyone would be scattering to their hometowns, other than Jake, who'd opted to stay on campus to work as a library assistant. He'd been stuck in his mom's apartment for an entire awful year, and he was in no rush to retread that contaminated ground.

Plus, he needed the money. Through Tanya's influence, Jake had convinced himself, and then his parents, to rent his own apartment next year rather than stay in the dorms. He'd lived in a single that year, anyway, and he could find someplace with a rent that was comparable to the school's room-and-board costs. So the difference was a matter of semantics: Adult; child. Free; not free.

It didn't take much coaxing for his parents to approve of the plan. His mom thought this experiment in self-reliance would be good for him. His dad didn't really care what he did, and he was happy to help Jake foot the bill if necessary.

Before Jake showed up at Tanya's apartment that final night, she'd told him that this gathering would involve something special. She didn't *warn* him, per se, but Jake was not amenable to surprises. He couldn't imagine a scenario in which this "some-thing special" was good. He'd kept himself up the night before with harrowing fantasies so intricate, so finely wrought with detail, that they'd veered into logistical: How would he get the pig's blood out of his hair?

As it turned out, no bucket fell on his head when he en-tered the apartment. The door was unlocked. Instead of the assortment of table lamps Tanya favored for her gatherings—the squat, mushroom-shaped red one on the kitchen counter; the blue-and-pink lava lamp the twins liberated from a yard sale all the way over in Bloomfield—Jake discovered a room illumi-nated solely by candles. Any candles she could get her hands on, it seemed. There was a Styrofoam square on the side table stuck with twisted pastel birthday candles. Over on the kitchen counter, a prayer-style pillar candle glowed purple, but in place of a saint on the label, Prince's visage gazed beatifically toward the heavens, both his ruffled blouse and his tower of curls ever more abundant in death. The scents of amber and vanilla em-anated from their host bodies and competed for dominance in the close air.

Everyone was already gathered in the living room, arranged on the couch and the two mismatched armchairs flanking either end. Only Nic remained standing in the corner of the room, just to the right of the couch. He was the only one who wouldn't acknowledge Jake when he walked in.

Tanya got up from her spot between the twins and handed Jake a glass of red wine. Then she locked the door behind him and told him to sit on the floor in front of the couch. Jake ob-served, in a vague way, that this was where Sasha had been seated when he'd first met her.

"Don't look so worried," Tanya said. "We're not asking you to participate in a séance."

"Or an orgy," Ariel said. Over the past few weeks he'd spangled his skinny arms in stick-and-poke tattoos. Jake knew he was supposed to think they looked cool, but he thought they looked like the random, mostly asinine scribblings on the back of a bathroom stall.

"Or a murder," Jess said. Her nails were extra long today, the edges sawed off into crisp squares. She clacked them together faux-maniacally.

Tanya gestured to the glass of wine. Jake hadn't touched it yet. "Have some of that," she offered.

"It's not spiked," Taylor said.

"That doesn't fill me with much confidence," Jake said.

Sasha turned to him. Her dark eyes went soft, like pools of melted chocolate. "Do you really think we'd do that to you?"

Sasha had only looked Jake full in the face a handful of times over the last few months, let alone talked to him at length. Jake didn't take it personally. He wouldn't be interested in making friends with him, either. But Sasha's reserve made those few moments of recognition even starker, more impactful. Jake felt ashamed, even though he couldn't identify what he'd done wrong.

Tanya held up a hand. "Guys, let's get back on track." She took a deep breath, as if preparing to dive into deep water. "No one's ever managed to figure out a graceful way of doing this, so I'll just come out and say it."

"That's not true," Ryan said. Jake's heart pounded so hard he thought he would vomit it out. A whole entire organ, right there on the rug. "Kate wrote me a poem in the same form and meter as 'The Tyger.'"

The name startled Jake. For some reason, he imagined that Ryan was talking about his mom, Kate. He imagined his mom sitting down to write a poem, referencing whatever poem Ryan had just mentioned—Jake had never heard of it—meticulously mimicking the rhyme scheme, counting on her fingers to get the sounds of the syllables exactly right. This filled him with tenderness, followed closely by more shame. He hadn't spoken to his mother in close to two weeks, and when he did talk to her, he was eager to get off the phone. He loved his mom, he really did, but something about the sound of her voice tugged him back down into himself, down into that dark place he'd been trying so hard to haul himself out of.

"She only wrote one quatrain, not six," Jordan said, pulling Jake back into the room, "and she also wanted to fuck you. That's not our primary motive here. Or even secondary. Or tertiary." Then she looked at Jake. "No offense."

"Oh, no," Jake said, haltingly, because he didn't know what else to say.

"Did you know that Paloma has secret societies?" Tanya said then.

It took Jake a second to register the meaning of her words. He ran his hands over the threadbare rug underneath him. It felt itchy. "No," he said. "I mean, I never thought about it. Isn't that more of an Ivy League thing?"

Beside Tanya, Jess rolled her eyes. "Those fucking Ivy Leaguers. They can't claim sole ownership over heritage academia."

"I see Jake's point, though," Jordan said. "Harvard was established over a hundred years before America was."

"So? Paloma was established in 1898," Ariel said. "That's legitimately old."

"Well," Tanya said, "Paloma does have secret societies."

"That's interesting," Jake said, trying to recapture the thread of the conversation.

"And we're all in one."

Well. That was news. But that did explain the bond among

them, which seemed to run so much deeper than other groups of friends. Jake had even suspected a level of telepathy among them, even besides the twins, who regularly said the same thing at the same time. Once, at lunch, he'd observed Jordan wordlessly switching plates with Tanya, and then each proceeded to eat their new meal happily, like it was what they'd each wanted the whole time.

"Don't worry," Tanya continued. "It's not culty. It's more of a social club. We basically do what we've been doing in front of you, in addition to a few rituals and discussions that you haven't been privy to."

"What kinds of rituals?" Jake asked. He wondered how they would've had the time to do anything that Jake wasn't there for.

A look of concern crossed briefly over Tanya's face. "I'm sorry, Jakey."

Jakey. That was the first time Tanya had ever called him that. He didn't quite know how to feel about it. Infantilized, for sure, but also comforted. Held. Involved.

"There's only so much we can tell you before you take the oath, if you decide to," Tanya continued. "Of course, that decision is entirely up to you. And we won't hold it against you if you say no."

"Why are you asking me, though?"

"Well, Nic and Ariel over here are graduating next week, which means there are two spots open. The group must comprise seven people. It's part of the rules."

Finally, Nic looked at Jake. He offered a quick smile, then looked back down at his beer.

"What about the other spot?" Jake asked.

From beside him, Sasha said, "That would be me." She said it so quietly that Jake had to strain to hear her. She added, somewhat formally, "I accepted the position yesterday."

"And you all want me in it, too?" Jake addressed the words to Nic, who resumed pretending that Jake didn't exist.

"We do," Tanya said. "The vote has to be unanimous."

"But why me?"

"Because you're an outsider. I mean that as a compliment." She shrugged. "And together, we transform into insiders. That's what our founders intended when they created this society in the thirties. Not to speak ill of the dead, but the formula is so obvious."

Tanya sat forward on the couch, resting her elbows on her knees. Her eyes glowed under the candlelight, magnificent and blue. Everyone else watched him, too, but Jake kept his focus on Tanya, because she was the one who made him feel safe.

"So, what do you think?" she asked.

Jake wondered if he'd taken this social experiment too far. He'd never intended to become an insider. He'd never wanted that, and he had a feeling that he never would.

Then again, he had a lot to lose by saying no. Everything, really. He had failed to build any kind of a life for himself at school, and then all of these people came along and conveniently built a life around him. Their presence had overwhelmed him, subsumed him, allowed him the opportunity to recreate himself into something new, or at least to pretend the person he had been before no longer needed to exist. Abandoning them would mean reverting back to aloneness. To nothingness. That prospect was unacceptable.

He took a sip of his drink. It went down the wrong way. He coughed into his hand; it came away splotched with red spit.

"Um," he said. He caught his breath. "Okay. Sure."

CHAPTER
FOURTEEN

"Personal matters," the floral woman said.

"Any chance you can tell me what these personal matters entail?"

The woman—her name was Fran—peered at Kate over her pink glasses and sighed. Kate smelled the menthol on her breath. "I'm just the office manager. I only know that this student took a leave of absence due to a mental health–related matter early in the semester." Fran pressed a hand to her mouth. "I shouldn't have even told you that much. There's just something about you."

"I think it's the desperation," Kate said.

Fran had hustled Kate to her office after Kate had shown her the photograph. *For privacy,* Fran had said, gesturing to the air around them, empty but for the receptionist over in the corner of the office, hunched over the copy machine, her purse slung over a shoulder.

Now Fran reached inside her desk and pulled out a box of orange Tic Tacs. She popped three into her mouth and chewed. "The past couple of years have been very difficult for these students," she said around the candy. "We provide as many resources

as we can here—our RAs are trained in crisis intervention, if
you can believe it—but these kids had the rug pulled out from
under them. Can you imagine being nineteen, twenty, twenty-
one when the world fell apart? And then coming back here and
pretending that nothing ever happened? I'm not saying *all* of
these kids are struggling, but so many of them are." She sighed
deeply again. "Every generation has their struggles, I suppose.
But this generation . . . They're so much more sensitive than
we ever were. Even us hippies and beatniks! And I get it. I do.
Sometimes I don't even recognize this world we're living in."

Well, that was certainly true. Kate thought back to the year
in isolation with Jake. There were so many good moments together. Sometimes, she even felt grateful for the excuse to spend
more time with him. They'd made banana bread together, then
sourdough bread, and then they'd preserved Persian cucum-
bers in a too-sweet brine. They'd watched six seasons of *Law &
Order: SVU*. They did jigsaw puzzles. They'd done a meditation
on finding peace within the shelter of your heart. One night,
over pantry pasta, Jake had informed Kate that the word *apoc-
alypse* meant "to uncover" in the original Greek. He'd said he'd
found solace in that; that an ending wasn't an ending at all but
the beginning of something else. The more brutal the ending,
the bigger the thing that was about to begin. That was the way
he saw it. (*But do you think it's something better?* Kate had asked.
Jake couldn't answer that, and neither could she.)

But then she took a closer look at that year, at the gaps she'd
conveniently leapt over, and in those crevices she found nothing. A heavy, bleating silence. During the day, she and Jake had
rarely seen each other; each had holed themselves up in their re-
spective work spaces—she in the office, he in his bedroom—and
they'd emerged only to eat or to go for a careful walk, each quiet
behind their masks. When they did talk, their conversations had

centered mostly on the state of the world, not on themselves. They'd cried together a few times, out of fear and frustration and that untenable uncertainty. But so had everyone.

She couldn't remember Jake exhibiting any signs of distress, beyond what was expected. Once, he'd even told Kate that he, too, felt a little grateful for the isolation. He was an inherently insular person, he'd confided, and it had taken him a long time to accept that—that he would never be like his father, gregarious and lucky, nor would he even be like Kate, who was not *loud*, exactly, but ferociously capable.

And anyway, Jake had continued, as Kate's heart had broken into a million little pieces, the isolation had given him an excuse to duck beneath the shelter of his introversion.

But Kate shouldn't have so blindly trusted him. He was only eighteen. He still used a Velcro wallet. His legs were still twiggy and knobbed like a baby deer's.

He was only eighteen, and she was his mother. She should have known him better than he knew himself. But she didn't, because—what? She was more invested in this fucking deal with MogenTech?

"Anyway," Fran said now, nodding toward the picture Kate held in her lap, "she found herself in a position in which she needed help, and luckily she got it, but how I wish she had gotten it sooner. I know we all feel guilty. It's our job to protect these kids. And we failed."

Kate knew Fran wasn't only talking about the girl—she was talking about Jake and Sasha, too.

"Can you tell me her name?" Kate said.

"I've already told you enough."

Kate's gaze landed on a framed painting, leaning against the windowsill behind Fran's desk. It was a finger painting of a butterfly, ostensibly, but like all finger paintings it was also a vivid,

Rorschachian smear. (It could also, Kate supposed, be a pair of lungs.) The painting looked new, the paper still a bright, crisp white. Fran was too old to have a child that small. But she was old enough to have a child with a child that small. Kate considered, not for the first time, that she would never be a grandmother.

"She was my son's friend," Kate said then.

Fran turned to the painting behind her, where Kate still looked. Then she turned back to Kate and shook her head sadly. Her face was a case study in pity.

"Tanya," Fran said, resigning herself to her generosity. "Her name is Tanya Gale."

Maybe it wasn't such a bad thing to be pitied.

Fran kicked Kate out of the office after that. She'd had to; the janitor had come by, keys in hand, warning them that if they didn't leave now they'd be locked in here until Monday. Kate used the walk back to Jake's apartment as an opportunity to look up Tanya Gale. She was getting pretty good at it now. Her process was seamless. She logged into Jake's Instagram account and typed Tanya's name into his followers. Kate found her instantly.

Her bio read: *tanya !! satan's little angle. rainbow emoji.*

Tanya's last post was from September 2nd. The image showed Tanya and another girl—this one also with bleached hair, but in a boyish cut—sitting on a white couch. Both stared, dead eyed, at the camera. The other girl's mouth was opened slightly, her red tongue lolling from her mouth. The purpose, it seemed, was to look intentionally vapid. The camera's flash burst against the mirror behind their heads, creating an orb of pure white light. The caption read: *cherry bombs.* Upon closer inspection, Kate noticed that Tanya had stuck a tiny cherry sticker onto her temple. The post had received 181 likes.

Kate tapped on the photo to see if the other girl was tagged. A black label appeared over the girl's neck: *jor_baby*. Kate navigated to her profile.

Jordan Noble. *paloma '24ish. my bones are made of delicate sugar.*

Kate flipped back to the picture of Tanya Gale and Jordan Noble on the couch and sifted through the background, looking for clues. There was a crispy potted plant on the left side of the frame. On the other side of the couch, beside Jordan, Kate could make out the melted throw of a pillar candle. Then her eye snagged on the mirror behind them, the frame heavy and gold.

Recognition lanced through her.

Kate pulled the sheaf of Jake's photographs from their pocket inside her jacket, found the image of the mirror, and compared it with the Instagram post. It was the same mirror.

Kate looked up to find herself in front of Jake's door and with zero recollection of how and when she had gotten there. She lingered on the sidewalk, too wired to go inside, because going back into that apartment would be like slamming into a brick wall. She needed to keep the momentum moving, keep the ideas flowing, and now she was pacing back and forth on the sidewalk, her fingers pinching and releasing inside the parka's deep pockets.

Another activity. Another body. Another mind to toggle between.

She pulled out her phone and texted Luna. Just to see if she was around.

Luna pulled up in front of Jake's apartment fifteen minutes later. Kate used that time to run back up to the apartment and grab the last bottle of wine from the fridge. When she got into the car, she didn't ask Luna where they were going, because she didn't feel like she needed to know. The part of her that craved control had unlatched at some point over the past week. Floated away into a nameless abyss.

From the passenger seat, Kate gave Luna a peek at what was inside her bag, unfolding the canvas just enough to reveal the bottle's screw top.

Luna laughed. "Thank god it's Friday," she said.

"Is it?" Kate said. "I honestly lost track."

Luna turned onto the highway but kept the windows open. Kate watched the speedometer climb steadily, then hover around seventy-five. The wind whipped their hair into cyclones. For the next few minutes Kate dropped into a daydream in which she used a palm-shaped plastic brush, pink like strawberry yogurt— the kind she'd had as a kid—to meticulously unravel the knots in Luna's long hair. She resurfaced to the sound of a Willie Nelson song on the radio, barely audible above the whip and crack of the wind. She turned the volume up louder, and she and Luna sang the rest of the song together, until Luna pulled off the highway and into a parking lot.

When they got out of the car, the air smelled like chlorine and seaweed. A sign arced above them: Pirate's Cove Mini Golf. The course sprawled beyond it, where a striped lighthouse strobed against the bright-green Astroturf and the horizon was stippled with netted masts. The Pacific loomed beyond its miniaturized imitation, like a predator's dark, open maw.

Kate couldn't remember the last time she'd played mini golf. They had never been a mini golf kind of family.

"I feel like I'm not having enough fun," Luna said, by way of explanation. "Fun is vastly underrated."

The course was busy. They followed a sprawling

amalgamation of families, seven adults and at least twelve kids among them, underneath the sign and toward a booth at the entrance, where a sullen, oily boy, no older than fifteen, exchanged clubs for cash. A stiff felt pirate hat was perched on his head at a slight angle, the accidental jauntiness an affront to his boredom.

Then they walked across a creaking drawbridge, stretched over a shallow, semi-stagnant river—the source of the briny stink—that wound weakly throughout the course. The first hole was simple, ten feet away and marked with a big black flag. Just a single stroke across the flat green. Boulders studded with barnacles cropped up along the sides of the green in a half-hearted reminder of the aquatic theme.

As they approached the first hole, Kate's phone buzzed in her back pocket.

There was a text from the anonymous number. This time, they'd sent an image.

Kate opened the text as soon as Luna was preoccupied with retying her high-tops. ("What is it about Vans shoelaces that always come undone?" she'd said, kneeling down to a lunge.)

Kate had to look at the thing twice to grasp what it showed.

It was her. It was Kate. The photo was taken from behind and a few yards away. It showed Kate standing at the ticket kiosk, with Luna standing beside her. The rounded top of the boy's pirate hat was just visible over Kate's head.

i see you :)

your friend is so pretty

Kate shut her phone off entirely and put it in her bag. Her hands were shaking. She twisted right, then left, a survey disguised as a stretch, but who was she looking for? She wouldn't know. She felt like she'd just stepped off a carousel.

Luna had stood up again, both sets of laces tied tightly. She slung her club across the back of her neck, then rested her wrists against either end. She nodded toward the hole.

Gallantly, she said, "After you."

The club felt too light in Kate's hands. It threw off her balance. She took her bag off her shoulder and set it down on the ground near Luna. "Guard that with your life," she said. From behind her, she thought she heard the violent *pop* of an old film camera, the kind midcentury paparazzi wielded against their glamorous prey. She flinched and turned and saw nothing, other than Luna, who had also thrown a glance over her shoulder to discover the nothingness that had frightened her. She honed her focus back on the ball and tapped it with attempted gentleness. The ball veered past the hole, rebounded off the brick ledge enclosing the green, and landed halfway between Kate and its target. Finally, with an increasingly delicate touch—so delicate it spun her into a near rage—she sank the ball in four more strokes.

Luna was better than Kate. So much better, in fact, that Kate suspected Luna came to this course regularly to practice. She shoved the thought away, because that thought was so pathetic, and Kate had always had a hard time coming back from that. Once, she'd refused a second date with a man after watching him eat a slice of pizza with a knife and fork, then dab primly at each corner of his mouth—first the left, then the right—after every bite.

"So," Luna said, after sinking the ball in two strokes on a particularly rugged hole involving a rusted rudder spinning treacherously halfway across the green, "what's going on?"

"What do you mean, what's going on?"

"Your energy," Luna said. Her fingers fluttered against the club's grip. "It seems scattered."

Kate fought against the instinct to defend. Who was Luna to comment on the state of her "energy"? This person didn't know Kate at all well enough to do that. But that buzzing she was feeling after receiving that text, that kinetic, directionless edge—it was quieting just a bit, being here with Luna, focusing simply on getting that infernal ball into that faraway hole. It was better than being alone. For the moment, gratitude drowned her irritation.

"It's about Jake," Kate shared. Luna remained quiet, waiting for Kate to go on. "I think his life was much more chaotic than I'd imagined it would be."

"What makes you say that?"

Then Kate told Luna everything she'd learned, and also assumed, albeit with certainty: That Jake was in a secret society called Stars & Spears. That two other students in connection with that society—Parker Deily and Sasha Williams—had also ended up dead. That another student in that society, Tanya Gale, had experienced some trauma so severe she'd had to drop out of school. And that that asshole, Dr. Lowman, was almost definitely gaslighting Kate about his own involvement in all of it. That maybe Sasha, or Tanya—or even Jordan, the girl in Tanya's Instagram post—was the unnamed woman Jake had referred to in his suicide note, who had seemingly played such a significant part in his life and in his death. (From memory, Kate recited: "She said: If you don't help yourself, then I can't help you. And then she turned away.") That even though she'd discovered all of this, she felt no closer to understanding what exactly—I mean *exactly*—had happened to make Jake feel the need to take his own life. What was the cause of his suffering, so that she might eradicate it from the earth. Fran seemed to believe it was the general state of the world that had done these kids in, and while the state of the world was objectively a hellscape, Kate was not inclined to blame everything on that simple fact. That was too easy. Wachs may have believed in

Occam's razor, that the simplest answer was the correct one, but Kate wasn't nearly so lazy, so Pollyannaish, in her thinking. At least her next move was now clear: find Jordan, and find out what she knew.

She only left out the anonymous texter who had just crossed the line into stalking, but only because Luna herself was now implicated in it, and she didn't want to scare her.

By that point they'd approached the course's final hole, an elaborate tableau starring a ship balanced on the razor edge of its hull like a beached whale, a cannon wound gaping clean through its side. The green ran straight through the hole, its path intercepted by stray bones and spilled doubloons. Kate and Luna lingered at the tee while a stray contingent of the kids they'd followed in attempted to pull the gold coins from the turf. They were glued to the spot. In his efforts, the veins emerged from one child's neck. Their parents were nowhere to be found.

"I'm sorry for harping on this," Kate said over the shrieking children. "It's the only thing I have room for in my brain."

"Don't apologize. I understand."

"Why?"

Confusion crossed Luna's face. "Why what?"

"Why do you understand?" Kate asked. Luna had been gracious and kind, and that was precisely what was making Kate so angry now. Kate actually wasn't the self-loathing type; she didn't think she didn't *deserve* friendship. She was merely looking objectively at the situation, and the evidence it bore could not have been clearer: Kate had nothing to offer anyone right now, and in the short time she had known her, she had offered Luna exactly that. Nothing.

"Why are you indulging me in this?" Kate continued. "Why are you pursuing this—whatever this is? This friendship?"

Luna regarded the horizon, her expression blank, unruffled. When she turned back to Kate, she said, "It's not enough to say that I like you?"

"I find that hard to believe." Kate gestured down at herself, as if she were coated in filth. "I'm not likable right now."

"That's exactly what I like about you," Luna said. "You're not trying to *be* anything. You're messy, and you're letting yourself be that way, and that makes me feel comfortable to be messy, too. I'm not scared that you'll judge me for it."

"You don't seem particularly messy to me."

"Well, you don't know me that well."

The kids had finally given up on their impossible task and scattered from the green, but Luna and Kate still stood there, silently.

Finally, Kate said, "Do you want to finish the game?"

Luna bounced her club from one shoulder to the other, knighting herself. She looked again toward the black ocean. "Not really," she said. Then she turned back to Kate and pointed with her club toward the bag drooping off Kate's shoulder. "What you have in there seems much more fun."

———

While Luna secured a spot at the picnic tables overlooking the ocean, Kate headed for the concession stand. She asked for two empty plastic cups, two hot dogs, and a boat of crinkly french fries, then swirled mustard and ketchup into two miniature condiment cups.

"It didn't occur to me to ask if you even eat meat," Kate said when she returned to the table, placing the tray between them.

"Is that a euphemism?"

Kate laughed. "A Freudian slip, maybe."

Luna grabbed a hot dog and dabbed some mustard over it.

"Well," she said, "I eat every kind of meat to which you may be referring."

Kate laughed and poured them each a cup of wine.

"I sometimes have a hard time connecting with people, so I tend to latch onto the ones that I do," Luna said. "According to my therapist, it's because my mom really suffered after my dad died. It was impossible for her to talk about anything other than him, or how fucked up she was about him. I grew up feeling chronically unheard. In some ways, I feel like I raised myself."

As she spoke, Luna peeled the outside of her hot dog bun, layer by layer, then placed each wafer of dough into her mouth. Kate was transfixed by her hands, which moved robotically, as if powered by muscle memory. Luna hardly looked down at them.

"Anyway," Luna was saying now, "suffice it to say I didn't have much in the way of parental guidance, and still don't, so all of my choices have been entirely my own, which I guess is liberating in some ways but terrifying in most others. After I graduated, I got some bullshit job as a blogger at a tech start-up in Oakland, but that lasted about three months, as it was slowly destroying my brain and also my will to live. After that I bounced around some of those elite tutoring agencies for a while, which paid stupidly well but still felt like a stopgap. So then I came here, because I always felt safe at school. Like, spiritually safe. I liked that my choices were spelled out so clearly for me. This is what you read; this is what you write; this is how you organize your days. I still have three more years left, but I don't really know what to do with myself after all of this is over. In some ways, I feel like my whole life has been spent in pursuit of this degree, of this feeling of safety and control, and I can't fathom what might come next."

Finally, she turned toward Kate, a beseeching look in her eyes.

"You're still so young," Kate offered. "You have more time than you think."

The platitude was not empty. By the time Kate was thirty, she'd relished any opportunity in which someone, anyone, had recognized her as young.

"Do you enjoy teaching?" Kate asked then.

"There's a part of me that does, but there's another part of me that would be perfectly happy to crawl inside a hole and never emerge again. Teaching is strange; it's both very intimate and very visible at once. I have a hard time with the visibility part."

By this point, Luna had skinned one-half of her hot dog bun down to its pale, fleshy center. Now she moved on to the second half. This time she grazed each flake against the small cup of mustard, letting it catch the barest hint of yellow, before setting it against her tongue and closing her mouth around it. Kate imagined her tongue pressing against the roof of her mouth, how that dash of bright mustard might burn the spot. The meat of the hot dog—of which Luna had taken one, cursory bite—remained nestled, unharassed, inside its gradually disappearing bun.

Kate only stopped staring when Luna's hands stopped moving.

"Sorry," Luna said. "I've been doing this since I was a kid." She hid her hands in her lap. "It's weird, isn't it?"

Yes, it was weird, but only objectively—that Luna did it made it eccentric, and that made it charming, and Kate was also aware of the whiplash-fast fluctuation in her feelings. Only a few days ago, she'd thought she would never see Luna again. Now here she was catching an intimate glimpse into her eating quirks—standard second- or third-date fare—and feeling intrigued, not repulsed. If this was indeed a date, Kate would count this moment as a victory.

And here the bottom line came tumbling toward her, its speed unchecked by either logic or circumstance: Kate was attracted to Luna. She couldn't stop being attracted to her.

She knew what she wanted to do with this information, and she knew what she should do with it, and the two were not the same. To solve this dilemma, she decided to just wait and see what came out of her mouth. This was a tack she deployed only in the most desperate of circumstances.

Now Kate poured the rest of the wine into their cups. "This might be the most wholesome date I've ever been on," she said out loud, and thus the choice was made. Kate turned out to be happy about the outcome. Even relieved.

But Luna chose not to comment on it; she merely smiled at Kate and took a sip of her drink.

When they were both finished—Luna's hot dog bun destroyed beyond all recognition as a former hot dog bun—they cleaned up their table and headed back to the parking lot. The ground beneath Kate's feet turned soupy.

"Are you okay to drive?" she asked Luna, who was fishing for her keys inside her bag. Kate felt the urge to walk closer to Luna, to know how the fabric of her sweater would feel against Kate's arm, and then even to pull her hand out of her bag and hold it in hers.

"Oh, sure," Luna said now. She gestured toward Kate's empty hands, where the ghost of that plastic cup still lingered. "That was mostly you."

When Luna started the car, they were startled by the sound of the music; the volume was still cranked high enough to block the wind from the drive here. Kate turned the knob down when they turned onto the highway, and she let the wind push against her face.

Luna pulled up to Jake's apartment a few minutes later. They idled in the car, where Kate lulled into the silence, the stillness.

"What are you up to tomorrow?" Luna finally said.

Tomorrow, Kate thought. What was tomorrow? What was today?

"Today is Friday," Luna reminded her, because Kate's confusion was that obvious. Or maybe she had said the words aloud.

"I'm getting drinks with John tomorrow night," she said, with no conviction. The prospect of them occupying the same space felt about as tangible to Kate as the nominal GDP formula she had copied down in Jake's notebook in Econ on Wednesday, whose explanation she had listened to with the care of a matriculated student—more care than most of the matriculated students around her, many of whom silently scrolled on their phones throughout the entire lecture—but which continued to elude her comprehension.

"I didn't know you knew anyone else in this town," Luna said now, in a joking kind of way.

"I don't," Kate said. "This is John. John John. Jake's dad, John."

"Ah," Luna said. "I didn't know he was in town."

"He's coming in tonight and staying for a week or two. I'm not really sure. I think he feels guilty."

"He should. He's left you alone this whole time."

Emboldened, Kate asked: "Are you jealous?"

Luna looked at her for a beat, then two. "Is there anything I should be jealous of?"

With a thrill, Kate thought: *Flirting. This is flirting.* She was flirting with a beautiful, interesting woman who liked her beyond any discernible reason, and this woman was flirting back, and it felt good. It almost felt amazing. It felt almost as if she were a whole entire human again, as if she had stepped back into the body she had mostly abandoned the second she'd learned that her son was dead. These good feelings were followed close on the heels by guilt, that ravenous mongrel, but now, more than ever before, she resisted the impulse to give in to its teeth. She wanted to chase it away. She only had to push herself a little harder, to run a little faster.

Also, there was the simple fact that she didn't want to be alone with a stalker on her back.

So she said: "Do you want to come up? Maybe have a drink?"

Luna hesitated for a moment, gazing straight ahead, and Kate watched her so intently she noticed Luna's thin gold necklace pulse against her neck. Finally Luna turned back to her, her mouth opened slightly, a silent question pouring out of it.

"Before you ask," Kate said, "yes, I'm sure."

Luna nodded once, a gesture bordering on transactional, so devoid of heat and promise that the fire building in Kate's core cooled, just a little.

But then Luna did something Kate never anticipated, and never really could have, because no one had ever done this to her before: Luna lifted Kate's arm from her lap, pushed the sleeve of her sweater up to her elbow, and grazed her mouth up and down the soft flesh. Against her arm, Luna's lips opened into a smile, her hard wet teeth pushing gently into the skin.

"Let's go up, then," she said, the words spoken so quietly Kate had to feel them, not hear them, to understand what they meant.

CHAPTER FIFTEEN

"How are you feeling?"

It took Kate a moment to locate the source of the voice, and then to recenter herself in relation to it. How did she feel? Too soon to tell. *What* she felt, though—she knew that. The ghost of some pressure between her legs, a whisper of stickiness along her belly. And then there was the smell, like saliva and crushed flowers, and a dull itch creeping down the left side of her body, where the couch's wool upholstery had imprinted its latticework upon her skin.

And then the memory of last night—really a few hours earlier; dawn hadn't broken yet—returned to her. How Luna had followed Kate up the stairs to the apartment, and the knowledge that Luna watched the way her hips rolled with each step. She savored the power Luna's attention gave her; she moved more slowly, with intention. Then falling into each other when Kate opened the door, redirecting Luna away from the bed and toward the couch (*At least I have the foresight not to fuck in my son's bed*, she'd thought to herself cruelly, and then kissed Luna harder to smother the thought), followed by the unsexy fumble when they took off their jeans—lifting the butt, arcing the chest, the pose of a child in the grip of a tantrum—and rearranging her body when Luna crawled over her, her tongue-pink nipples grazing lightly over Kate's chest, then lower and lower, pushed on by an inevitable force (*an object in motion remains in motion*), and watching her golden head move, slowly and deliberately, between her butterflied thighs.

She had forgotten herself, those minutes or hours Luna spent crouched over her, and then all over again in altered shapes. Kate was not her current self, nor had she animated one of her former, younger iterations, pulled forth from a time when she was freer and dumber and unsaddled by the years of being imprisoned within herself, the many disappointments and frustrations that had wrought. Last night, with Luna, her body had met every challenge and pleasure with perfect grace, like it was born for this, which in the grip of certain moments she believed that it was. She was unburdened by judgment. She knew what she liked and what she didn't like, and she flowed along the lines of that simple binary.

But then she came one final time, and everything she'd lost returned with such force. All the memories, the awareness of her body. The *her*-ness of her returning was like a slap in the face. The sting of it brought tears to her eyes, and she'd hidden them by unpeeling herself from Luna's skin and turning her face away.

And here she was, hours later, her nose inches from the couch's back cushions, exactly where she had left it. She must have fallen asleep. The list of things she needed at that moment was long. Water, Advil, clothes, to brush her teeth, to sleep in a bed, and probably a shower, too. But she remained where she was. She was so tired.

Then she felt a hand—Luna's hand—touch her knee. The touch was light but firm, reassuring. Luna said her name. Kate couldn't not answer it.

163

She rolled over to her other side to find Luna standing over her, a glass of water held out toward her. Kate sat up and accepted the water, holding it against her lap.

"Are you okay?" Luna asked again. She got down onto her knees to get on eye level with Kate.

"I'm fine," Kate said. "I'm good."

"Okay." Luna sounded unconvinced. "I'm sorry to wake you up, but I thought you wouldn't want to sleep on the couch the rest of the night. Want to get in bed?"

There were so many reasons why it was a bad idea to go to that bed with Luna. But Kate was too tired to say them. She followed Luna into the bedroom. She got in, on her usual side, and lay down gingerly, so aware of the space around her. She felt like a stranger in her own bed. Though this wasn't really her bed. It never was.

"Even though Fran knows me now, I don't think she'll give me Jordan's class schedule. I might have better luck going to the cafeteria on Monday morning and hanging out there for a few hours until she comes by, hopefully. Or until a security guard finally gets suspicious and kicks me out." Kate offered this information without warning, and only to rebalance the scales of perception by bringing Jake back to the fore.

"What?" Luna said.

"Jordan Noble," Kate clarified, bolstered by the clarity in Luna's voice that signaled she was just as awake as Kate was. "The girl I found on Instagram who was friends with Tanya Gale. You know that photograph Jake took? With the gilded mirror?" The flow of her thoughts was imprecise, Kate knew, but she trusted Luna to follow.

But Luna turned onto her side, facing away from Kate. "How do you plan on doing that," she said, her voice monotone and far away.

"What's wrong?" Kate said.

"What do you mean?"

"You clearly don't want to talk about this."

"No," Luna said. She turned back to face Kate, the planes of her face gradually revealing themselves in the brightening room. "I don't."

Kate felt her heart sink. "Why not?"

Luna flipped onto her back and spoke, with renewed force, to the ceiling. "I want to talk to you about these things, I do, but not right now. Literally anytime but now. My mind is a million miles away from all of that, and honestly, I'm shocked that yours isn't."

"'All of that'?" Kate said, anger mounting within her. "What is that supposed to mean?"

"This 'investigation,'" Luna said. Kate could hear the scare quotes around the word. "Don't you think you're getting a little carried away with it?"

"Of all people." Kate paused, trying to hide the hurt in her voice. She knew sex changed things. That it lifted the veil from your eyes, and with that cleared vision rendered the person before you either more beautiful or repulsive. Sometimes it took a moment for the former to reveal itself—you'd know it when they left and you wanted them back—but the latter always emerged instantly, with a violence that made you want to bury your head beneath your pillow and wish them gone, even perhaps that they never existed.

The guilt she'd felt a few minutes earlier, when she was peeled awake—that had nothing to do with Luna and everything to do with herself. The circumstances. She didn't regret what they'd done. She didn't want Luna to leave. And she hoped—a rare, sparkling fairy of a feeling—that Luna felt the same way.

But that didn't seem to be the case. Luna continued to stare at the ceiling, her body seeming to edge even farther away.

"Of all people," Kate continued, "I didn't think you would discourage me from finding out what happened to Jake."

"I'm not trying to discourage you. I'm only trying to help you find some separation between yourself and this . . . pursuit."

"I'm sorry you don't understand," Kate said. "But there is no separation. This is my *life*." She put a hand to her forehead, shading her eyes from the blinding vision of everything she had lost. For a moment, the room was so quiet she could hear Luna breathe, her throat working in a swallow.

Finally, Luna said, "You're delusional if you think this is a life."

"Get out," Kate said, but she was the one who got up from the bed, trawling the floor for her sweater, her underwear, a pair of shorts, anything to conceal her nakedness, which seemed so egregious now, in the cold light of misunderstanding.

"I'm sorry," Luna said. She sat up, the blanket draping across her lap. "I didn't mean to upset you. I just want the best for you."

"You don't even know me."

"But I could. If you would just let this go, even for a few moments, I could really know you."

Kate didn't trust herself to say anything else, so she just stood there, bleating with anger, until Luna rose from the bed, quietly dressed, then stood before her. Waiting.

The room had turned from dust to sepia: Another day. Another whole day. The prospect of it, looming, made Kate want to retch.

"I'm sorry," Luna repeated. Her whole body, her whole spirit, was dripping in apology. But Kate couldn't hear it. She heard nothing but the blood rushing into her ears.

Then Luna passed a hand, so lightly, over Kate's arm. And then she left.

Kate moved back to the bed. There was a divot on the other side, which she smoothed flat with a quick brush of her hand. She picked up her phone from the nightstand.

your girlfriend's cute
she know ur a crazy bitch?

She shut the phone off and stuck it in the back of Jake's closet.

———

John looked good; she had to give him that. His dark hair was still thick, shot through with a peppering of silver at the temples, his skin tanned to a rich walnut. Technically she had seen John just a few weeks ago, at the funeral, but she hadn't really *seen* him then. Then, she had been a senseless mass of vital organs, in possession of the bare minimum of awareness. Just enough to get from bed to funeral home to gravesite and then, carried by a stream of proffered elbows, back home again.

Now, at the hotel bar, with her only slightly clearer vision, she supposed that John had lost some weight, just as she had, thanks to Richard's so-called grief diet. But where the sapping of vitality rendered Kate's face gaunt, even sickly under some lights (fluorescents, the sun), John, cradled between the tea lights on the slick cherrywood bar and the amber pendants hanging low above it, looked mysterious. Grizzled. Even alluring, to a certain type of person.

Fucking men.

She laid a hand on his shoulder as she approached him on a barstool, alerting him to her presence. She let her hand linger against the buttery-soft suede of his navy jacket.

The corners of his eyes crinkled when he smiled at her.

"Katie," he said. His voice was low and rich and edged in regret. Since they'd broken up, her name always sounded a little mournful when he said it, but that was compounded now, a million times over.

"Johnny," she said, because she couldn't help herself, couldn't help but feel the comfort in being addressed by her nickname. She was still reeling from what Luna had said, the uncrossable rift that had opened between them. After Luna left, Kate had spent the rest of the day stewing in her distress, too wired to fall asleep. She'd tried to read Jake's notebooks to refocus on what mattered— the investigation—but Luna's words kept ringing in her ears. The text, too. They undermined everything Kate was doing. Those messages—both of them—made her feel so pathetic, like she had completely wasted the past few weeks chasing an elaborate fiction.

And maybe she had. Maybe Luna and Wachs were both right: maybe she should let this whole thing go, accept the objective reality, and properly begin the grieving process.

But eventually she'd fallen asleep, sitting upright in Jake's desk chair, and when she awoke, she was confronted with Jake's even, geometric hand, and she was struck with such yearning (she felt compelled to press the page to her cheek), and it became clear, once again, that she was not capable of giving up her investigation. The longing was so intense it threatened to kill her. She had to see this through.

But not before she got some real sleep. She'd spent the rest of the day in bed, waking up and drifting off until five p.m., at which time she'd stripped the sheets, replaced them with fresh ones, turned the phone back on and checked it a single time— no word from Luna; she'd reminded herself that she didn't care, that her silence was for the best—and sent a selfie to the anonymous number. *Still here*, she added. *Still crazy.*

Then she showered and dressed and made her way over here, at her and John's agreed-upon meeting place at the agreed-upon time, where she now ordered a vodka martini, extra dirty with three olives, and considered an answer to the question John now put to her:

"How are you?"

"This is the second time someone has asked me that question today," Kate said, "and the second time that I have no good answer for it."

"Understandable," John said. "It's an impossible question to answer."

"For you, too?"

"Why wouldn't it be?" The bartender delivered her martini. He was clad in a waistcoat, sleeve garters, and a gleaming, well-oiled handlebar mustache, a relic of the historic hotel's Prohibition-era heyday. Kate drowned her response in a sip of her drink: cold, biting. Looked like a fool, made a good drink.

"I'm a wreck too, you know," John continued. "Even if you refuse to believe it."

"They say seeing is believing."

"Here I am," John said. "I'm here, with you." He gestured down at himself, the physical body sitting in a physical chair, as if that alone were enough to comfort Kate.

Kate shook her head. It was always the bare minimum with him, but at least now she didn't expect anything more. "I don't doubt that you're devastated."

"But."

"But I don't think you feel the same way I do. You're not a mother."

"That's a terrible thing to say," he said. "I didn't know the mourning of our child had become a competition."

And Kate knew he was right: it was a cruel thing to say out loud. But she didn't mean it as an accusation—it was just the truth. John hadn't carried Jake inside his body for the better part of a year. He hadn't labored for thirty-two hours to bring him into the world, for twelve of which the baby had banged his cheek against his rib cage, emerging red and dented like a pumpkin dropped from a not-unremarkable height, and John didn't watch the baby plump and fill and grow from the sustenance he had produced from his own body, just for that baby.

For Kate, a mother, the loss of a child was a physical failure. She had done the work to create him from nothing, the blood and bones and spirit. It was a betrayal of her body that she couldn't keep him alive.

"I'm sorry," Kate said now. She took a deep breath. "We started off on the wrong foot. That's not how I wanted this to go."

"You had ideas about how this would go? I didn't know you gave me that much thought." He didn't wink at her—John was never so uncouth—but he might as well have. And that was just like John, too—to brush off the trouble as if it were a piece of lint on his two thousand dollar calf suede jacket, and to do it so smoothly, magician quick, that Kate found herself covertly studying the spot, wondering if the filth was ever there in the first place, or if it had merely been a trick of the light.

It was only later, well after they'd separated and begun down the road to divorce, that Kate had realized that this wasn't an innocuous charm. This was lying. John's grasp was less a stranglehold, more an ether mask placed gently over her face, but she'd wriggled free of it so long ago now that she could see the shadow of an arm looming overhead. And she knew to slink in the other direction.

Now, she said, "How long are you in town?"

"I have a deposition next Monday, but until then I can work remotely."

"And what do you plan to do for the next week?"

"Ten days, actually." With a single finger, John motioned for the bartender to refill his drink—Basil Hayden's, neat. "I'd like to see Jake's apartment before it goes, to start."

"You're inviting yourself over?"

John looked at her sharply. "It's not your apartment, Kate. It's Jake's. Or technically," he continued, accepting his fresh drink with a nod, "it's mine. I paid, what, eighty percent of that rent?" John cut her off before Kate could launch her defense. "It's not a criticism. Not in the least. As long as Jake was happy, I was happy. And I thought living on his own made him happy."

They fell into a reflective silence, in which John surely wondered what Kate might have weeks ago: Was *that* the thing that had made Jake so unhappy? (Though the word *unhappy* fell mortally short of what Jake had been.) But now, Kate knew better. Thoughts of Dr. Lowman's milky, unreadable face hovering over her pulled her deeper into her silence, and it wasn't until John tapped her hand—just the pinkie finger; a tentative gesture—that she realized she had abandoned the conversation.

"I'm here," she said.

"Are you?" John twirled his finger above his head in the shape of a tornado. "Seemed like you were up there."

For a moment, Kate again considered telling John what she had actually been doing here all this time. Quickly, she decided against it. Her previous attempts at confiding in another person had repeatedly shot her in the foot. It was better for everyone if she kept this secret.

"Other than visiting Jake's apartment," Kate said, "what do you plan to do here?" She steeled herself, expecting him to say something unacceptable like *spend time with you.*

John shrugged. "Same things you're doing here, I suppose. I want to feel connected to Jake, to understand him a little bit better." John looked at Kate, his eyes soft. "You know the first thing I did after I got the call from Wachs? I went down to the storage unit and pulled out Jake's old sheets. You remember the Batman ones, from the Greenbriar house? I took them out and wrapped them around myself and stood in the middle of my kitchen. I was probably standing there for an hour, if I had to guess, because when I went down to the basement, the sun was out, and when I regained consciousness, it wasn't. But you know time lost all meaning after we got that call."

"I didn't know you took those sheets," Kate said quietly. John had picked out those sheets when Jake was three, on the eve of his graduation from the crib to the big-boy bed, but Jake didn't actually see a Batman movie until a few years later, when John rented the Michael Keaton movie, planted Jake in front of the TV, popped it into the VCR, and proceeded to completely terrify their child—thus began a series of waking nightmares involving an axe-wielding Joker hiding underneath his new bed—but even then, even still, Jake loved those sheets. Absolutely swore by them. He'd refused to change them until he was eight, at which time John had insisted that he was too old for cartoon sheets, and anyway, the divorce was finalized and they were selling that house. Kate had an inkling that Jake loved them because his father had picked them out for him. Or maybe they reminded him of a time when both his parents lived under the same roof.

"I wanted to have something of his from when he was a baby," John said now. "I absconded with them when no one was looking."

"You could have told me. I would've given you something better."

"What could be better? Those sheets served me well that day. I'm glad I have them. Another one?"

It took Kate a moment to realize John was referring to her empty drink. With her teeth, she slid each olive off the pick, washed them down with the last sip, and flagged down the bartender to order herself another round.

John scoffed. "Your self-sufficiency is showing."

"Oh, I'm sorry—are you offended that I can order my own drink?"

"It's not the *can*, it's the *needs to in order to assert my supreme independence.*"

"Pot, kettle."

"Okay, we're both proud. That's why I loved you."

"That's one of the many reasons why we imploded."

"Who was it?"

"What?" Kate said.

"Who was the other person who asked how you were today?"

"You don't believe I have other people in my life who care how I am?"

"I don't know much about your life now, true. But I know you quit your job, your parents are dead, and over the course of our near-daily conversations you've mentioned a friend maybe twice. That leaves very few potential candidates."

"I have friends," Kate said. She was unable to hide her defensive stance—the change in tone; the quarter turn away from John—and thus, like a rookie, showing her cards. But John was kind of right. She did have friends, mostly from college and law school, but she tended to attract people who were just as "self-sufficient," to use John's veiled insult, as she was. And career oriented. And married and/or with children. And they were the kinds of friends with whom she didn't need to spend every single night to feel connected to—they'd known each other for so long they could always pick things right back up from where they'd left them, even if it had been weeks, even months, since they'd last spoken. And her friends had been there for her since Jake, texting her, calling her, bringing her homemade meals and books of simple, comforting poetry, but she had made it clear to them, lovingly, that what she needed right now was solitude.

And she knew she was making excuses for herself, that John

knew precisely where her buttons were and how hard to push them, and he had a way of making her hate herself, and that was why she fucking hated him, too, and also why she already found herself stumbling toward her third martini.

She considered the empty glass, which she didn't even remember draining, nor had she bothered with the olives.

"How long has it been?" Kate said, staring down into the crystal eye at the bottom of the empty glass. It blinked at her once, twice. A signal: yes or no. But it could've only been light overhead, catching a glimmer in that trace of murky liquid.

"Since you finished that drink?" In her periphery, Kate saw John shake his watch free from his cuff. "Twenty seconds."

"No," Kate said. With her fingers she unskewered an olive, fat and slimy, then dropped it back down into the glass, blinding that moving eye. "Since you were happy."

"That has to be a rhetorical question."

"Let's pretend Jake was still with us."

"Kate," John said. Her name was a warning, but she chose to ignore it.

"Then when?"

John shifted on his barstool to face her fully. Kate shifted slightly toward him. Close enough that their knees touched. "I was happy with you and Jake," he said. "I was happy when the unit remained intact."

Kate resisted the urge to roll her eyes. *Still full of shit, after all these years?*

"If you were happy," she said, slowly, "why did you avoid us?"

"What are you talking about? When did I ever avoid you?"

Over in the lounge area, a few paces behind them, a pianist took up his bench and began to play a song, melancholy and slow, the aural equivalent of a wooden spoon dripping molasses. It suited the room nicely—the evergreen velvet, the dark glazed wood, the red silk wallpaper that absorbed the candlelight—but she sensed a heaviness come over the room, a turn in the chatter from sparkling to conspiratorial. Kate felt her own tongue loosening, her inhibitions shedding like an overcoat.

"Did you ever cheat on me?"

"What?"

"I've always had this inkling about you," Kate said. "Like you were hiding something."

"I thought you wanted this to go well."

But Kate barely heard him. "I was too afraid to confront you when we were married because I didn't want to ruin Jake's family," she continued, "and even after the divorce I was still afraid to ask, because I was afraid that I was right. That I would've allowed my husband to live a double life right under my nose. That you'd been fucking her, whoever she was, and then you would come home and kiss our child and lie down next to me and sleep the deep, dreamless sleep of the unpenitent sinner."

"I don't know where this is coming from," John said, clearly tempering his anger, "and I didn't know you were such a poet."

Kate ignored his attempt at levity, just another of his diversion tactics. "All those late nights? All those work functions you made me believe I didn't have to join you at? All those business trips you suddenly needed to extend another week?" John began to say something, but Kate put up a hand, erecting a wall between them. "Don't try to tell me I'm crazy. I've had enough of people telling me I'm crazy." Finally she put her hand down. She held her glass to her lips and tipped her head back, letting the olive fall into the trap of her mouth. "Anyway, it doesn't matter now. Nothing matters now."

John sighed deeply, staring into his own empty glass. For the first time tonight, he looked precisely as devastated as he'd claimed he was. Speaking directly into his glass, he said, "I

should've known I would come here and suffer your abuse."
A small smile crept across his face, and when he looked up at
Kate, his eyes were glittering and singularly focused. Kate sud-
denly wished she looked better. She wished she smelled better.
The thoughts materialized with the violence of a shove. "But
it feels like home."

Kate was swept with disgust, but in its wake it left behind
a trail of something else—something deeper, richer, pulsing.

It was desire. Desire for him, or his familiarity, or merely a
perversion of her resentment, a chunk of coal under immense
heat and pressure and mutated into a diamond.

Even though coal didn't actually transform into diamonds,
outside metaphor. Kate knew this. Coal remained coal. It would
always be a dirty rock.

Either way, she couldn't stand for it. She'd already allowed
so much of her judgment to slip free of her grasp. She had to
wrangle some of it back in, if only to prove to herself that she
still could.

"It was a woman," Kate said. She met John's gaze, willing
the light to gutter. "The person who asked how I was this morning. It was a woman. I just started seeing her."

Was Kate still seeing her? Probably not. But John didn't
need to know that. The tactic worked, anyway—John's expression shuttered.

"You're seeing someone?" he said.

"Is that so hard to believe?"

"Yes," John said. "The timing is awful, Kate. Are you sure
you're ready to be in a relationship?"

"Please don't try to give me relationship advice."

"God, no. Even I can admit I'm the least-qualified person
on earth to give you relationship advice. Except maybe that guy."
John gestured over to one of the small tables near the piano,

where a portly older man, red faced in a navy blazer with gold buttons, leaned into the ear of a woman who looked to be in her twenties, squeezed into a black dress, her chestnut hair pouring down across the back of the velvet chair. Kate watched as the man's thick hand hovered above her knee, then came to a rest. When Kate turned back to John, his disgust was etched into every line and muscle in his face.

"Anyway," he said, coming back to the conversation with a deep, labored sigh, "if you're happy, that's great. But I couldn't imagine committing to a relationship right now."

"So I don't understand your decisions, and you don't understand mine."

"It's almost like we're on the same page. Who is she?"

Kate considered lying—she knew how the story of their meeting would sound—but she had enough self-respect left in her to tell the truth. A version of it, anyway.

"We met on campus."

John coughed against his drink. "And what, dear god, were you doing on campus?"

"Same thing you said you wanted to do. Feel more connected to Jake."

"Please don't tell me she's an undergrad."

"She's a graduate student and an entirely respectable thirty years old."

"That's a hell of a lot younger than you, Kate."

"Don't pretend you've never slept with someone ten years younger than you."

John cocked an eyebrow. *Only ten years?* But he let that one go.

"Slept with is one thing. A relationship is quite another," he said.

"It's new," Kate said vaguely, "and we're still getting a handle on each other. And she lost her father when she was young," she added, as if that fact would excuse all of her objectively poor decisions, "so she understands what I'm going through."

"Well, I'm very sorry to hear she lost her father," John said, "but for whatever it's worth, I believe this is one of the poorer decisions you've ever made."

"Lucky for me, your opinion isn't worth anything."

Then John raised his glass, angling it toward her. "To being together," John said, catching her gaze one more time, "and no longer being able to hurt each other."

Kate hovered her glass near his. "To Jake," she amended. "The only good thing we've ever done."

It was only two hours later—after finishing up her drink, brushing off John's request to pay for her eighteen-dollar Uber, falling back into bed, and beginning to drift off to sleep—that Kate bolted upright, her heart in her throat, and realized that John never denied that he'd had an affair.

CHAPTER SIXTEEN

By three a.m. she'd given up on falling asleep. Even attempting to do so was foolish. The black screen behind her eyes was plagued with images of John entangled with a faceless woman. Hands gripping hips, a fist in her long, thick hair. The images clicked into place in a steady procession, repeating in an unending loop. Sometimes a rogue slide, culled from another movie, would slip its way into the projection.

The woman had Luna's face. The ground fell out from under her. She slipped on a pebble. The hands—they pushed her.

The hands held a baby in a soft blue blanket. The baby was fragile, a raw egg.

Kate picked up her phone and scrolled back through her most recent texts. John. Luna. She could never escape them.

Then she noticed a text she had missed from late last night—a response to her selfie from the anonymous number.

wow. you look like shit

She scrolled back through their conversation. Another mystery she couldn't unravel.

i'm dead fucking serious.

She lingered over that phrase. It unsettled her, but not in the way the sender intended. If she were wielding a threat seriously, she thought, her inner contract editor emerging, she wouldn't have used the words *dead* and *fucking* as modifiers. Concision in a text held power. Formality did, too. Whoever sent this text was hedging. There was no verve behind the words, which led Kate, again, to the conclusion that this person sent these messages on someone else's behalf.

And that person had to be Dr. Lowman. Dr. Lowman sent a student—a child—to do his dirty work. The thought was maddening. She stared at the screen, wishing for a new message to come through. One minute, two minutes, three. It wasn't going to happen.

I don't believe you're going to hurt me.

She sent the message, set her phone face down on her belly, closed her eyes, and counted backward from one hundred. Then she picked up her phone again.

Follow me if you want, but I'm going to continue with my work until I find out why my son died. If we happen to run into each other over the course of my investigation, I hope you won't attempt to obstruct my progress.

Backward from fifty, this time. She picked up the phone and called the number, though of course she didn't expect an answer. She didn't get one, nor was there a voicemail message.

This is the final text I'll be sending you. I ask that you respect my privacy and do not respond to this message.

By five a.m. she gave up on lying down. She got out of bed, rootled through Jake's closet, and pulled out the plastic bag of Jake's possessions that the police had given her after they'd found his body. The clothes had been too destroyed to keep—waterlogged, muddied, eaten at by rocks, teeth, pincers—but somehow, his shoes had remained on his feet, and only slightly warped by the water but in relatively good shape. Now she balanced one in the palm of her hand and held it up to the desk light, taking stock of the pattern of the laces, the canvas uppers brittle and mottled. A jeweler counting a diamond's occlusions. If she had a loupe, she'd use it.

Then she set the shoes on the ground and slipped them on.

They were too big, but only by about a size and a half—Jake was five feet ten, and she was five feet five. If she wore thick socks or even layered two pairs, she could get away with wearing them.

She spent the rest of the day on the couch, reading William Blake and accidentally dozing off. When she became too hungry to put off eating anymore, she went downstairs to Tony's and ordered a takeaway, whatever Richard recommended for her today. Today was a day of no decisions and no action. It was a day to recenter herself for the week ahead. If Richard noticed the shoes, he didn't say so. But he did throw in an extra order of french fries on the house.

Then she brought the food back up to her apartment and ate her chicken souvlaki with a plastic fork that snapped midway through the meal. Eventually she fell back asleep on the couch. The next morning she awoke feeling more energized than she'd been in days, though her feet felt stiff and damp, encased within that petrified leather.

———

She looked down into her bowl of Cocoa Puffs, the tiny spheres bobbing in a pond of beige milk. A spoonful, then another. Her third bowl in as many hours. It was already eleven a.m., and still no sign of Jordan. It was a long shot, expecting to see her here (who knew what her schedule was like; who knew if she even ate breakfast?), but Kate was running out of options. Like she'd told Luna on Saturday (she shook her head, as if to physically remove any thoughts of the woman from her mind), she didn't want to exploit her in with Fran at the registrar's office, or to pique her suspicion. No, it was better to forge ahead on an untrodden path.

She still had three hours until her classes began for the day—Econ at two, Shakespeare at four—but she was beginning to become restless. And people were starting to look at her. It would only be a matter of time until one of the security guards finally kicked her out, as she'd also shared with Luna (an image of the flesh of her breast tucked into the curve of her hand, a thumb rolling over a nipple, followed by some frantic spoonfuls of cereal—bury it, bury it, bury it).

And indeed, here she came now, rounding the corner of the entrance and heading straight for Kate's table: the security guard who'd waved her through a few hours earlier, her once-innocuous expression now grim. Kate wondered whether she had become fully psychic. She closed her Econ notebook and slid her tray to the side, telegraphing to the security guard— Ronda Curtis; she was close enough, now, for Kate to read the name tag pinned to the chest of her gray short-sleeve shirt—that she would participate in her ejection from the school grounds with whatever dignity she could muster.

"I was just leaving," Kate said, before Ronda even had the chance to ask her to leave. She said the words quietly, so as not to draw further attention to herself, even though, with a glance around her, she gathered that most people in the half-full cafeteria were already looking at her. Wondering who this middle-aged person was, this outsider puncturing their sacred space. Wondering if she was a threat, or just lost.

"Take your time," Ronda said. She laid a hand on the table. It was a gentle gesture, made to make Kate feel less threatened.

"Do you know who I am?" Kate asked, keeping her voice down.

"A student alerted me to your presence."

"Why not ask me to show you an ID?"

Ronda raised an eyebrow. "Do you have an ID to show me?"

Kate huffed a laugh. Ronda remained silent as Kate packed up her things, draped Jake's parka over her arm, cleared her table, and allowed the guard to escort her out of the cafeteria. As soon as Kate left, she felt that the room had released a collective sigh of relief.

But here was the problem: Now that she'd been caught, she would no longer be allowed to roam free around campus. She couldn't get into her classes, the student center, the cafeterias—anywhere the people who knew Jake would be. She didn't imagine Ronda would let her do such a thing; even now, she spied the guard pulling her walkie-talkie from her belt, likely preparing to alert campus security to her presence. Panicking now, Kate looked around her, seeking an out.

She saw it just to her left. The restroom, that millennia-old escape route.

"Before I leave," Kate asked Ronda, who'd already shot her a raised eyebrow, "may I use the restroom?" She gestured to the door beside her, to prove to Ronda just how close it was, and just how little havoc she could possibly wreak by entering it.

"Fine," Ronda said. "But be quick about it, please. I'll be right here."

———

Someone was peeing in the stall beside her. She tried to be quiet, but her breathing had become labored. She laid her hand over her heart, willing it to be still. She didn't know what to do next, but she knew that she couldn't leave this cafeteria. Not yet. Then there was the sound of the toilet paper unfurling and snapping, the brush of a pair of pants pulled up and zipped, a flush, the door creaking open. When the faucet turned off, the paper towel snapped, the door handle pulled down, Kate finally emerged from the stall and was met with a very tall girl with cropped blond hair, one-half of her body already disappearing to the outside world. Her retreating foot was shod in a scuffed brown Chelsea boot, the nails gripping her leather shoulder bag blazing in green polish.

Familiarity radiated through Kate, the clang of a heavy bell. Jordan Noble. That was her.

She booked it out of the bathroom, where Ronda was waiting to haul her out. Kate set the pace, hurrying out the entrance, where she shook Ronda off as politely as possible ("Take care," Kate said, to which Ronda offered some kind of warning about not being found in school facilities again) and made a beeline toward the girl, who was heading diagonally across the quad and thankfully tall enough for Kate to spy amidst a crowd of students rushing through the green between classes. Soon the girl disappeared inside the Classics building. Kate pulled a blue baseball cap out of her bag, initially brought in case of rain, and slipped on Jake's big parka, because Ronda had probably given security her description. Then she followed the girl inside the building. She paused before the locked turnstiles. She tried to swipe Jake's ID card. The turnstile jammed against her upper thighs. They must have finally deactivated the thing. But the girl was loitering in the lobby, just beyond the turnstiles she herself had floated through, texting intently. Kate still had time to catch her, if she could figure out how to get past that barrier.

Honesty. That was the way to get inside.

Kate approached the security guard's desk, assuming a pose conveying both humility and capability; a pose with which she might have approached the bench, had she ever been a litigator.

"Hi there," she said. The security guard was resting his chin in his hand, a position which he did not alter when Kate greeted him. He acknowledged her presence with an upward flick of his gaze, already soaked in skepticism.

But Kate pushed on.

"I'm the mother of a former student here," she continued. She assessed the guard's expression, seeking any hint of a thaw. None. "Who passed recently," she added. It earned her a pursed lower lip and slow, downward nod. "I met with my son's professor, Steve Lowman, last Thursday. He told me to come back to his office today so he could lend me a book."

Well. *Some* amount of honesty.

Scrambling, she continued, "It was something that helped him work through the loss of one of his students years ago, he said. I'm not remembering the title now." She put a palm to her forehead and closed her eyes, fake-racking her brain. "*Blue Nights? Blue Moon?* I'm not sure. Anyway," she said, opening her eyes again, letting herself ramble on, hoping the nonsense would lull the guard into submission, "he asked me to stop by the office today to pick it up from him."

She glanced toward the elevator—Jordan was already gone. Anxiety coursed through her in great, nauseating waves. She wondered if she'd be able to jump the turnstiles and make a break for the elevator. But she turned back to the guard, hiding her shaking fingers inside her coat pockets. "Okay if I head up there?"

The security guard assessed her for a long moment. "Let me just give him a call," he said, after a pause protracted enough that Kate doubted whether he'd even seen her, or heard her, or whether she was even occupying this physical space at all. It was possible that none of this was happening. That she would wake up at any moment in her bed in San Francisco, disorientated but whole, in the darkest hours of the earliest morning, and she would scrub her eyes into sharper focus and pad down the hall to Jake's room, where the door would be shut—his door was always shut—and she would press an ear against it and discover, just beyond it, the deep, steady bellows of his sleeping breath.

But for now, Kate tried not to vomit as the security guard picked up the phone and called Dr. Lowman's office. On the other end of the line, Kate heard the phone ring, and ring, and ring.

"He's not picking up," the guard finally said, placing the phone back in its cradle. Kate felt her sinuses prickle. Tears. She was actually going to start crying. The guard looked down, shuffling a stack of papers, keeping himself busy. "But why don't you go on up and wait for him. Third floor."

"What?" Kate said. She rubbed at her eyes.

The guard kept his focus on the stack of papers and flicked a hand toward the elevators. "Third floor," he repeated.

Kate couldn't risk lingering any longer, so she thanked the guard and hightailed it up to the third floor. Had it only been last week that she'd first come here and first discovered Dr. Lowman's connection to all this death? She thought back on herself then, and she was moved by a sense of protectiveness for that other, ever-so-slightly younger version of herself. She didn't know much more now, that was true, but this past week had been a gauntlet. And she was only partway through it.

A flash of yellow-white shook Kate free of her memory. Jordan had taken a seat at the nearest end of the row of rounded plastic chairs lining the wall. Kate pulled her baseball cap lower over her face and slunk toward the seat at the other end, nearest the wall, then reminded herself that this girl didn't know her, and also she had a right to be here. The security guard himself had let her up. But still, she felt a need to hide, to camouflage, so as not to startle her into attack.

She pulled out her phone and bent her head low over it,

watching Jordan in her periphery. The girl opened a spiral notebook. Her lumpy brown bag sagged on the floor beside her like
an obedient dog.

At that moment, it dawned on Kate that she had no idea
what she was doing to her. Would she confront her? Would she
continue to follow her all day? She had no plan, no direction.
Flying by the seat of her pants, as she'd been doing all week. It
was becoming exhausting.

Before Kate could make a decision, Dr. Lowman peeked
his head around the door of his office. Kate dipped her head
lower over her phone, hiding her face.

"Jordan," Dr. Lowman said. "Why don't you come on in?"
The girl lifted her head, stood with balletic grace, then gathered
her bag and followed Dr. Lowman into the office. The door
shut with a soft click.

Over the next five minutes, Kate strained to hear the conversation on the other side of the door, but all she could hear
was Dr. Lowman's cloudy, muffled intonations—that was
what she heard the most—punctuated occasionally by Jordan's
higher tones. There was a pleading edge to her inflections, and
a chastising bent to Dr. Lowman's words. But maybe Kate was
imagining it.

Kate was startled when the door opened. Jordan headed
toward the elevator, her long, purposeful strides whipping
up a breeze behind her. Her gaze was fixed on her phone,
her fingers skittering quickly over the keyboard. As far as
Kate could see, her expression was grave, her lip caught between her teeth.

Quickly, Kate followed her toward the elevator, but at
the last minute, when Jordan drew her attention toward the
control panel, Kate veered toward the exit stairs and flew
down the three flights, dizzy with speed and gravity, nearly

tripping over her feet and face down to her death or mauling at least twice. Outside again, she caught Jordan heading back across the quad. Kate followed her path, which she quickly discovered led off campus and into town. Kate remained a few paces behind her and across the street, trying to keep her steps, clumsier than usual today, as quiet as possible. She tried to read Jordan's expression, but the distance and angle made it impossible; there was only the pale jut of a cheekbone, the squarish tip of a long nose. The profile brought to mind the severed marble heads of the ancient goddesses, their smooth blind eyes and closed set mouths creating fickle expressions—haughty and placid at one angle, stormy and murderous the next.

Jordan turned on Willow Street and slowed when she reached the health food store. Kate crossed over to her side of the street but remained a few paces back, watching as she lingered outside a door beside the store's main entrance to type something on her phone. Then she put her phone in her bag, turned her back toward Kate, reached into her pocket, and slid something into her hand. Kate ventured another step forward. Another. Soon she was so close she could smell the ginger and turmeric wafting from the juice bar at the back of the store.

Finally Jordan stilled her movements and turned toward the door. But then she whirled to face Kate, baring her fist, which was clad in a gleaming, spiked knuckle-duster.

Brown, Kate thought, in the slice of a second before terror slammed into her. Jordan's eyes weren't white and unseeing. They were polished walnut and gleaming with rage.

"Who the fuck are you," Jordan said, "and why the *fuck* are you following me?"

"Please don't be afraid," Kate said. She put her hands up slowly, baring her palms. "I'm Kate, Jake's mom."

For a moment, Jordan's face morphed into recognition, then shifted quickly back into anger, though a milder version of her former rage. She lowered her weaponized fist.

"I was told you were here." She said it so quietly Kate wondered whether she'd heard her correctly.

"What were you doing in Dr. Lowman's office earlier?" Kate asked gently. She took a slow step forward. No sudden movements.

"I'm in his class," Jordan said.

"No, you're not," Kate said. "Jake and Sasha were. But you aren't."

Jordan's mouth opened in disgust, and Kate didn't blame her for it. Her obsession with this investigation was objectively disgusting, but only to those who didn't understand it and weren't directly implicated in it, which comprised everyone else on earth, now that Luna, the one other person who defied those classifications, had found her way to disgust all on her own.

And that, she discovered now, was liberating. Kate was beholden to no one and nothing. She had no job, no family, no visions of the future. She had no social code to follow, no costumes of civility to assume each day and shuck each night, finally free to descend into her weirdness. She *was* her weirdness. She could do anything she wanted.

"Were you talking about Jake and Sasha?" she said now, bolstered by this newfound freedom. "Or Tanya?" She took another step toward Jordan, then a couple more, until she was so close she could see the girl's winged eyeliner—the wing on the left side was longer and thicker than the right— and the olive undertones in her brown lipstick. "Were you talking to Dr. Lowman about what happened to them? Were you talking about how you abandoned him when he needed you the most?"

"Hey," Jordan said. "You can accuse me of whatever crazy shit you want; do *not* accuse me of abandoning Jake. We let him in—we *trusted* him—and he turned his back on us."

"So that's why you weren't at the funeral," Kate said, realizing now that Rex was the only one of Jake's college friends to be there. The only one she now recognized, anyway.

Jordan looked at her intently. "I don't think he would've wanted us there."

She said: If you don't help yourself, then I can't help you. And then she turned away.

Again, Kate thought back to the line in Jake's final note—the line that had haunted her most. If Jordan was telling the truth—that they had welcomed Jake in, and he had been the one to abandon them—then the girl Jake referred to in his note couldn't have been Jordan, or Sasha, or even Tanya.

Then who was she? And how did she connect to Sasha's death, too?

"What about Sasha?" Kate asked.

"Sasha was an accident waiting to happen," Jordan said. Kate thought back to the girl she had seen in the diner. The haphazard clothes, the wild eyes. "She hated the idea of becoming a doctor and saving the world. She hated the pressure. She hated her life. But she couldn't find a way out of it." Then she added, "We tried to help her. We just didn't know how."

"Do you think Sasha killed herself?"

The girl shot her an icy look. "I think she was too fucked up to know her own name."

"So you think it was an accident."

"What else would it be?"

Could the girl who'd come into the diner have been on

drugs? Possibly. Kate's experience observing people on drugs other than weed, which she didn't think counted, was admittedly limited.

Regardless, Sasha had certainly been acting erratically, and she was obviously paranoid. It would make sense.

But something wasn't sitting right with her.

Then she noticed a figure approaching Jordan from down the block—a tall, hulking boy in cropped corduroy pants, a mustard angora sweater, and a pair of gold wire-frame glasses, too small and delicate for his face. He looked like a bear in a squirrel costume.

Jordan turned and saw him, too. She held up her hand in a wave, though it could've been a signal to stop. The boy paused to lean against the storefront a few paces down and scrolled on his phone.

Jordan turned back to Kate. Her gaze, once defiant, now softened. "I know it sounded like I was shit talking Jake and Sasha, but I wasn't. Jake is . . . he was kind. Gentle. That's really hard to come by in boys."

"I didn't mean to scare you earlier."

Jordan nodded, finished with this conversation. Kate turned back the other way and headed down Willow toward Main Street. When she was a safe distance away, she looked back over her shoulder to find Jordan hugging the boy—even she, who must have been close to six feet tall, had to stand on her toes to get her arms around his neck—and then leading him through the door beside the health food store, pushing him gently with a hand against the middle of his back.

Pushing.

A push.

Kate stopped dead in the middle of the sidewalk. On her phone, she pulled up Sasha Williams's death announcement from the *Sutter Point Courier* website and scrubbed to the bottom of the article.

> *The spokesperson confirms that the SPPD ruled Williams's death accidental. A toxicology report concluded that there were no controlled substances present at the time of death.*

Sasha was sober when she died.

Someone was lying.

CHAPTER SEVENTEEN

At precisely twelve forty-five p.m. Kate found Wachs exactly where she knew he'd be: sitting at the counter at Tony's, nursing a coffee (milk, no sugar) and a turkey sandwich (lettuce, mustard, no tomato). The timing worked out well. She'd only had an hour to kill between her run-in with Jordan and Wachs's regularly scheduled lunch, during which time she walked a loop around town—Main Street to Washington to South Drive to Elm and back again—reading over and over Sasha's death announcement on her phone, and consciously avoiding the health food store on Willow Street, despite the fact that every bone in her body, every ringing alarm bell, was summoning her back there. Back to Jordan. Kate may have declared herself free from social constructs, but it was personally important that she keep her promises. She didn't want to scare Jordan again. Even if the girl likely wasn't completely innocent, she didn't deserve to be stalked.

Now she slid onto a barstool beside Wachs.

"Of all the open barstools in all of Tony's," Wachs said through a mouthful of rye, barely turning to acknowledge Kate, "she sits in the one right next to me."

She caught Richard's eye at the other end of the counter, who presently came over and took her order. He always asked what she wanted, even though she rarely ordered for herself.

But she didn't want to look weak in front of Wachs. Couldn't betray any lack of critical thinking skills. She had to be in full control over herself and her choices.

"I'll take a grilled-chicken salad," she said, even though what she really wanted was a fat slice of that devil's food cake glistening in the pastry case.

"Cold out there today," Wachs said, as Richard poured Kate a glass of ice water. "Chance of rain."

When Richard was safely out of earshot, Kate said, "I want to talk to you about the Sasha Williams case."

Wachs dropped his sandwich and brushed the crumbs off the front of his shirt. "The Sasha Williams case is closed."

"How did you determine that her death was accidental?"

He took a deep breath, closed his eyes, then reopened them after a beat. Kate had to hand it to him—he knew how to temper his impatience. "We evaluated a number of factors, which ultimately ruled out either a homicide or a suicide. There were no signs of a struggle, as one example, and we didn't find a note."

"Did you look at footage from the security cameras in the stairwell?"

"I can't tell you that."

"Did you at least interview her friends? Get a handle on her mental state before she died?"

"Of course we did," Wachs said, keeping his voice low.

"And no one told you anything that might lead you to believe she was under immense pressure. That perhaps she was carrying an emotional burden too heavy for her to handle."

Wachs cocked an eyebrow. "What are you saying, Kate?"

"If I truly wanted to kill myself, I'd choose a more foolproof method than throwing myself down a single flight of stairs. Hy-pothetically speaking," she added.

"Our investigation turned up no evidence of foul play," Wachs repeated.

"But her tox report came back clean, right?"

"Her shoes were untied; it was late. Trip and falls happen all the time."

They quieted when Richard delivered Kate's salad, then re-mained silent for another minute as Kate moved some pieces of chicken around on her plate. "I spoke to Sasha's friend," she finally said. "She told me she'd been drinking heavily in the weeks before she died. Or doing drugs. Or both, seems like."

Wachs picked up his sandwich and took another bite. "She didn't need to be under the influence to trip and fall."

"Her friend was convinced that she was."

"The tox report doesn't lie."

"But people do." When Wachs stared at her silently, his ex-pression betraying nothing other than a consuming blankness, she continued, "I think Jake and Sasha both knew something. Something damning that they threatened to leak."

"You can't make those kinds of claims unless you have con-crete evidence."

"That's what I've been trying to show you," Kate said. She paused and swallowed, bringing her voice back down an octave. "But there's only so much I can do on my own. I think you need to seriously consider reopening the case."

"That's your opinion?"

Kate nodded firmly. "That's my opinion."

Pointedly, Wachs looked down at something on the ground, or underneath the counter. His gaze remained fixed, waiting for hers to follow.

Finally, she saw it: the sneakers. They hung off her feet,

stained and misshapen like a pair of fossils. She'd forgotten that she'd put on Jake's shoes this morning. Just like slippers, but more sentimental. And she'd forgotten that she'd forgotten to swap them out for her own shoes before she left the house.

When Wachs looked back up, his expression was no longer blank—it was confident, couched in the comfort of his own sanity.

"Have you gotten in touch with Terri Conover?" he said.

"Who?" Kate said. It was an effort to peel her gaze from her feet. Her damning feet. But when she did, braving a glance toward Wachs, she noticed a shade of pity in his look, though he also couldn't seem to help the corner of his mouth from lifting in a smirk.

"The psychiatrist I referred you to."

"Please don't try to undermine me." Kate couldn't keep the pleading from her voice. She wanted to be believed. She wanted this over with. Mostly, she wanted to take off those goddamn shoes. They were too precious to be out in the world, anyway. They belonged under glass.

"I could say the same to you," Wachs said. Then he stood from the stool and slapped a few bills on the table, throwing Richard a wave as he walked out the door.

When Einstein was stuck on a physics problem, he dropped the problem and instead picked up his violin, believing that engaging a different part of his brain would fire up new connections.

Wachs wanted concrete evidence? Kate would give it to him. But she couldn't keep doing what she was already doing. Her leads were dried up, her usual tactics squashed. She needed to do something so unexpected that the firing of her synapses would spark a fucking miracle. She needed to pick up her metaphorical violin.

So she picked up her phone instead.

"I wasn't expecting to hear from you so soon," John said on the other end of the line.

"I wasn't expecting to call you so soon." Kate tried to keep her voice light. She was still pissed at him for his lie by omission, but on balance, her disgust for the Luna situation outweighed her disgust for John, and since those were her only two options, well, here she was.

"What's up, Katie?"

Kate put John on speaker and laid the phone beside her on the bed. She leaned down and slipped off the sneakers, placed them back in their plastic bag, and tucked them into the back of the closet.

"I've found myself with a free day," she said, picking up the phone again, "if you can believe it."

"Taking a day off from rigorously roaming the campus?"

The gibe hurt more than Kate expected it to. "I think you're right," she said. "I think I need to get out of this apartment."

"That's a good idea. You want me to help you pack up?"

A lash of panic. "That's not what I meant," Kate said. "That's not what I meant at all. I meant I need to get out of the apartment for the *day*. I'm not ready to *actually* leave it. I'm not ready to go back."

"Okay," John said, in a low, soothing tone. "Take a deep breath."

"Don't patronize me."

"Who's patronizing? I'm asking you to breathe. And also to wrap your head around the fact that you need to be out of that apartment in a week. Either way, it's a very straightforward request."

"Okay," Kate said, on the tail end of a sigh. It actually did cool her down a little bit. "Let's table that discussion."

"I think we both need a distraction." A rustle of papers on his end of the line. "According to *Sonoma Today*, there's a photography exhibit at the Franklin Gallery up in Sonoma that, I quote, 'simply cannot be missed.'"

"Well, if *Sonoma Today* insists."

"*Our Stolen World: Landscapes In Peril.*"

"Sounds lovely."

"Might be small-town, but it's something to do."

"Don't be a snob."

"I can't help who I am. I'll pick you up in a half hour?"

Kate wiggled her toes in her socks. She'd been wearing them with the shoes for almost an entire day.

"Give me an hour," she amended. "I think I need a shower."

California was burning. The smoke was shirred and plumed like a torn feather pillow, an eldritch monster of a thing. It had a density to it, a gravitational pull; Kate searched its bottommost layers, the edge of the formless mass, expecting to spot a row of houses stuck to its invisible tentacles.

Kate squinted at the tiny text of the description, hanging just to the left of the massive print. *The Camp Fire of 2018 was the deadliest fire in California history, taking eighty-five lives, injuring seventeen more, and destroying 153,336 acres of land. Though it was ignited by an electrical transmission line and kindled by dried vegetation, the season's drought conditions exacerbated the devastation it wrought.*

"A bit morbid, don't you think?" John approached Kate from behind, keeping his voice respectfully low. They were the only two people occupying the narrow gallery, not including the administrative assistant behind the desk, an older woman with an electric-blue buzz cut and Wellington glasses to match, who currently sipped from a thermos—tomato soup, from the smell of it—and gazed placidly out the windowed walls.

"His subject is climate change," Kate said. "What *should* the mood be? Jubilant? Tranquil?"

"You can shut your thesaurus now."

They moved on to the next image, which depicted a drowning New York City block, the waterline nearly rising to the low brick building's black iron awnings.

"It's morbid that he *actively seeks out* images of climate-induced destruction," John responded. "Chasing the ambulance."

Kate glanced at him sideways. Tension radiated from him. "Why are you so disturbed? You work in historical art. You know some of the most effective art is created under the worst circumstances."

John shook his head, like a shiver. Kate followed close behind as he paced before the next image, then the next, taking cursory glances at each of them. "I don't know," he said, finally pausing in front of a blank wall between frames. "How could we have ever been so presumptuous as to bring a child into this world?"

There were a million reasons for it, Kate thought. Because we wanted him more than anything. Because we weren't enough for each other. Because our reserves of excess love were threatening to drown us both. Because we wanted to create something beautiful, but we had no talent; we didn't know how to use paints, or instruments, or a camera or a pen. So we used each other, and what we created dwarfed us in its brilliance.

"Because we needed him," Kate finally said.

They were silent for a moment, standing in front of that

wall of white nothing. Kate felt the gallery assistant drag her gaze, curious now, from the windows and over toward them.

John cleared his throat. "I'm ready for a drink," he declared, and when he spoke again, any trace of vulnerability was gone, the mask of bluster slapped back on. The quick-change: one of John's best acts.

Without another word, he walked out of the gallery, picking up a program from the desk and offering the assistant a wave and a smile on his way out—the kind with eye contact, disarmingly warm—and headed out to the car parked in the lot across the street. He didn't turn to check on Kate once; he simply expected her to follow.

They headed back down toward Sutter Point, stopping along the way for a beer and an artisanal sourdough pretzel at a local brewery, and then, a few miles later, for two to-go cups of pinot noir at a family-owned vineyard. Appetizers, John declared, taking hold of the steering wheel with a palm and a knee. It was close to five when they returned to Sutter Point, at which time John declared a craving for a proper martini.

"To complete the holy trinity," he said, turning onto the side road that led to the hotel, and the bar inside. "Wine, beer, vodka. One of the holy trinities, anyway."

Kate didn't care where they went or what they drank. She just wanted to be somewhere warm, drink in hand. She'd watched the temperature on the dash drop to fifty when the sun began to disappear.

Inside, they opted for one of the small tables in the lounge area, close to the piano. The room was nearly empty at this early hour, and close to silent, with the piano free of its player. They ordered their drinks from a server, still tying an apron around her waist, then settled back into big velvet chairs. Over at the bar, the mustachioed bartender worked a shaker like a power tool.

"Waiting on someone?" John said.

He nodded toward Kate's lap, where Kate held her phone. She didn't even remember pulling it out of her bag, or how long she'd been staring at its dumb blank face, bearing no new messages. Not from the mysterious texter, not from Luna.

The silence was better, she reminded herself. The silence was what she'd requested. But the silence was deafening, and it made her restless.

She switched the ringer off and tucked the phone back into her purse.

"No," Kate said. "No one at all."

"What about your new . . . whatever you want to call her."

"We're putting things on pause."

"What, that happened overnight? You just told me you were excited about it."

Kate rubbed her hands over her face. "I could've been lying."

"About the whole thing?"

Kate shot him a glare. "No, not about the whole thing. Just about how well it was going."

"Well, I'm sorry."

"No, you're not. You told me so."

"I'm sorry if anything is adding to your unhappiness."

Kate laughed loudly, puncturing the silence in the room. "I wish it were as simple as unhappiness."

"You know what I mean."

"Well, you were right about something," Kate said, after the server delivered their drinks. "I am not ready to be in a relationship." She took a sip of her martini and felt the vodka trail a soothing burn across her throat.

"Do you want to talk about it?"

"Not really."

"Good. It still feels strange to think about you with some-one else."

"You liar. I bet you love thinking about me being with a woman."

All swagger, no bite. Guilt sluiced through her at the thought of what'd happened with Luna.

"I can't say I *never* thought about it after you came out to me," John said.

"If you can call it that," Kate said. In truth, she'd never of-ficially "come out" at all. She'd never seen the point. She'd told John about a month into their relationship, when it'd become apparent that things were quickly becoming serious, but that was only because that was the point at which she'd revealed all kinds of intimate facts about herself—the facts that made her a whole, dynamic, complex person. That was also around the time she'd rolled out that her longest relationship had lasted a little under two years, ended because the guy had fallen in love with someone else. If John had rejected her for her sexuality, fine, he could fuck off. It'd happened before. But John had merely nodded, and smiled, and said: *Interesting.* And then they'd con-tinued to talk about whatever it was they'd been talking about, rolling right along.

Kate hadn't counted his seeming disinterest in understand-ing her sexuality as a red flag; she'd taken it as a sign of his cool lack of judgment, acceptance, even—a trait he'd need, if he were to succeed in his chosen field. And at least he wasn't like so many other men she'd dated, all of whom, to a man, had asked either if they could watch or if they could join. That was, if they didn't scoff outright, assure her that bisexuality was a phase, or declare it a layover to being a full-blown lesbian.

Anyway, the subject had rarely come up over the course of their marriage. Why would it? They'd tacitly understood that they were married, not dead, and that they would likely continue to find other people objectively attractive, at its easiest; or at its most challenging, they would really *want* to sleep with other people. Gender notwithstanding, in either paradigm.

But Kate had never intended to fulfill the latter. And perhaps John did. Perhaps it *would've* been better if they'd been more honest with each other. If they'd cared a little more about what went on behind their proverbial closed doors.

Though Kate doubted it. Even when she'd put the question to him bluntly, just last night, John had artfully deflected an answer. A liar was a liar was a liar. Better to accept it.

Or: better to divorce it, and *then* to accept it.

Now Kate mirrored his smirk, finally climbing up onto higher ground. When the server returned, John switched to whiskey, and Kate stuck to vodka. The pianist arrived, and the guests did, too. Over the course of their next two drinks, they talked about their lives, their voices growing more confident and relaxed. The cities they lived in, the cases they worked on, the son they had loved, spoken about in the present tense. Together, they worked a spell: a bit of denial, a pinch of alcohol, a dash of delusion, and thus emerged from the bubbling elixir the illusion of normalcy. The spell was seductive, but it was fragile: reality loomed just beyond the fantasy, hammering down its gossamer door.

Eventually, Kate knew she needed to let the fist fall.

She looked straight into John's eyes, but for a moment, less than a moment, Jake's face flickered over his—the illusion's dying breath.

"You don't even know what I've been doing this whole time," she said. "I've been on a reconnaissance mission."

John's usual teasing smile faltered; he was suddenly aware of the change in her tone. "A reconnaissance mission," he repeated. Kate nodded. "I found something." She pulled her phone out, navigated to her photos, and landed on the one she needed. Then she handed her phone over to John, screen first.

She watched in silence as he scanned over the image, watching his expression morph from confusion to devastation. "What am I looking at?" he asked after a few moments, even though, by the end, Kate was sure he knew exactly what it was.

"It's Jake's suicide note." She'd taken a picture of it before handing it over to Wachs. Even though she'd memorized it, she knew a copy would come in handy.

"Where did he leave it?"

"In one of his notebooks. It fell out when I was reading it."

"Why were you reading his notebooks?" His voice was tired, expressionless.

"So I could find out why he died."

John laid the phone on the table between them, pushing it a half inch away from him. "The police already declared it a suicide. Now we know for sure. What else is there to find out?"

"Well, now we know he took his own life. But I think there was a reason why."

"This is so dangerous, Kate. We could spend our entire lives trying to find out why. We could drive ourselves insane with it."

"No," Kate said. "Did you even read the note? He talked about blood. He talked about 'telling the truth.' What did he feel so guilty about? No," she repeated, shaking her head, "this situation is different. Jake didn't take his own life because he was suffering from depression. I read his notebooks, I remember our conversations, and I know my child. He took his own life because he felt that he needed to."

For a moment, Kate's words hung heavily between them. It

wasn't until the server returned to their table that one of them—John—dared to alter the silence to order another round.

When she left, John sighed deeply and said: "I agree that this note is concerning. And I agree that it doesn't sound like the Jake we knew. But we also couldn't have fathomed, in our most horrific nightmares, that the Jake we knew would ever have done what he did."

"That's not all, though. Jake was friends with Sasha Williams, the other student who just died, also under mysterious circumstances. I've found out that they're both in a secret society and—"

"Stop right there." John held up a hand, squeezing his eyes shut. "Just stop it, Kate."

"I've asked Wachs to reopen Sasha's case."

"Shut the fuck up, Kate."

Kate sat back in her chair, startled by his anger; John mirrored her, startled, too. The woman at the table beside them looked over at Kate, concern marking her expression.

"I'm sorry," John said, lowering his voice again. "I didn't mean to scare you."

Kate scoffed. "It'd take a lot more than you yelling to scare me."

"I'm still sorry. But Kate . . . I just don't have the strength for this. Jake is *gone*. And this"—he waved a hand over Kate's phone—"this is only making that harder to accept."

Kate gathered up her phone again, hiding the offending information it carried inside her purse.

"That's fine," she said. She hadn't expected that John would help, anyway. "If you don't have the strength for this, I can find enough for us both. It's what I've been doing for weeks."

John gave her a searching look. Searching for what, Kate didn't know. Recognition. Sanity. All of the above.

"I'm worried about you," he said.

"I'm not."

John tried a laugh. "You wouldn't be. But I'm glad I'm here."

"Are you?"

"Someone has to look after you. And to be honest, it'd be nice to have someone looking out for me, too."

"What makes you think I'm that person?"

"Don't be difficult."

"Fine," Kate said, sighing. "I can look after you. Only because you're the father of my child."

"Always have been, always will be." He looked at his watch.

"You have somewhere else to be?" Kate said.

"Yeah," he said. "Bed. I'm still on Bali time. Or New York time. I don't even know anymore." The server delivered their drinks then, but John requested the check before she left.

"Last call?" Kate said.

"On my tab, yes. But you're free to do whatever you want after that."

John was right, though: it was getting late, and Kate was tired—and a little drunk, she realized when she finally stood ten minutes later, her final martini drained. Quickly, John shot over and caught her arm. Stumbling. She was *stumbling* drunk.

"I can't let you go home like this," he said, keeping hold of her arm and leading her around the table and toward the door.

"I've been drunk before, you know," she said, but when she did, she was aware of an inability to separate the *d* from the *r* in the word *drunk*, and it also felt so much easier to drop the *you* and stick with the *y*. *I've been runk before, y'know.*

"Humor me, then," John said. Somehow, they were in the lobby now. The marble floors were so polished Kate could make out her reflection in them. Almost. Mostly it was a darkish blob.

"Stay in my room for the night."

"Ugh. I don't want to sleep with you."

"God, no. No, no. You take the bed; I'll take the couch."

"You don't need to sound so horrified by the idea of sleeping with me."

"All right, I'm done with this conversation."

John led them across that spotless white floor and to the elevator bank, keeping a light hold on her arm. She might have drifted off to sleep standing up in the elevator. When they reached his room, Kate fell onto the bed. She felt her bag and coat lifting from her grasp, her shoes being slipped off, and the covers—clean, pressed, divine—snuggling up around her shoulders. Even with her eyes closed, she sensed John's face so close to hers. She remembered the smell of him and the feel of his warm breath against her mouth. She remembered having once found a home in them.

Before she registered what she was doing, she cupped a hand around the back of his neck and pulled his mouth toward hers. It couldn't have even been called a kiss—it was a brush, a grazing. The barest hint of skin against skin.

But John pulled back firmly, sliding Kate's hand off his neck.

"I'm sorry," she said. Her mouth felt gluey.

"It's okay," John said. His tone was so gentle. It only made Kate feel more ashamed. "Don't worry about it. Just go to sleep. I'll see you in the morning."

She thought she said something else to him—*I'm sorry*, or *I have no idea why I did that*, or *Why did you push me away like that; are you really so disgusted with me that you can't bear to barely even kiss me?*—but she couldn't be sure. She descended quickly into blackness.

There was a bulldozer in the room. Kate shot upright, struck by a toxic cocktail of nausea and a pinch of memory loss. The former returned to her when she looked across the room, lit by a thin column of sunlight emerging through a crack in the drapes. It revealed a sleeping silhouette. The dark head was cocked awkwardly in the crook between the couch's rolled arm and an overstuffed cushion, the socked feet hanging off the other end. Its arms were crossed across the chest, fists stuffed into armpits. Then a snore, the approximate decibel of an earthquake, startled it into a change of pose; it rolled onto its other side, back toward Kate.

It was John. He was the bulldozer.

Kate lay back into the pillows. She pinched the bridge of her nose, trying to stop the pounding behind her eyes. What had she done last night? Bits and pieces of the conversation floated up from the bog of her memory. She vaguely recalled swapping memories of Jake—his first steps, which both of them had missed, the information relayed by the nanny when Kate had relieved her for the day. The trip to New York when Jake was six, where they'd taken him to see the lighting of the Christmas tree at Rockefeller Center, and the pure joy in his face, the reflection of those brightest lights in his eyes, had reduced John to tears, he'd said. (Kate remembered it differently. She remembered Jake in tears, completely overwhelmed by the crowd and the lights and the sheer size of the tree, cut from the roots and transplanted in this unnatural, unyielding home, put on display like a freak show act. John, as Kate remembered, was reduced to frustration, unable to understand why his son had to be the way he was.)

Now, she remembered telling John something about the investigation last night—she didn't know what—and she remembered showing him Jake's note, and that was when the turn had happened.

And now she was here. With her ex-husband. She grabbed her phone from the nightstand, pushing aside John's watch, his pill organizer, his glasses case, his book. (It was a memoir by a father who'd lost his teenage son to suicide—Kate had read it, too.)

There was a missed call from Luna, plus a missed text. Both had come in earlier this morning. It wasn't even seven thirty.

Kate sat up again, more slowly this time, and opened the text.

Hey. Give me a call if you can.

Kate snuck into the bathroom, shutting the door softly behind her. Luckily, the toilet was in a separate little room—John had splashed out on a suite—so she closed the lid and sat on top of it, shutting that door, too. She dialed Luna, her heart in her throat.

Luna picked up on the third ring.

"Hey," she said, panting a little.

"You okay?" Kate said. "You sound like you're in the middle of a workout."

"What? Oh, no. I just ran across the room to pick up the phone. I was grading some papers."

"At seven thirty in the morning? I'm impressed."

"Needs must. Thanks for calling me back, though. I wasn't sure if you were going to. I just feel so bad about how we left things."

Outside, in the bedroom, the snoring came to an abrupt halt, followed by a yawn. "Kate?" John said, his voice inching closer to her little locked room.

Shit. Kate didn't want him to find her here, corralled in the bathroom, whispering into her phone like a guilty teenager.

Over the phone, Kate said, "Can I call you back later? Now's actually not a good time."

"Oh," Luna said. "You're the one who called me back now."

"I know, but something just came up."

John said her name louder this time, followed by a knock on the door. "Are you with someone?" Luna said.

"That was John," Kate said. "Long story."

Luna was silent for a moment, then said, "Sorry to interrupt your day with John. I'll leave you two to it."

Then she hung up. A few seconds later the phone buzzed in Kate's hand, delivering a text from Luna.

I'm gonna lie low for a bit. I really need to focus on the thesis, and I think you need to focus on this thing with John. Text me when you feel ready.

Kate stood and slid open the door. She went over to the sink, the gleaming tiles cold beneath her feet, and ran some water over her face. Her skin felt inflamed. She lifted her head to confront herself in the mirror, her vision blurred with water. A dark figure appeared in the mirror behind her, lurking in the doorway. With a start, she turned.

"Whoa," the figure said. Kate's vision cleared then. John. Of course, it was John. She lowered her right hand, which in her terror she had raised in a fist.

"Sorry," she said. "Jumpy today."

John brushed past her toward the sink, laying down a bead of toothpaste onto his toothbrush.

"First you want to kiss me," John said around the toothpaste, the corners of his mouth mossed in fine foam, "and then you want to punch me." He spit precisely into the sink, a pale-blue bullet. "Never a dull moment."

"What are you talking about?" Kate said. But as soon as she said it, she remembered—the attempted kiss. The aborted kiss.

Her breath came in shallow jags, dark spots marring her vision.

She left the bathroom and quickly gathered up her things. By the time John came back into the bedroom, she was putting her parka back on. She could mostly see clearly, but her heart still pounded.

"I have to go," she said, pocketing her phone.

"Don't be upset," John said. "I know you didn't mean anything by it."

John actually looked disappointed. Maybe he was just as lonely as she was. But that didn't mean they needed to be together. And that wasn't why she tried to kiss him, if that was what she had even done—he was her closest link to Jake, and she needed to feel closer to him. That was all.

"I just need some space," Kate said. Being alone was probably the last thing she needed right now, but being here, in this hotel room, with her ex-husband, was only confusing her more. She was such an idiot. Why would she have ever thought that doing the unexpected would spark some brilliant new idea? Of course that wouldn't work. That never worked.

Going by the book worked. Digging worked. Logic worked.

On her way out the door Kate threw a final glance behind her to find John leaning against the doorframe to the bathroom, arms crossed over his chest, his eyes closed against her.

CHAPTER EIGHTEEN

They called themselves Stars & Spears.

"As in the William Blake poem," Tanya said. "When the stars threw down their spears / And water'd heaven with their tears." She grabbed a handful of popcorn and stuffed it in her mouth. Jake watched her chew and swallow. "Don't worry," she added. "You'll have it memorized, too."

"You'll have to," said Ariel. They'd changed positions and rearranged themselves in a seemingly intentional pattern; now, he sat to the left of Tanya on the white couch, with Ryan on his other side.

"Or else," said Taylor. She was on Tanya's right, and then Jess squeezed between her and the arm of the couch, and Jordan and Nic flanked either end, standing with their arms crossed like a pair of bodyguards. Nic had moved the coffee table over to the side of the room, replacing it with two folding chairs produced from the hallway closet, where Jake and Sasha had been summoned to sit.

Tanya had dubbed this their "orientation," now that he had officially accepted their invitation, but between the bootleg chairs and the weight of Nic's steadily hostile gaze, it was feeling more like an interrogation. Tanya had also dragged her gooseneck desk lamp out here from her bedroom and aimed the spotlight directly over Jake's and Sasha's faces. That didn't help, either.

Now Tanya clapped her hands once. She tended to do that a lot, Jake was noticing. "Story time," she said. She gestured to Jordan, who roused from her gargoyle pose and cleared her throat. Her arms hung loosely by her sides, her hands curled into fists, like she was a kid in a school play preparing to recite their single line.

"Our society was founded in 1933 by a cohort of English majors, inspired by William Blake's poem 'The Tyger'—"

"Don't blame them," Taylor interrupted. "It was the interregnum ennui."

"—whose speaker," Jordan cut in, louder this time, "questions how god, the creator, could have made a creature so vicious as a tiger, and then so gentle as a lamb. How can we reconcile living in a world that contains such horror and such beauty—and, by extension, good and evil—in equal measure? The only reasonable response is to accept the awesomeness of the creator's powers and the inscrutability of its will. This is what the society's founders called 'perfect balance,' and the society formed in its pursuit."

Then Jordan took a half step backward, resuming her stoic position.

"But in order to settle into that balance, we must first expose ourselves fully to both good and evil." Jake was startled by the sound of Nic's voice, cutting through the silence Jordan left behind. "This pursuit is solely symbolic, mainly through discussion and theme parties," Nic added. Through the shadows, Jake could just make out a smirk breaking across Nic's face. "And some bonding rituals."

"We pride ourselves on being less elitist in our approach to membership than other university societies," Jess said, picking up the thread. "The people we tap aren't necessarily those with the best leadership skills, the richest parents, or even the most high achieving, academically. Though they can be, obviously," she added, shooting a glance toward Sasha. "We base our membership decisions off chemistry."

"Vibes," Taylor said.

"We trust our gut," Tanya added, training her focus on Jake. "That's why I tracked you down in the bookstore. I noticed you from across the room, and something just clicked."

"Pinged," Ryan said. He nodded his chin toward Sasha. "That's how it felt when I saw you in Rice."

Jake hadn't actually known how Sasha had come to join the group. He'd never asked. He'd barely even considered it. There was something irreducible about the particular makeup of this group, like they had all been born together, and would maybe even die together, too.

He still didn't believe he was fully enmeshed like the others were—didn't really feel it—but he trusted Tanya more than anyone. And that was enough.

"So," Tanya said, "if you want to back out, now's your chance. Speak now or forever hold your peace."

The room fell silent, all seven pairs of eyes falling heavily on the two figures in the flimsy metal chairs. Jake braved a glance toward Sasha. She remained completely still, the only movement a quick flick of her thumbs against each other—a nervous habit Jake had noticed her doing before. She looked serious. More serious than he was. But if she wasn't saying anything, he certainly wouldn't, either.

Jake nodded at Tanya. She smiled, then again clapped her hands together a single time, in place of a gavel. "Excellent," she said.

Then she looked to Jordan, who disappeared into Tanya's
bedroom, then reappeared with two door-stopper books. Cere-
monially, she handed one each to Jake and Sasha. *The Complete
Poetry & Prose of William Blake.* They were brand-new copies,
not borrowed from the library. He felt a little guilty that they'd
spent money on him.

"Until your initiation is complete, you must carry this book
with you at all times," Tanya said. "If any of us see you without it, you'll receive a demerit. Three demerits, and you're out."

"But we'll still love you," Taylor said.

"We'll reconvene at the start of next semester. Your first task
will be to recite 'The Tyger' from memory. If you mangle the
recitation, you'll get another demerit."

"Don't be fooled," Ariel said. "It's not as simple as it seems."

"Be on your guard," said Ryan.

"Roadblocks may arise," Jess added, gravely.

"Any questions?" Tanya asked.

Jake and Sasha remained silent; Sasha out of obedience,
most likely, Jake out of complete fear.

Tanya smiled. "That's our cue, then." She raised her hand
and wiggled her fingers. "See you next semester."

Jake didn't mind working in the library. It was pleasant, a cavernous retreat from the hot, loud world. He liked the abandoned
campus, which made him feel free. The emptiness gave him time
to think, but not in the bad kind of way—it was the spacious
kind of way, like he'd felt as a kid sometimes, playing in his
room alone with the angels watching over him, when the ceiling
suddenly vaulted to the heavens. He started journaling again,
not creatively, but just as a place to put his looping thoughts.

And he was still taking photographs with the disposable cameras he'd gotten into the habit of picking up at the drugstore. They were small enough to slip in his pocket, and he liked the ritual of waiting to see the results. Everything instant stressed him out. (Earlier that semester Ryan had performed an amateur past-life regression on Jake, courtesy of some really good weed, and discovered a lifetime in which he was a nun, circa eighteenth century in northern France—Jake, too, saw a placid wrinkled face cradled by a cornflower-blue habit, an arthritic hand curled around a white pillar candle, the creak of his supplicant knees. *Should've stayed there*, Jake had said, when he'd emerged from the half-waking dream.)

When he wasn't working, roaming, journaling, waiting in line to get his photographs developed, he was memorizing "The Tyger." It only took him a week to get it down pat, the cadence so ingrained it matched his gait, but the group's warnings had struck fear in his heart. What would they do to him if he failed? Maybe that was when they'd break out the pig's blood.

And the more he recited the poem, first only in his head and then out loud—timidly, and then with confidence, embarrassment be damned, letting his voice boom across his apartment—the more committed he felt to the project of joining the society.

And he'd tried to tell Tanya that, to express his gratitude for the invitation and the opportunity to be a part of something bigger than himself, and also to apologize for his silence during the orientation, which could have been construed as hesitation (it was), but all of his texts went unanswered. First a day, then a week, then two went by with no word back. It got bad enough that he'd actually picked up the phone and tried to call her, but that, too, went straight to voicemail. He'd texted everyone else in the group, too, and he'd received the same silence.

At first he panicked. Had they changed their minds about Jake? What unforgivable gaffe had he committed to make them recant their friendship? Was it that time he hadn't understood Nic's crypto joke? Or that one time he'd turned down their invitation to go kayaking on the Scotia River? (He hated getting wet, but he would never tell them that—instead he'd pled three papers, all due within the week.)

Or was it something more dire than that—was it simply his essence, his very soul, that didn't fit right? Had they all finally caught a whiff of that putrid thing inside of him? Had they become so completely repulsed by him, and then by themselves, for ever having been foolish enough to think him worthy of friendship? Had they all agreed that, actually, the ping Tanya had felt when she first saw him had been a fluke? Or, hang on a second: Had they all *died*? (A checkup on their TikToks and Instagrams, all still active, quickly disabused him of that notion.)

Somehow, though, he'd emerged from the gauntlet of his increasingly morbid ideas, and from the ashes emerged a new, more optimistic thought experiment: Maybe the silence was a test. A test of his commitment. He should want to be a part of Stars & Spears enough that he didn't need to be coaxed along the road to belonging.

Eventually, he texted Sasha. It was his first text to her ever, not counting the group texts—not because he didn't like Sasha, but because they didn't seem to have much in common. They did, however, both sign up for Lowman's Classical Mythology course for next semester, at the urging of the group. Every single one of them had taken his course—even the hard science majors among them, to Sasha's relief—and Jordan, the only actual Classics major present, had taken the professor on as an unofficial mentor.

Sasha confirmed his suspicions: she, too, had been flat-out

ignored. And she, too, had doubled down on her Blake studies, even going so far as to memorize a few more of his poems, just in case that was one of the "roadblocks" Jess had cryptically warned them about.

that's why you're the resident genius, Jake texted.

lol, Sasha texted back.

Then they made a pact: they'd memorize all the same poems—"London," "Jerusalem," and "The Lamb," because they were his most famous, and therefore the most likely to be requested for recitation, assuming the group wouldn't go nuclear and ask for *Milton*.

Because if they were to commit themselves to this society, then they would also commit to each other. If one went down, the other would go right down with them.

———

July yawned into August. The days got hotter, the nights darker. Signs of humanity trickled back onto campus. Jake's trolley of books to restack grew taller. The line for the canteen in the library basement extended to one other person, then three, then five. The welcome emails from Jake's new professors charged into his inbox one morning, bearing syllabi and last-minute requests that consumed Jake with dread, right down to the bottoms of his feet. (*Please come prepared to discuss Act 1, Scene 1 of* As You Like It. *Please read the Minotaur myth from* Classical Mythology *and write a one-page analysis, addressed to your TA. Please be prepared to share a fun fact about yourself!*)

At eleven p.m. one night, a week into the new semester, Jake was sitting on his bed, deep into Orlando's spar with Charles, when his phone buzzed once, then twice, from his desk across the room. And then, like an afterthought, it buzzed a third time. Carefully, he closed his book, paced across the room on cold bare feet, and flipped his phone over, revealing its lit face. Tanya had finally texted him.

Meet at the wayside tomorrow at midnight
download signal and delete this message
wear black

———

Jake and Sasha hiked up to the Wayside together, using the flash-lights on their phones to light their path. At the last minute, before leaving his apartment, he'd slipped his camera into his pocket, just in case; now, as the incline got steeper, the edge of it jammed against his upper thigh.

Sasha had received the same texts from Ryan the night before, though in a slightly different order (*tomorrow midnight meet at the wayside / wear all black / delete these messages and download signal*), and now they used the twenty-minute hike to cram in a few more recitations of "The Tyger," one final re-hearsal before taking the stage, their books of Blake tucked under their arms, their steps and voices matched up like a piece of paper folded perfectly in half.

There was something to this, Jake thought—finding align-ment with another person. He'd never really seen the point of it until now.

Then, a few paces from the summit, they spied the light and crackle of a fire through the thinning trees. They paused and looked at each other—a bid for good luck, or a silent *what the fuck*. And then they continued on.

They emerged into the clearing to find a raging bonfire. Seven figures were arranged in a semicircle around it. Every-one wore black togas, black kerchiefs tied around their noses and mouths, their own books of Blake's poetry held in their left hands. Jake's Air Jordans glowed, stark white, against the fire. He was such an idiot. Why wouldn't he have thought the all-black memo would apply to his shoes?

Then the tallest figures—Nic and Ariel—stepped forward. From Jake's vantage, it looked like they were stepping directly onto the edge of the fire, lighting up the visible parts of their faces. Beads of sweat ran down Nic's forehead.

"Welcome," Nic said, "and congratulations. By accepting this invitation, you've agreed to leave behind the known world and enter the unknown. Here, you will unlearn yourself and come to learn yourself again. Here is a world of great good and great evil. Here you will learn the art of alchemy as a means of transcendence. Here you will supplicate yourself to the art of not-knowing. Here, you will kneel at the feet of your id."

Jake tamped down an urge to laugh. It was all so . . . performative. Hard to suspend his disbelief and take it all seriously, same way he'd never quite been able to ditch his secondhand embarrassment and give into the spectacle of live musicals.

Then Ariel raised his right hand in the air, holding his book like a torch. The five people behind them removed their togas and face coverings, revealing the white clothes that had been partially visible beneath. Only Ariel and Nic remained in their black togas, the curves of their naked shoulders gleaming in the firelight.

"Do you accept the call?" Ariel said.

Jake stole a glance at Sasha, unsure how to respond. She nodded once, her gaze fixed on Ariel. Jake mimicked her. From behind Ariel, Tanya smiled.

Finally Nic lowered his arm, and together, the group intoned:

When the stars threw down their spears
And water'd heaven with their tears:
Did he smile his work to see?
Did he who made the Lamb make thee?

When the silence settled, Ariel redirected his focus to Jake and Sasha.

"According to the dictates of our founders, your first task as initiates is to recite our banner text." He jutted his chin toward their arms. "Drop the books."

They did.

Then he turned behind him, gesturing to Tanya, who went over to the mansion ruins and returned bearing an armful of objects, made visible when she resumed her position near the bonfire: two handles of vodka and two wooden diadems, spiked with thorns.

Jake had never seen a thing like that before—a weaponized headpiece. The whole thing started to become less funny.

Then Ariel gestured to Jess. She reached into the pocket of her dress and produced a small white baggie, wiggling it a few times.

A wicked smile broke across Nic's face. "*Nemo saltat sobrius,*" he said. "Nobody dances sober."

CHAPTER NINETEEN

Two days after her night with John, Kate received a call from the Sutter Point Police Department.

"Detective Wachs wants you to come down to the station today," Felix said.

Kate dropped her spoon in her bowl of minestrone, a small puddle of brown liquid splashing onto the counter. She couldn't risk sneaking back onto campus, so she'd spent most of her time over the past few days here at Tony's, rereading the book of Blake poetry and Jake's journals, exactly where she'd started. She hadn't been holding out for a miracle, per se—she'd lost her faith in such occurrences—but with every recitation of every journal entry, and every parsing of every scribble in the margins of the poetry, Kate felt herself tugged back, back, back in time and space. It was as if the momentum she'd experienced over the past couple of days had never even happened.

Kate tore off a corner of her paper napkin and placed it over the wet spot.

"What time?" she said. She watched the paper expand and pulp.

"How soon can you be here?"

Kate was the only person in the café, other than Edith, another of Tony's regulars who'd claimed the table in the back corner of the room. Even Richard leaned against the counter, chin in hand, swiping idly through his phone. Orange and black garlands hung in neat, evenly spaced swoops on the wall behind him; this morning, she was greeted by a flock of bat decals gliding across Tony's front door. Richard had decorated the place last night, he'd told her earlier, only in order to appease the town's board of commerce, who'd raised a stink after Richard had declined ("Forgotten, technically," Richard had confided in Kate) to decorate the diner in keeping with his neighboring establishments, per the unofficial edict that the town "promote a collective sense of unity," the president had told Richard, who'd silently noted the redundancy and morally bristled against it. The decals, the garlands—it was Richard's half-assed, last-minute attempt to stave off the president's bureaucratic wrath this year. Now he was staring a hole into the front door, as if the heat of his gaze could peel those tacky decals clean off the glass.

Halloween. Which meant that Kate only had four days before she needed to vacate the apartment. Four days to wrap this up.

Over the phone, she said: "Twenty minutes?"

"I'll tell him that," Felix said. "Oh, one more thing—he said to bring the photographs. I assume you know what he means."

———

Kate watched Wachs open the Styrofoam box, pick up the slice of marble cake encased in plastic wrap, then place it back into the container.

"What is this?" he said. He looked puzzled.

"It's a piece of marble cake," Kate said. For clarification, she added, "It's from Tony's."

"But," Wachs said, "why?"

"I wanted you to have it."

At the last minute, before getting the check from Richard, she'd asked for a slice of cake to go. It'd been staring her in the face the entirety of her three-hour stay, mocking in its heft, and she was suddenly overcome with the feeling that something bad would happen if she didn't liberate it from its plastic display case. She'd ordered it for herself, but when she walked into Wachs's office and found him slumped behind his desk, she was compelled to give it to him instead. The sugar, the gift, the sustenance, the pleasure. He seemed to need all of it. Despite her misgivings, she'd actually come to care about this man.

"Well," Wachs said now, closing the lid on the box and pushing it gently to the side of his desk, "that wasn't necessary, but thank you anyway."

Kate tried not to feel disheartened by the sight of the abandoned box, closed like a mute mouth.

Wachs cleared his throat and smoothed the crease between his brows. He hesitated for a moment before speaking again, but Kate noticed the quick flicker of his gaze across her person, scanning for signs of possible insanity. She sat up taller in her seat and crossed her legs, conveying a cool self-composure and a total lack of urgency that she did not actually possess. At least she was wearing her own shoes today.

Apparently satisfied, Wachs continued, "We took another look at the security camera footage from the night Sasha Williams died."

Kate's stomach dropped. "The security footage from the stairwell," she clarified.

"That's the one."

"The footage I recommended that your office evaluate."

"Yes, and which we *did* evaluate." Wachs straightened his tie. "But our conversation reminded me of something: We never looked at the security footage from the fourth-floor hallway. Before I reviewed the new tapes, I wanted to take a closer look at the stairwell. Are you ready to see this?"

Wachs turned his laptop toward her. The screen was split, showing two sharp-focused images pulled from the Thurgood security cameras. The left side of the screen showed the empty stairwell between the fourth and third floors; the right side showed that same stairwell, now with a body crumpled at its foot. Kate's hand caught her throat, but she nodded at Wachs, signaling that she was okay.

Then Wachs pointed at the time stamp at the top right-hand corner of the first image.

"This image was taken at three thirty-one a.m.," he said. Then he moved his finger to the time stamp on the second image.

"Three thirty-nine," Kate said. "You think someone scrubbed the footage taken in between?"

Wachs nodded. "The same pattern applies to the footage from the fourth-floor hallway," he said. "That chunk of time is just—missing."

"How is that possible?"

"It's not so hard to hack into security cameras these days, unfortunately."

"Is there any way to track down who did it?"

"You might be able to help me with that."

Wachs turned the laptop back to him, typed, then swiveled the screen back to Kate. This image showed a bird's-eye view of the hallway, the camera stationed at the entrance and aimed toward the vending machine at the end. The time stamp read *3:15 a.m.* On the right-hand side of the hallway, near the back, Kate could just make out Sasha following another figure out of the emergency door. Sasha was taller than the other person, obscuring most of the person's frame, but the left hand and a back slice of the head remained visible. Most likely female, based on the stature.

Kate produced Jake's photographs from her pocket and laid them out, side by side, across Wachs's desk.

"You catch on quickly," Wachs said. He came around the other side of the desk and sat in the chair next to Kate. They studied the photographs in silence.

Then Kate gestured to the photograph depicting the eight toga-clad people standing in a line. She pointed to the figure off to the left, her close-cropped hair white with the flash, a scuffed Chelsea boot just visible amidst the dark ground. "That's Jordan," she said.

"Too tall," Wachs said.

She moved on. "Tanya."

"Hair doesn't match."

Then she moved on to the final female figures in the photograph, standing at the end of the line. The twins. She knew they were twins, even with their faces covered, but she'd never been able to identify them. Never managed to find their social media profiles. It was like they never even existed.

Kate brought the image closer to her face, then farther away, trying to find focus. Wachs reached into his pocket and handed her a pair of reading glasses. She gave him a skeptical look— *Aren't you too young for these?*—to which he responded with a shrug. *Nope.*

Now, with the glasses, she studied the twins' left hands. One was bare, the other encrusted in rings and a stack of bracelets extending halfway up her forearm. She gestured for the security footage on Wachs's screen.

Reading her silent request, Wachs grabbed his laptop and zoomed in on the figure leading Sasha into the stairwell. Her left arm, the only one visible, gleamed in the hall's low light, and another magnification revealed a tangle of bracelets.

When she looked back up at Wachs, she couldn't keep the hint of triumph from gleaming in her eyes.

CHAPTER
TWENTY

Jake was floating. Or, no, he wasn't floating—he was *vibrating*, buzzing at such a high frequency that the soles of his feet lifted from the ground, the pitch so ethereal that dogs could probably hear it.

He didn't ask what was in the powder that Jess produced from her pocket, dug out with her fingernail, and placed beneath Jake's nostril, then proceeded to do the same with everyone else present, ending with herself. No one else questioned her, and now that he'd managed to clinch their trust, he didn't want to lose it. Taylor had assured them that it was clear of fentanyl— they'd used the test strips to make sure—which meant it was either coke or ketamine or molly. He'd only done coke once at a party freshman year, just the tiniest bump rubbed into his gums, and it made him feel like he'd never not loved anyone or ever had an intrusive thought in his life, but the high wore off after an hour or two, and by then the reserves were gone. He'd been too scared to try the other things, though he'd watched the others do them a bunch of times. Taylor and Jess usually supplied both, Ariel and Ryan couldn't say no to either, and Nic,

Jordan, and Sasha occasionally did molly before a show. Tanya refused all of it.

But she didn't refuse it now, and that made Jake feel better about his own decision not to, either. There was a taste like chemical sludge in the back of his throat, and the blue core of the bonfire had transformed into a sprite in the shape of an hourglass, all tits and ass and thighs. She beckoned him closer; he reached out to poke a tendril of her waist-length hair, but then someone pulled the back of his shirt, forcing him back toward the cool black ground.

"Not so fast," they said.

Jake turned to find a giant stag. The stag spoke with Nic's voice.

Jake reared back, prepared to bolt, but then the stag decapitated itself and there was Nic, the real one, holding the animal head in his hands.

"Relax, man," he said. "It's just a mask."

A violently realistic-looking mask, with life-sized horns and gnarled, matted fur, but okay. Then Nic grabbed Jake by the shoulders and positioned him beside Sasha, who stood completely still, gazing intently at the fire. Did she see the sprite, too? Did she also want to touch that long, long hair, to noose it around her wrist and give it a tug?

Jake watched Sasha rouse when Tanya appeared before her with the vodka. Tanya steadied the base of the bottle with one hand, and with the other she tipped the neck against Sasha's lower lip to nudge it open, their faces so close Jake thought they might kiss. Sasha dutifully drank, choking all the way through, and then Tanya moved on to Jake. When she held the bottle out toward him, the waft of the alcohol strong enough to make his eyes water, he wanted to say, *I love you so much.* He wanted to say, *I'd do anything for you*; he wanted to say, *I would probably die for you, if there was a bullet I would take it for you, if there was a train I would jump in front of it for you.*

Instead he just drank, but most of the sip ran in burning runnels down the sides of his mouth and onto his chin. His clumsiness earned him a smile, the kind that made her lioness eyes glister like a chunk of amber, but then Tanya shuttered them, snuffing the light, teetering a bit, and for a moment Jake feared that she would fall back into the fire. But then she opened them again, and smiled with her pointy teeth, and rejoined the others on the far side of the bonfire.

Then Ariel said something, but it wasn't Ariel; it was actually a bear with Ariel's skinny arms and dumb tattoos. *A mask*, Jake remembered, catching himself before he could run. *They're wearing masks.*

Then Sasha took a step forward, leaving Jake behind to fend for himself, but she turned, the fire rimming one side of her face in an evilly bright silhouette, and she said: "Roadblocks." Jake had no idea what she meant. She gestured for him to step forward too, so he did, and they both looked at the bear, who nodded his head, but the nod was barely visible, he barely even had a neck, and then Sasha looked at Jake again and said, "Ready?"

Ready for what, he wanted to ask, but then Sasha grabbed his hand and opened her mouth and began to speak.

CHAPTER
TWENTY-ONE

Jordan lived about a mile away from campus in an apartment on Chiswick Street, in a newish midrise building sandwiched between a parking garage and a gourmet grocery store. Kate buzzed the apartment number she'd given her—3F—and the front door opened with a click.

Kate had called Jordan an hour earlier, having found her information on PalomaGate, and asked if she could come over and talk with her.

You can't be fucking serious, Jordan had said. But Kate had been prepared for her aggression. She'd have had the same re- action if the person she'd recently caught trailing her across a private campus had invited herself into her home.

On the phone, Kate had remained silent. This was the most facile tactic, but it almost always worked.

Do you know, Jordan had eventually said, her voice like sandpaper, *how exhausted I am?*

Yes, Kate had said. *I think I'm the only person in the world who really knows it.*

Waiting it out had worked. Now Kate climbed the three

flights of stairs to Jordan's apartment. 3F was at the far end of
the hallway, which was painted the color of clay and bathed in
pallid industrial light. It smelled of weed and cooked onions.

Kate knocked three times. Jordan opened the door a crack,
closed it again, undid the door chain, and opened it again, standing off to the side to silently welcome her in. The apartment was
small, probably a one-bedroom, consisting of a living room, a
wall of kitchen appliances off to the right and demarcated with
an industrial steel island, and a desk at the back, facing a large,
single window. There were two doors off to the left side, likely
leading to the bedroom and bathroom.

Jordan gestured to the couch, a puffy, worn maroon leather.
There was a holographic glass ashtray on the coffee table and a
thin paperback book. Clarice Lispector. In lieu of a TV, an array
of colored pillar candles, frozen in varying degrees of melt, were
collected on the console table across from the couch.

Jordan sat heavily in the armchair diagonal from the couch.
Kate noticed that she was wearing the same outfit she'd worn in
an Instagram post from last spring: a lace-trimmed camisole in a
red floral print, a chain belt slung low on her hips, and a pair of
oversized cargo pants with exaggerated pockets tucked into her
Chelsea boots. It was like seeing a cartoon character in the flesh.

Jordan scooched herself forward in the chair. Then she tipped
her torso forward into her lap, covering her face with her hands.
She breathed deeply a couple of times, then straightened again.

Jordan set her mouth into a tight line.

"Fine," she said. "What do you want to know?"

CHAPTER
TWENTY-TWO

It was "The Tyger" they wanted. It couldn't have been any other way. Still, all the studying, the memorizing, the repeated, mantra-like recitations—all of that preparation had paid off. Jake and Sasha reeled off the poem in perfect tandem, their voices clipped together like a latched bracelet. It had to have been muscle memory, at that point, because the roadblocks did arise—Jake was wasted, he was hardly even present in his body, and even though Sasha seemed to be her usual reserved self, utterly composed, the words streaming from the dark O of her mouth like dancing ribbons, Jake had seen her get fucked up right there with him.

When it was over, she let free a cackle, a spiky little nugget of a sound.

And then the party began.

There was some dancing, because someone had had the fore-thought to bring a Bluetooth speaker. There were professions of love. There were alleged sightings of the ghost of the Wayside's late inhabitant, but it only turned out to be Taylor, dashing behind the chimney with Nic, a streak of white in her pale dress. Jake even felt bold enough to pull out his camera and document the scene:

All of them lined up in their ridiculous black togas, which they'd put back on at Jake's request. Sasha and Tanya and Taylor, holding their books over their mouths. (Jordan doubled over, in actual pain, after the flash went off—he hadn't realized he'd kept it on.)

And there was a conversation with Tanya, a very important one, but after everything happened, Jake could only remember scraps of it. He remembered that he told her that he loved her—that was the most important thing—but not in the sexual way, not even in the romantic way, but in the way of the most intimate of friendships, the kind that grew up between two kindred spirits who asked nothing of each other except for their presence. Or something like that. He remembered, too, that Tanya didn't seem to hear a single word of what he said. She stared directly over his shoulder, her eyes glassy, her mouth parted like a fish drowned in air. It made her look stupid, and that wasn't right.

"Did you hear that?" Tanya said suddenly. Something dark crossed her face, obliterating whatever spark still smoldered behind her eyes.

He didn't register when Tanya got up, stumbling toward the thing that had so preoccupied her, but then he was alone. The sprite in the fire had grown fangs. He was overcome with a desire to call his mom. They hadn't spoken in a week, and he missed her so much.

That was when the animal wailed. It was the sound of pure agony, like nothing he had heard before. He became aware of a commotion growing over by the mansion ruins, and Jake roused from his reverie, following the crowd toward the source of the sound. On his way over he felt a hand clutching his wrist. The hand belonged to Sasha, catching up with him. Her eyes were glazed, but behind the fog winked the unmistakable flash of terror. He interlaced his hand with hers, and they followed the wail.

Jake tried to make sense of what he beheld there, in the remnants of the mansion's great rooms.

At first he thought it really was an animal, though nothing born of this earth—it would've been some nightmarish creature, long limbed and pale and uncannily dexterous, its many digits flexing and pinching at the black dirt. But the head was too far away from the limbs. It lay discarded, horned and open mouthed, at least a foot away from one of the arms.

When the panic dissolved, Jake's senses fine-tuned, and then he thought that it was two people fucking. Because it turned out that there were *two* figures there, undulating against each other, and the moans were coming from both of them, and one of them was Tanya. She straddled the figure below her, the hem of her dress bunched up around her hips to reveal the bare expanse of her left leg, mottled with dirt and something deeper in color and thicker in consistency.

Jake's perception detached. He hovered an inch or two above his body. He watched himself watching. He watched the others watching, too, the audience transfixed, held captive by the players on the dimly lit stage. Someone had turned on their phone flashlight and arranged it face up, reducing their faces to a vague arrangement of shadows, like a painting assembled of negative space. With the scene exposed now, Jake could see that it was Ariel on the ground, and he was bleeding, from somewhere around his head.

Sasha clutched Jake's hand harder. Jake wanted to turn to her and ask her what the hell was happening, because even though Sasha was just as much of an outsider in this situation as Jake was, she still knew everything. But he couldn't drag himself away from the two figures writhing on the ground before him.

Finally, Nic stood from where he'd been huddling with the others. He laid one hand over his heart, and with the other he gestured toward Tanya and Ariel, who had stilled their movements as soon as he'd raised himself from the ground. Jake was reminded of the statues of the ancient Roman emperors, eternally caught in poses conducting magnanimity, virtue, harmony, grace. And how wrong that was, considering the chaos he lorded over.

"The battle between good and evil," Nic said. His voice sounded even louder now, amplified, cutting a path clear across the silence.

Jake remembered this immersive theater experience his dad had taken him to in New York, years ago, in which the actors were indiscernible from the attendees until they did something drastic to move the story along—breaking into monologue, releasing a scream, shoving another actor in disguise hard enough to force the other to their knees. Jake couldn't help but feel vindicated when the hoax was revealed. *You see now?* he'd wanted to cry to the stunned audience. *None of this was ever real.*

Jake didn't know what he was witnessing right now, not exactly, but it reeked of an attack. But all of them—Nic, the narrator; Tanya and Ariel, the leads; and all the bit players that brought the illusion to life—had engineered this entire scene. This was all part of a bigger plan.

But that didn't explain why Tanya gazed down at Ariel, still pinned between her legs, with a volatile combination of violence and bewilderment, as if he had stolen something from her. And it seemed like Jake was the only one who had noticed it.

Then Nic nodded at Jess—or maybe it was Taylor; even sober and in daylight Jake occasionally confused one for the other—who crawled a few paces behind her and reached for something resting on one of the mansion's foundation walls. There was the sound of a zipper opening, then closing, in quick succession. There was a breath caught in a cough: it came from Ariel, still prostrate and heaving beneath Tanya. Then the twin crawled back over to Nic, who reached down to take the thing she now held in her hand.

Jake was not shocked to discover that it was a knife. Why
wouldn't it be a knife? He had clearly stepped into a dreamworld,
and even though the dream had turned out to be a nightmare,
at least it followed its own perverted logic. At this juncture in
the story, it would only make sense that Nic would be wielding
a knife in his outstretched hand—not a slick little steak knife,
but a thick, angular slab of metal, the kind made for hacking—
and that he would now be using the tip of that knife to point
directly at Jake, and then at Sasha, and then would say:

"Now, who's going to play god?"

Sasha dropped Jake's hand.

"What are you asking us to do?" Sasha said.

Jake would've asked the question himself, but he was too
afraid to speak. Generally, it seemed unwise to ask questions of
a person who was aiming a knife at you and was also fucked up
on mysterious substances.

Nic lowered the knife. He seemed vaguely irked. "The
ethos," he responded, "dictates that the commingling of the
blood of good and evil creates perfect balance."

Jake was listening to Nic as he spoke, but he couldn't stop
looking at Tanya: She'd begun moving against Ariel again, swaying to the syncopated beat of a strange little tune she hummed
to herself. Her gaze remained fixed ahead of her, into the trees
that encroached upon the ruins. Ariel remained mostly still,
but his hands had gravitated up toward her hips. He seemed
to be enjoying this. Jake felt his face flush, equally in shame as
in horror.

"The drawing of blood," Nic was saying, "is the final act in
our ritual, and the most important." He mimed a slice at the
palm of his hand with the knife, silently conveying what he was
asking Sasha and Jake to do: a cut in Tanya's palm, a cut in Ariel's—deep enough to draw blood—then joining them together.

Jake blanched. He understood the secret society shtick—up until a few minutes ago, he'd even been enjoying participating in the charade—but he was simply incapable of enacting harm on another person, even if it was consensual. Especially if that person was Tanya. The idea of it—the phantom weight of the knife in his hand, then the snap and drag of the skin breaking under its blade—sent a ticklish shudder through his arm and straight to his heart, leaving his whole body weak.

No. He wouldn't do it. If it meant that he lost these people, then so be it.

Because there was at least one other person in his life who loved him, and whom he loved in return. And that person could be enough, if it came to it.

Apparently, Sasha had a similar idea. "I'm not doing that," she said.

Her bravery was a buttress. Finally, Jake felt strong enough to speak. "I'm not either," he said. "That's just—disgusting."

On the ground, Tanya whipped her head toward Jake and raised herself to her knees. "Pussy," she spat.

Jake didn't know whether to laugh or cry. He knew he shouldn't take the denunciation seriously. Tanya was not herself. Sober Tanya never would have said that to him.

Still. The word aimed directly at the tenderest part of himself—the part that blinked painfully at the barest flash of light, that shuddered at a harsh word, that wanted only to retreat deeper into itself until it collapsed. The part that he had scrambled to keep locked away, ever since it had revealed its duckling-soft head.

What could Jake even say in response? *No, I'm not? You hurt my feelings? How could you say something so cruel to someone who told you they loved you?*

Of course he couldn't say that. That was schoolyard shit,

and anyway, it would only feed directly into the curse she'd launched at him.

Instead, he said, "You're a crazy fucking bitch."

It was the best he could do to rise to the occasion, and even before the last word sprang forth, he wished, so badly, that he could return to the past. For a moment he was struck by the deep unfairness of linear time. It was only a second ago that he'd said what he'd said, barely even the past, so close he could raise a hand and still feel the words pushing against his palm, like he could gather them up and stuff them inside his pocket.

But he'd said it. He couldn't unsay it. The words worked their dark magic. Tanya shoved Ariel's hands away from her hips, stalked toward Nic, and grabbed the knife. Nic's grip must have been loose; it slid too easily from his hand.

Tanya looked at Jake. She was a stranger.

She said: "If you won't do it, then I will."

Everything happened so quickly after that.

Tanya moved toward Ariel, who'd propped himself semi-upright on his elbows, and threw a slash across his cheek. Kneeling over him, she bared her left wrist toward herself and used the length of the blade to slice a line, horizontally, across the flesh. She moved the knife to the left hand, the ruined one—it was shaking, now, the blood pooling inside her grip—and did the same to her right wrist. Through it all Tanya's face remained expressionless, her movements smooth and considered, but her breathing turned jagged when she dropped the knife on the ground, her work finished, then held her wrists upright and away from her body, watching the thick rivulets of blood drip down her forearms.

Then Ariel curled back into the dirt, clutching his face with his hand, and the spell shattered. Someone screamed. Jake plummeted back down into his body. He followed Taylor and Jess over toward Nic, who'd carried Tanya over to the other side of the mansion's ruined wall, back toward the fire, while the others peeled off and rushed toward Ariel.

Taylor and Jess crouched at Tanya's feet to wrap their discarded togas around her wrists, pressing down hard to stanch the blood. Nic wrapped his other arm around her shoulder, rubbing it in soothing strokes. Tanya kept her face buried in Nic's chest, squeezing her eyes tight. The pain must have set in.

Jake stood behind Taylor and Jess, his role unassigned.

"We need to take her to a hospital," Jake said. Over the ruin's wall, he could just make out Ariel's face. Even from this distance, he could see that it was half-coated in blood. "Both of them," he added.

Taylor turned and assessed Jake. "No," she said. "They can't know we gave her anything. She was already on something."

"What kind of something?" Jake asked. Had they taken something before the ritual? Tanya rarely did any kind of recreational anything—she wasn't even a very big drinker. It didn't seem like her to double up in one night.

"Tanya's on medication that might interact with certain kinds of drugs and alcohol," Jess said.

"What kind of medication?"

"Tanya has bipolar disorder." Taylor looked at Jake quizzically, but without a shred of sympathy. She was seeing him for exactly who he was: an interloper. "She never told you that?"

No, she never told him that. Jake suddenly felt like he knew nothing at all. He felt like he knew no one. He didn't care that Tanya had bipolar disorder—he didn't give a shit about that—but why hadn't she ever told him? What was wrong with him that she didn't feel she could trust him with this information?

"I don't think the hospital will care about who gave her the drugs," Jake said now. "They just need to stabilize her."

"We can't risk it," Taylor said, with renewed force. "Our parents would literally disown us if they found out about this.

And think about what the school would do. They'd probably expel everyone implicated, which is all of us."

Then Ryan, Jordan, and Sasha came over, bearing Ariel's weight between them. The left side of his face was a mess of blood. It dripped down his chin, his neck.

"We need to get them back down," Ryan said. He was panting a little, from fear or exertion or adrenaline, Jake didn't know.

But Tanya lifted her head and turned toward Ariel, slowly and deliberately. Even in the dark, Jake could see the challenge blazing in her eyes.

"You deserved it," she said.

"What the fuck are you talking about?" Ariel said, his words garbled by his swollen lip.

"You know what you did."

Jake's stomach dropped. He tried to think back to that period of time between talking to Tanya by the fire and hearing that animal wail. He'd lost track of her, and he couldn't remember seeing Ariel anywhere, either. Could something have happened between them then? It was possible. Jake hadn't known Ariel to be violent, but there was something about him that Jake had never quite trusted, like he was carrying a lipstick-sized pistol.

Whatever Ariel might have done to Tanya—had that sent her over the edge?

Or, Jake thought, with a bolt of horror, was it his own words—hateful, untrue, spewed in a moment of weakness—that had also aimed directly at Tanya's softest parts? Was that the flick that unlatched her latent rage?

Now Ariel released a laugh. "You really are a crazy fucking bitch."

Then Nic stood, erecting a physical wall between Tanya and Ariel, but Tanya continued to bellow behind him. "That wasn't part of the script," she repeated. "That wasn't part of the script."

"You need to get him away from her," Nic said to Ryan. "She can't get more worked up."

Ryan hooked his arm around Ariel's shoulders, and Ariel made a play to shove him off, but the fight was drained out of him. Eventually, he let Ryan lead him back toward the ruins, out of sight again.

"They both need medical attention," Sasha said when they were gone. "We need to take them to the hospital."

Jake was relieved that she'd said it. The violence of that exchange between Tanya and Ariel . . . It was all wrong. And he wasn't—none of them were—equipped to handle the fallout.

They needed professionals. They needed adults.

"I agree," he said now.

"No," Nic said, and with that word Jake deflated completely. "Taylor's right. No one can find out about this."

"I know where we can take them," Jordan said then. "Dr. Lowman. His wife is a nurse."

"Wouldn't he tell the school?" Jake said.

Again, Nic only said: "No."

"There was another incident, years ago," Jordan finally said, sensing Jake's and Sasha's confusion. "An S&S student committed suicide."

"Parker's death was completely unrelated to the society," Nic said. "Nothing like . . ." He gestured toward Tanya, who was now silent and had retreated beneath his arm.

"The society used to include someone from the faculty as an honorary member," Jordan explained. "They were mostly there to moderate their discussions. They didn't come to the parties or anything."

"That was Dr. Lowman," Jake guessed.

Jordan nodded. "Steve still felt responsible for Parker's death," she continued. "He and Parker were close. He felt like he should've seen the signs. So after he died, he took a step back from the society, and the remaining members decided not to continue the tradition of involving a faculty liaison at all. It was just easier that way."

"And now you're implicating him in another potential scandal," Sasha said.

"We can trust him," Taylor repeated.

"What makes you so sure?" Sasha said.

"The longer we wait, the worse this is going to get," Taylor responded. She nodded at Jordan. "Just make the call." Jordan disappeared, heading down toward the trail to pick up cell service. Then Taylor nodded at Nic. "You're sober enough to drive, right?"

"I can be," he responded.

"We need another driver for Ariel," Taylor said. She dispatched Jess to find out from Ryan whether he was good to drive, then redirected her attention to Nic. She would be a great commander, Jake thought. The lines of her body had expanded and glowed when she'd stepped into her authority. "Nic, you'll take us to Steve's. I'll call Ryan when we're on the way; then he can take Ariel and the others down and head over there. We shouldn't let Tanya near him again."

Jordan and Jess reappeared then, and the plan clicked into place. Steve and Mariah were ready for them, Jordan said, and Ryan gave the okay to drive.

Nic and Taylor helped Tanya up while Jake hung back, trying to catch Tanya's eye. But she was unreachable. She had abandoned him—abandoned all of them—completely.

Jake followed them to the car and helped Tanya into the back seat. Taylor and Jess sat on either side of her, and then he climbed into the passenger seat. When Nic had peeled out of the parking lot and turned onto the highway, Taylor called Jordan, giving her the go-ahead to bring Ariel down to the other car.

And then it was silent. The dark road unspooled before them.

Jake looked down at his shoes, tucked inside the shadows below the passenger seat. Somehow, in the confusion, they'd become mottled with someone's blood. Tanya's, probably. He couldn't help but feel his heart sink. It would be impossible to get them clean again, and he'd never be able to tell his dad what had happened to them. He would be so upset with Jake.

"What do you think she meant?" he asked quietly.

"What who meant?" Nic said.

Jake glanced back at Tanya. He didn't want to invoke her name and break this fragile peace.

Nic shook his head. "Who knows? She's beyond fucked up."

"She's more than fucked up," Jake said. "I'm fucked up, you're fucked up, everyone is fucked up, but no one else is slashing their wrists and attacking people's faces and accusing them of—"

"Accusing them of what?" Jess interjected from the back seat.

"You heard her," Jake said.

"No, I didn't," Jess said. "I have no idea what you're talking about."

"Assault!" The word slipped out like a hand grenade. He waited for the explosion for a minute, then two, until it was clear that it would never come.

He looked in the rearview mirror. Jess's face was stoic, serene. No one else said a word.

"Why are you doing this?" Jake finally said.

"We're protecting ourselves," Jess said. "That includes you, too."

Then Taylor cleared her throat. "It goes without saying that no one can say a word about this." Taylor met his gaze in the mirror. "Not a single part of it."

He knew what she was doing; he *knew* that what he saw

between Tanya and Ariel was not exactly how the bigger plan was supposed to go, even though that plan was one thousand kinds of fucked up.

But he couldn't shake the feeling that he was wrong.

Even if he was right, he couldn't stomach the consequences if he spoke up. Maybe Tanya wouldn't press charges, but even still, the school would probably launch an investigation, and even if that investigation couldn't necessarily result in expulsion—Ariel had already graduated, safely outside the school's jurisdiction—it would spell crushing humiliation, the tainting of reputations. Not just Tanya's but the entire society's. The society itself would probably grind to a halt. He would destroy everything. He would lose these people. He would be trapped with himself.

No. He couldn't do it.

He knew this made him a bad person, possessed of every shade of weakness and cowardice and disloyalty.

But he'd known this anyway. Even if, to a casual observer, he seemed like a fine person, relatively innocuous, he had always known that there was something wrong with him.

And there was something delicious about sinking into his worst nature, now, to offer himself something to point to and show the world: *Here I am. What you see is exactly how bad I feel.*

In the back seat, Tanya's ragged breath had smoothed. A quick look behind his shoulder revealed her sleeping form, slumped across Jess's lap.

It was almost like nothing had ever happened. Like she had snared them all in some unthinkable dream.

CHAPTER
TWENTY-THREE

"We promised not to tell anyone about what happened that night," Jordan said. Over the past hour or so she had shifted forward in her chair, talking animatedly, full armed. Now, returning to the present, her energy dimmed, bending under the reality of everything she had just said.

"You made a pact?" Kate said.

"I wouldn't be so melodramatic about it. We just came to a mutual agreement."

"But Tanya still took a leave of absence," Kate said. "The school must have known that something had happened to her."

"She dropped out," Jordan clarified. "And yes, the school and her parents knew she'd experienced a . . . mental break. But Tanya never told them what triggered it."

"Did Tanya ever press charges against Ariel?" Jordan shook her head. "And I can only assume she never followed up privately, either."

"I don't know if she did," Jordan admitted. "I doubt she even remembers what happened that night."

"But you do."

Jordan's eyes blazed with anger. "I know what you're trying to accuse us of," she said, "but you should know better than anyone that people are innocent until proven guilty. And we have no evidence suggesting that Ariel did anything to provoke her before the incident. He swears up and down that he never touched her. We know Ariel. We trust him. Why wouldn't we believe him?"

Kate took a breath. Technically, this was true, but her gut was telling her something very different. But this wasn't the time to hunt down that feeling.

"And Dr. Lowman?" Kate asked.

"He respected our wishes to keep this a secret."

"And I was going to leak that secret," Kate said. "That's why you sent me those anonymous texts."

The revelation had dawned on her days earlier, but Jordan's story validated her suspicion.

"Dr. Lowman told me you'd asked him about the society. I got scared." Jordan shrugged, conveying the justification she couldn't articulate. But Kate didn't need any further explanation. She had acted emotionally. She was twenty-one years old. Kate had forgiven Jordan for those texts as soon as she'd seen how defeated the girl had looked when she'd opened the door for her. How sapped of joy.

"But what did Tanya want?" Kate said now. "Did Tanya want to keep it a secret?"

"Of course she did. She wanted what was best for all of us. Mariah cared for her and Ariel overnight, but she insisted that Tanya should get more intensive medical attention once she was stabilized. Tanya actually agreed to that. I called her parents myself to let them know what was happening, and later she and her parents decided together that she would take the rest of the semester off. Possibly the rest of the year. Forever. I don't know." Jordan sighed deeply. "She's in pretty intense therapy right now. I haven't really been able to speak to her."

"But she's okay?" Kate said.

"I honestly don't know what to say to that."

"I spoke to Jake's friend Rex," Kate said, after a moment. "He said that Jake began to pull away around that time. He stopped journaling, too."

"Didn't I already tell you that?" Jordan said, her frustration seeping through the cracks. Kate didn't have much longer with her; she needed to get her answers and then get out. "Jake and Sasha both pulled away from us after that night. We all had each other's backs, and neither of them wanted any part of that. Not that I blame them. They just . . . weren't as close with us as we were with each other." Finally Jordan collapsed back into her chair. She was done. "Is that all you wanted to know?"

"One more thing." Kate passed Jordan her phone—earlier, in Wachs's office, she'd captured images of the security camera footage when he wasn't looking. She didn't feel bad about this.

Kate pointed to the braceleted arm of the figure disappearing into the exit stairwell, Sasha trailing behind.

"Can you identify this person?"

Jordan looked at her, pleadingly. "Please don't make me say it." But Kate held her stare. "Taylor," she finally said. She put a hand to her mouth, as if she were trying to force the name back inside.

"You're positive?"

"As positive as I can be."

"Had she and Sasha been arguing?" Jordan nodded. "Because Sasha threatened to tell the school about what really happened that night."

"Yes."

"What about Ariel?"

Jordan shot her a sad look. "I already told you. We don't know what he did to Tanya, if he did anything at all."

The pieces clicked together. "But Sasha knew," Kate said.

Jordan nodded.

"She spoke to Tanya?" Kate asked.

"I don't think so," Jordan said. Quietly, she added, "I think she saw what happened between them. If anything happened at all."

"So everyone was protecting Ariel," Kate said. Anger crested like a wave. Tanya was the one who'd needed protecting—not Ariel. It wasn't clear whether Ariel had attacked her, and Kate knew she should stick to the presumption of innocence principle. But instincts were a lawyer's best asset, second only to a knack for creative interpretation. And her instincts were blazing.

Jordan stayed on the defense. "We were protecting *all* of us," she said. "And Sasha never told any of us what she saw or what she knew."

"Did Ariel wipe the security footage?"

"Nic," Jordan said. "He did it for Taylor."

"And Taylor did what she did for her sister, because Jess supplied the drugs."

"You have to understand that it was an accident," Jordan said. "They got into a fight, it got physical, Taylor pushed her, and Sasha lost her footing and fell down the stairs. But Taylor knew the cameras would've caught everything, and she panicked."

"And she knew Nic would've done anything to protect her."

"Nic watched the footage himself," Jordan said. "He swears it was an accident."

"You know I'm going to have to bring this information to the police," said Kate. "They're going to question you again. All of you."

"I know."

"Thank you again for your help. You've been instrumental."

"Instrumental," Jordan repeated. "Great."

Kate busied herself with putting her phone back into her purse, reaping these last few moments she had with her.

Finally she stood. Jordan remained in her chair, staring at nothing. But Kate couldn't help pushing a little bit further.

"Do you remember the last time you saw him?" Kate asked.

Jordan didn't look at Kate when she answered. "Earlier this month. It was at the Levee, a dive bar a few towns over. I hadn't seen him since everything happened. His back was turned to me, but I knew it was him. I wanted to go over to him, to say something—I don't even know what, just to acknowledge him—but he looked like he was deep in conversation."

"He was there with someone?"

"I don't know who she was," Jordan said. "I didn't recognize her."

"Do you remember what she looked like? Hair color, height, skin tone, anything?"

"I'm sorry," Jordan said. "It was dark; it was late. I was drunk."

"But it was a woman," Kate said.

"Female presenting," Jordan corrected.

"Right," Kate said. "But . . . how did he seem?"

Jordan's gaze snapped back onto Kate. "He seemed like he wasn't even there."

Kate didn't wonder at the contempt in Jordan's voice when she said it.

———

Outside Jordan's apartment Kate paced across the sidewalk, taking stock. Jordan had vindicated her suspicions about Sasha's death. She virtually confirmed that Jake died by suicide, a decision triggered by an inability to handle the weight of the secret he'd been holding on to—possibly worsened by the pressure from the group. All the questions she had held so tightly since the moment she learned that Jake was dead—all were disappeared, and now she was returned to herself.

But doubt still lingered. She still felt like she was missing some crucial piece of the puzzle.

She didn't call Wachs. There would be time to field his anger for sneaking around with witnesses (tempered, Kate was sure, by her imminent disappearance from his town forever). Eventually, there would be time to relish the opportunity to prove that she was right.

Well, she was right that someone had been killed. But it wasn't the person she'd thought.

For now, she needed to reflect. To metabolize. To figure out what the hell to do with herself, now that she no longer had a clear purpose.

Really, there was only one person who would care to talk to her about this. She pulled out her phone and sent her a text.

Jake jumped. Nothing more to it.

I know you asked for space, but I wanted to tell you that.

She received her answer soon after.

Kate - I'm so happy you reached out to me.

I was planning on a hike tomorrow at noon. Want to come?

CHAPTER
TWENTY-FOUR

The Jungle poster. The Cure poster. The Kandinsky poster. The Jim Jarmusch poster. The *Psycho* poster. The Cocteau Twins poster. Kate unpeeled them all from the wall, careful not to tear them, and rolled them into tight cigars and stacked them in a pyramid beside the front door. She lifted the framed Hockney print from its mount and set it against the wall. She emptied the drawers and put the clothes in the Bankers Boxes she'd bought in bulk at the hardware store, folding everything first. Then the books, the desk lamp, the things in the nightstand. She threw away the toiletries moldering in the shower, but first she ordered two bottles of his peppermint soap on Amazon and had it sent to her apartment in SF. The shoes and laptop and phone were wrapped in layers of newspaper and placed into their own individual boxes. The sheets, she would deal with later. All of the furniture would stay, per the deal John had struck with the landlord almost two weeks earlier.

I'm proud of you, John had said when they spoke over the phone last night and she'd told him that she was finally beginning to pack up Jake's things. Then he'd invited her to dinner, but Kate declined. For that night—one of her last nights—she needed to be alone.

He hadn't asked what had prompted Kate's sudden acceptance of her inevitable fate, and she was glad about that, because she couldn't tell him. Not after the way he had reacted when Kate had shared with him the barest hint of what this investigation had entailed—that there was an investigation at all.

John probably thought the steady sway of his mere presence had been the impetus for Kate to begin to behave in kind. Kate didn't care. She was no longer in the business of caring what John needed to believe in order to make himself feel better.

She'd begun packing at five in the morning, and now it was eleven, an hour before Luna would arrive to take her on the hike. She popped down to Tony's and was relieved to find her usual seat empty. The ritual took on a new importance, now that it was reaching its end.

Richard came over with a laminated menu and a pitcher of ice water.

"You look good today," he said, pouring her a glass.

"Why do you seem amused?" Kate said. She'd seen his smile.

"Not amused in the slightest." He placed the menu before her. "Happy."

"That makes one of us." She made a show of glancing over the menu while Richard pulled out his pad and pencil. "I suppose I feel more . . . settled."

It was true: Though she had expected to be in hysterics while packing up Jake's apartment, what she had actually experienced felt closer to a flow state, a trance. She hadn't really known what she was doing over the past week—each step of her investigation had revealed itself slowly, a figure emerging, limb by limb, through a slowly clearing mist. She had almost forgotten what it felt like to take control over her actions: to set a goal and complete it, each step clearly defined and executed with total confidence. She had to admit, too, that packing forced upon her the sense of finality that she had resisted facing. Now she cautiously welcomed its arrival. In her head, she'd even begun drafting the email she'd send to Tracy, begging for her job back.

"Does that mean you'll be staying in Sutter Point a little longer?" Richard asked.

"The opposite, I'm afraid. I'll be leaving in a couple of days."

"Time to begin to live," Richard offered.

Then she looked out the window and saw Luna outside. Kate checked her watch—Luna was ten minutes early. Kate asked Richard for two cream cheese bagels to go, plus a chocolate croissant and two coffees, then spent the next five minutes watching Luna pacing across the sidewalk in front of her parked car. Back and forth, back and forth. She never ventured past the tip or tail of her car.

When she joined Luna on the sidewalk five minutes later, breakfast in hand, Luna seemed startled to see her.

"Nervous?" Kate said.

Luna smiled, but she looked weary. She gestured to the diner's windowed wall. "No chance you saw me from in there, right?"

"We all have our quirks."

"Hm." Luna looked at Kate for a beat, then two. Kate couldn't quite parse what she saw in her expression: Fondness? Skepticism? Regret? Kate hoped it wasn't the latter. What Luna had said the last time they'd seen each other had hurt, but it wasn't unforgivable. And she didn't want to leave either this woman, whom she liked, or this godforsaken town, which she both hated and loved, with any bad blood. She needed a clean break.

Wordlessly, Kate handed Luna a bag and a coffee—a peace offering—and got into the passenger seat. Luna followed after her, peeling off the sidewalk and heading toward the highway.

As Luna drove, Kate filled her in on what she'd discovered about Sasha's death, and what had happened to cause it.

"I spoke to Wachs on the phone last night," Kate continued. "He thanked me for staying on his ass about this, and he actually accepted that he was wrong to discourage my interest in Sasha. Turns out I'm not crazy."

"I never thought you were crazy," Luna said. "So, you know what happened to Sasha. But what about Jake?"

"I suppose there's nothing more to know." Luna was silent. After a while, Kate said, "But I still have this feeling that I'm missing something. I still don't know who this girl is he referred to in his note."

"He mentioned a girl?" Luna said. "What did he say about her?"

"The whole letter was centered around a girl, actually. I think he'd become close with her after he left the society and confided in her about what had happened. It sounded like she wanted to help him, but maybe she didn't know how to."

"Couldn't it be someone from the society? Sasha, maybe? It sounds like they were on each other's sides."

"It can't be Sasha," Kate said. "In the note, Jake writes that this girl asked if he took a blood oath. That means she wasn't there, at the ritual. She didn't see what had happened. She was an outsider." Kate looked out the window for a moment. "Jordan mentioned that the last time she saw him, he was at a bar with a girl she didn't recognize. It could be her, whoever she might be."

"It could be," Luna said, turning into the dirt parking lot at the base of the trail. "But does it really matter who she was? The upshot is the same."

That was when Kate noticed where they were: the trail that led up to the Wayside. She should have assumed Luna would take them there—it was her favorite hiking trail—but she hadn't considered the logistics. She'd just been happy that Luna had answered her text.

"Are you ready?" Luna said.

Kate was stalling, peering out the windshield, through the tree cover and up to the invisible ruins beyond.

She took a deep breath. She could do this. The closure might even be good for her.

"Let's go," she said.

They were quiet on the way up. Kate imagined retracing Jake's steps that night, imagining his fear and innocence. There was nothing she wouldn't do, she thought now, to stop him from reaching the summit of this trail that night. She broadened the scope of her reflection to encompass all the kids coming up here, naive to the fact that something horrible was about to happen. And that the horrible thing would reap even more horrible things.

"I'm really sorry about Jake," Luna said, breaking Kate's musings. "I know I've told you that before, but I feel like I need to say it again. I need you to know that."

"Of course I know that," Kate said. "Thank you."

"You don't need to thank me for stating a fact."

Then they reached the summit. A pair of hikers sat on the low stone wall over by the ruined mansion's chimney, engaged in a quiet conversation, and another, lone hiker stood near the edge of the cliff, hands on his hips, surveying the view.

But Kate barely even noticed the view. It was that lone hiker that Kate was drawn to most.

She left Luna by the mouth of the clearing, moving closer to the person at the end of the trail. The lines of his body were shadowed by the sun that hung like a coin directly above him, but Kate couldn't help but feel that she knew him.

And then he turned around.

Kate took a step back, physically recoiling from the person she saw. It was so unlikely that he would be here—this trail was under the radar, best known to locals and avid hikers, of which he was neither—and his presence, in that sacred spot, bordered on the uncanny.

That was when John noticed Kate, too.

But his gaze flickered quickly to Luna, who had now come to stand beside Kate.

And his gaze rested there, on Luna. Recognition dawned on his face, quickly blotted out by horror.

"What are you doing here?" he said.

He wasn't talking to Kate. He was talking to Luna.

CHAPTER
TWENTY-FIVE

Her mother always told her that one parent was enough. But her mother was a liar, because then her mother died, and Sophia was left with nothing, and nothing was not enough. Nothing was the antithesis of enough. There was a reason why it took two humans to create a child. Children needed a spare. Especially children who turned into thirty-year-olds, with nothing to their name other than a Nissan Altima, an admin job at a food-services company in Queens that catered to public schools and jails, and a rented apartment in Rego Park, shared with a blue betta fish and an aloe plant, both three years old and refusing to die.

Sophia had a father, of course, but her father had been little more to her mother than an accidental sperm donor and a bank account since he'd knocked her up when he was a smart, cocky senior at Bayside High School. Claudia was the daughter of the drugstore owner in town. She'd caught John's eye stocking the shampoo shelves. She had been one year younger, also a student at Bayside High, but too quiet for John Cleary to ever notice her in the halls.

According to the lore, John and Claudia had spent one

summer together. By the time Claudia discovered that she was pregnant, John had already shipped off to Cornell, without even leaving a phone number or an address. Which was just as well. Claudia was confident that she could raise her baby alone, even after her parents kicked her out of the house and she was forced to make her own way with odd jobs—waitressing mostly, but there was also a stint as a maid at the Marriott in Fresh Meadows, a teacher's assistant at the preschool at the conservative synagogue, and a remote customer-service representative for an insurance company based in Kentucky—and charity from sympathetic friends (of which she had very few) and coworkers (of which, over the years, she had many).

John didn't find out about the child he had sired until that child was three years old, and even that wasn't Claudia's choice. John and Claudia ran into each other in downtown Bayside when John was home for Christmas his senior year of college. By that point, Claudia's parents had thawed enough to cautiously request visitations with Sophia, their granddaughter, but not enough to offer Claudia any kind of help—either financial or emotional—or even really to look her in the eye.

Claudia had been on her way to her parents' house, Sophia in the stroller in tow, when she saw John for the first time since the last time they'd seen each other, three years and eleven months earlier. John was walking toward her on the sidewalk, his arms loaded with grocery bags. He stopped short when he saw Claudia, then blanched when he saw the baby. Sophia looked nothing like John—she'd inherited Claudia's corn silk hair and her fox-like chin and her high, fluting laugh—but even at three, she'd already adopted the steady, disarming gaze that her father had used to snare her mother.

It must've been that stare that'd drawn John in, too. Like called to like.

John didn't even ask Claudia if Sophia was his. The question might as well have been scrawled across his face. Claudia nodded, a silent answer to a silent question, and John veered over to the trash can in front of the laundromat and vomited.

Then they went to the Taiwanese restaurant next to the laundromat and ordered hot sake and three-cup chicken, and by the end of the meal John had promised Claudia he would do whatever he could to help. Claudia refused, John insisted, and Claudia wasn't so proud or stupid to refuse him a second time.

So the story went.

The "help," of course, referred to money, which was not much at first, then a little more when John completed law school, and then enough to become insulting when he pivoted from big law to a private practice. (Doing what, Claudia never knew; it was Sophia who had later thought to ask.)

From the start, John never indicated that he was capable of being present in Sophia's life, nor that he was particularly interested in that kind of dedication. That was just fine with Claudia, and Claudia made it be fine with Sophia.

But it was not actually fine with Sophia. Annual birthday cards stuffed with cash and a dashed-off note did not a father make.

And as much as her mother would have liked to believe otherwise—a borderline-clinical condition that, later, after checking out Leon Festinger's theory on the topic from her high school's library, Sophia diagnosed as chronic cognitive dissonance—something vital and essential was lacking in their home. This probably began and ended with the distance between the two people occupying it. Claudia worked constantly, for which Sophia could not begrudge her. But she *could* begrudge her mother for the ways in which she chose to spend the dearth of her downtime. Quilting, watching glorified soap operas on Bravo, smoking one pack of Marlboro Ultra Lights per day. None of the above activities involved Sophia, both because Sophia had no interest in any of those things (she preferred baking, surfing porn-adjacent Tumblrs, and rereading Chuck Palahniuk's entire oeuvre) and because Claudia had never invited her daughter's participation.

A father, Sophia thought, might warm the place up.

On her sixteenth birthday, Sophia made an executive decision to contact John on the phone—a heretofore-uncharted mode of communication—without consulting Claudia first. Sophia knew Claudia would warn her against the overture at best, confiscate her cell phone at worst, and she believed she was making the adult decision in avoiding yet another unnecessary fight with her mother.

It wasn't hard to find John's cell phone number in Claudia's address book. It wasn't like Claudia had purposefully hidden his contact information from Sophia—Sophia was, after all, in possession of all the addresses John had occupied over the past thirteen years— but it *was* hard to get him to answer his phone. She tried him three times that day, three times the next, and four times the third. By that point, she was starting to worry. Was John sick? Was he dead? Had he changed his cell phone number without bothering to tell Claudia? Sophia couldn't decide which was the sadder answer. Or was it sadder that she needed to ask herself these questions at all?

Finally, on the second ring on the fourth day, Sophia got through to someone on the other end.

But it wasn't John. It was a woman.

"John can't come to the phone right now," the woman said. She sounded harried and pretty. Sophia had no idea whether John was married or dating or in any kind of relationship at all, and now Sophia felt real fear, the kind her ancestors' ancestors must have felt when they were being chased by wild animals.

She didn't really know why. She knew that this woman was not a threat to her livelihood. She could claim no real ownership over John Cleary, other than the biological, and logic would dictate that that wasn't evidence enough.

Then again, biology usually trumped logic.

Sophia considered hanging up. But her curiosity overtook her panic.

"Is he okay?" Sophia said. She tried to keep her voice steady, to make herself sound older than she was, but it still wobbled on the last word.

"He's fine," the woman said. "He thought he lost this phone, he went and bought a new one, and of course I find the old phone now."

"Where was it?"

"In our son's toy chest," the woman responded. "Can I ask who's calling?"

"Sophia," said Sophia.

There was a pause on the other end. "Is there a last name?"

Sophia's stomach dropped. There was a woman in her father's life. There was also another child. Neither had any idea that Sophia existed.

"Harding," Sophia said, because there was no point in lying.

Another pause. "How do you know my husband?"

That was when Sophia hung up. Let John's wife believe he was having an affair. Let them fight over it, let them divorce over it, let them ruin the son's life. Surely it wouldn't be Sophia's problem. Sophia might even sleep better at night, knowing that justice had been served, and so poetically, too.

———

Sophia didn't sleep better at night. She slept much, much worse. She couldn't stop thinking about the wife, but mostly, she couldn't stop thinking about the kid, living in the lap of luxury, with two parents who loved him and gave him a chest for his toys and probably a big house to live in, too.

One night, some unseen force delivered to her an image of the boy being dropped on his eggshell skull and splattering yellow goo across a white nursery carpet. The thought returned the next night, and the next, and the next it was followed by the image of her, Sophia, pushing her thumb into the boy's fontanel like it was a little pot of Gak, and then of the boy alone on a park bench at night, surrounded by dense forest teeming with untamed beasts and wild-eyed wanderers.

A hand reached out from the darkness. It tugged the boy's head back in a single hard jerk. His white throat, a baby's throat, was doughy and ringed.

She filed the thoughts away, overcome with shame, but the things kept shaking loose.

And other, attendant thoughts plagued her, too. These thoughts were less violent, but they were not less disturbing.

For instance: Did the boy look like her? Did he talk like her? Did he have their father's eyes?

Sophia couldn't know. If her father had his way, he would keep her ignorant forever. That was not acceptable.

In freshman-year bio, tracking dominant and recessive traits across a Punnett square, Sophia had discovered, to her humiliation, that she'd been born with a collection of genetic traits that could not be traced to her mother and thus must have been inherited from her father. So it was from these traits, culled by process of elimination, that Sophia formed a kind of Frankensteinian image of her brother.

Her brother, as it turned out, thought brussels sprouts and arugula tasted like soap. Her brother could not roll his tongue into a burrito. Her brother had just one dimple. Her brother did not have a hitchhiker's thumb, and when he folded his hands together, his right thumb settled over his left, just like Sophia's did, and which her mother's did not.

—————

John never called Sophia back. Sophia decided it was because his wife never told him that Sophia had called, not because she had told him and he decided to ignore her. This was the explanation she could live with.

—————

Sophia never stopped thinking about her brother. Over the ensuing years of her adolescence, and then well into her early adulthood, this ersatz version of him took up a regular residence in the part of her consciousness that she kept hidden from others, but which took on an outsized role in her inner monologue, much the same as a child's imaginary friend would. In this way, her brother accompanied her on dates, job interviews, and trips to the grocery store. He weighed in on the movies Sophia should rent on demand—he had clearly defined opinions about directors. And also about the routes she should take to work to avoid traffic. He suggested that she not send an angry text to the person she'd been seeing for three weeks who'd then ghosted her. He suggested that she not cut bangs. He suggested that she not feel sad that their father had moved back to New York, and not to feel ashamed that John had not reached out and asked to meet, even though he now lived so close that Sophia could practically see his high-rise glittering across the East River. He suggested that she give her mother a call every now and then, too. Sophia never heeded that advice,

and she let him know just how offensive she found it that he
had an opinion on her mother at all.

⸺

Either luckily or unluckily—even later, she could never decide
which—the brother Sophia had created was dashed to pieces
with the advent of social media. Sophia would google her father's name on a semi-regular basis over the years, and those
searches bore no tantalizing fruit.

Until one night, a few years ago, after coming home from a
particularly soul-crushing first date, she'd opened an incognito
window on Chrome—as the ritual always commenced—and
typed in her father's name, expecting the usual stale lineup of his
contact information at the firm preceded by unusable information pertaining to John and Jon Clearys who were not her father.

This time, though, she navigated to the Images section—the
second step in her ritual—and was confronted with a photograph she had not seen ten thousand times before. It showed
an older man with his arm around a teenage boy who looked
somehow both bored and bewildered. Both were dressed in
button-down shirts, blazers, and khaki pants, but the boy's
shirt was noticeably rumpled, hanging a little too loosely off
his skinny frame. The boy had dark hair, like John's, with the
kind of wavy texture and noncut that defied taming with a
brush. He probably had an inch or two over John, but he held
the extra height uncomfortably, like a gift he never asked for
and now didn't know what to do with. In the background was
a rolling green lawn dotted with round tables, all of which were
laid with white tablecloths and tight floral centerpieces. Layers
of high-rise buildings surrounded the space like a green-screen
backdrop, obstructing the sky.

Sophia clicked on the image. The three gin and tonics Sophia had downed earlier threatened to repeat themselves across her keyboard. She was redirected to an article published a month earlier in an online-only magazine covering upscale social events in Manhattan. She scrolled down to the image and read the caption: *John Cleary and his son, Jake Cleary, attend the 42nd Annual Hodgkin's Lymphoma Research Gala at 620 Loft & Garden.*

Jake. Her brother's name was Jake. Somehow, over the years, she had never bothered to give him a name—she'd come to think of him less as a person who lived and breathed in the real world, more an extension of her own personality.

From there, she easily found Jake Cleary's Instagram, which was private, and then his Facebook, which was public.

And then the gaps filled in easily, quick as an undammed river.

Jake was a senior at a fancy prep school in San Francisco that, according to her research, was regularly ranked within the top ten private high schools in the state. He was headed to Paloma College in the fall. A few people, mostly his parents' friends, judging from their formal typing style, wrote their congratulations on his wall. He went to basement parties. He often wore a black-and-white T-shirt from the band Brainiac. He seemed to undergo a massive growth spurt between his freshman and sophomore years of high school; during that time, his Adam's apple also became legible. There was a collection of photos taken in a backyard that belonged to someone named Elsie Walters, a short redhead with big boobs. (Sophia also looked up Elsie Walters— she was gay and went to Berkeley.) Jake had gone to Peru with his mother his junior year. There they were, that tight little duo, perched atop a pair of spangled llamas with the verdant shadow of Machu Picchu standing sentinel behind them.

Jake's mother. John's wife. She was real.

And she was on Facebook. Her name was Kate. She was the general counsel at a technology company called Chalice. She was just as pretty as Sophia had suspected, all those years ago, when she'd spoken to her over the phone.

That was about as much as Sophia could take. She shut her laptop, headed for the bathroom, and stuck her finger down her throat.

———

It didn't come as a surprise when Claudia died three years later. Less a surprise that it was lung cancer that did her in, caught at stage four because Claudia had done nothing, over the preceding few years, to investigate her hacking cough and chronic chest pain, nor to quit her pack-a-day habit.

After Claudia received her diagnosis, Sophia packed up her fish and her plant and moved back into the bowels of Long Island to take care of her. At first her mother had refused her ministrations. Then she grew too weak to fight her off. In some ways, those last couple of months with her mother were the most peaceful they'd ever spent together.

The day her mother died, Sophia wrote to John to let him know. Underneath her sign-off, she left him her cell phone number. *In case you want to give me a call*, she'd added, passive-aggressively. It wasn't the first time Sophia had thought to give John her number. But before now, she hadn't been truly desperate—only curious.

A week later, she was packing up her mother's home, preparing to list it on the market later that month (she'd gotten in touch with a real estate agent as soon as Claudia started coughing up blood), when she received a call from a 917 number. She knew who it was before she even answered.

"Is this Sophia?" John said. His voice was higher pitched than she'd imagined it would be, but smooth, routinized. It was like he was taking a call with a colleague. One he didn't even care about that much.

You're psychotic, Sophia thought. "Yes," Sophia said. "This is she."

"I'm so sorry to hear about Claudia," John said.

"Thanks," Sophia said.

"I have some really fond memories of your mother," John said.

Liar, Sophia thought. "Like what?" Sophia said.

"We had a lot of fun together," John offered vaguely. "I remember thinking that I wished I'd met her earlier. But by the time we became friends, I was already weeks away from heading up to Cornell."

"Were you dead?"

A confused pause. "What?"

"Did you die when you went to Cornell? Were you dead for the intervening thirty years between getting my mom pregnant and calling me ninety seconds ago?"

"No," John said. "I wasn't." Finally, some contrition. After another, prolonged silence that Sophia vowed not to fill—it was not her job to fill it—John said, "I'm sorry for the absence. I just didn't know how to do all of this. I was young; I barely knew your mother. I didn't even know if I wanted to have children at all."

Sophia wouldn't tell John she knew about Jake—it wasn't the time to wield that particular weapon. Instead, she said, "Thank you for the money. And the cards."

"It was the least I could do."

"Literally, the least." John actually laughed at that. She wasn't trying to be funny. "It's more than many absentee fathers do, I'll give you that."

"Was it terrible?"

"Which part?"

"The end."

"Yes. It was all terrible."

"Did you have anyone to help?"

"No," Sophia said. "Both my grandparents died when I was a teenager."

"Friends?"

"None close enough to deal with this shit."

"Boyfriend?"

Sophia snorted. Of course this boomer would assume that she was straight. (That he was technically a Gen Xer and correct-ish about the present state of her sexuality didn't matter.)

"None to speak of," she said.

No, none to speak of. No one since Shane, her Big Ex, had left her almost two years ago for a woman who looked like a sideways version of Sophia, a woman named Shayna—no joke—who favored the same espadrille brand as Kate Middleton and had an important job as a physician assistant at Queens Hospital Center. Sophia checked up on both of their Instagrams daily via a phishing account (brandon_seaton09837940111). Shane had grown out his hair long enough to wear it in a topknot. It looked bad. *He* looked bad. She couldn't understand how she had ever been attracted to him. The thought of fucking him made her feel physically sick. And she was stuck forever with his stupid handwriting tattooed on her wrist.

"Well, if you ever want to talk, I'm here," John said.

"Thanks," Sophia said. A half-hearted response to a bullshit offer.

"What do you plan to do now?"

What *did* Sophia plan to do now? She hadn't taken the time to think about it. The prospect of returning to her sad apartment and her nothing job filled her with bone-deep dread. There was nothing keeping her here. And it was a seller's market, the agent had told her; assuming she could give the house a deep clean, patch up the water stains, toss or hide all those weird, depressing quilts, and add a ficus or two, she could get a good chunk of change for it. Enough to bridge the gap—miles across, miles deep—that she toed right now.

But actually, she wasn't so scared, gazing into that limitless abyss. Not as scared as she should be.

Mostly, she felt free. So much of her identity had been constructed beneath her mother's scaffolding. Now that the scaffolding was destroyed, the true face of the structure could finally be revealed.

And who was she, really? She didn't know. But she wanted to find out.

Sophia glanced toward her laptop, where she'd kept Jake's Facebook page open since she'd first discovered it years earlier. In his profile picture, he stood dwarfed at the base of a redwood tree. Even though the photo was taken from a distance, Sophia could still detect the shadow of her own face lingering in his—the distance between the eyes; the shape of the teeth.

"I'm moving to California," she finally said.

Within the space of ten days, Sophia quit her job at the food-services company, vacated her studio in Rego Park, signed a lease on a one-bedroom in Sutter Point, dumped the aloe plant and flushed the fish, and landed a job at Paloma College as an administrative assistant in the admissions office, secured with a fawning cover letter, two professional references wrangled by calling in long-standing favors, and a Zoom interview with the outgoing admin assistant, a young woman named Brooke with wet lips and a shiny forehead who, even from the shoulders up, looked to be about forty-seven months pregnant. Sophia wasn't even planning on landing at the college itself—wasn't there a dearth of university jobs?—but a local search on Indeed led her straight to that listing. That she was actually semi-qualified for the role led her to toy with the possibility of maybe one day believing in an abstractly beneficent universal force.

She rented a U-Haul, packed up the Nissan, and drove for three days straight to get to California.

Her training wouldn't start until two weeks before classes began, which was not for another two months, but she still asked Brooke if she could procure a pass to campus. *To familiarize myself with the layout*, she'd said. Brooke did her one better: with the help of IT, she also bestowed upon her a Paloma email address and access to PalomaGate, the school's universal portal used, for different purposes, by students, faculty, and staff.

Thusly she procured the back-end information on Jake that she previously wasn't privy to with a basic Google search. There were his class schedules from all four preceding semesters, plus the upcoming semester; his major (English), his birthday (a Libra), his social security number (673-90-7879), his emergency contact information (Kate Cleary, mother), his home address (a Pacific Heights condo that sold for $2.5 million in 2013, per public records), and his GPA (a respectable 3.64).

This all worked to solidify, for Sophia, the reality of Jake-the-human, and to weaken the perception of Jake-the-avatar, in anticipation of meeting him in the flesh.

Because that was what she was going to do, of course—that was the reason she was here. What she would do when that happened, though, Sophia had no idea. She'd had plenty of time to formulate a plan on her drive out to California, buffeted by

the backdrop of the West's ever-unfolding spaciousness, my-
thologized for triggering epiphany. But she'd failed to harness
either resource. Every time she approached the thought of meeting Jake, she instantly retreated. Told herself she would think
about it tomorrow.

But that promised tomorrow never arrived. She accidentally
found Jake in the library the day after she moved to Sutter Point.

She was tucked behind a study carrel on the eighth floor, re-
viewing Jake's syllabi for the upcoming semester, when she heard
a groan and a squeak approach from behind her. She turned to
find someone emerging from the stacks at her back, pushing a
trolley piled with books across the runway at her side, and disappearing into the stacks in front of her.

It was Jake. She knew this in her gut, even though she'd only
caught the barest glimpse of his profile, half-obscured behind
a mop of dark hair.

Abruptly, she stood. Her mind emptied of thought. She followed his slow pace toward the last stack in the room, watching
the lines of his back shift beneath his white shirt. The trolley
was heavy. He'd angled his torso forward over the handlebar,
arms tucked against his chest, and his feet had gone slightly
pigeon toed with the effort.

"Excuse me," Sophia said. They were the only two people on
this side of the room, but still she kept her voice low. It wouldn't
be right to be overheard.

Jake stopped and stood to his full height—unremarkable,
five feet ten at most, but perfect nonetheless.

Then he turned around.

When Sophia saw her brother's face for the first time, everything clicked into place.

Sophia loved him and she hated him. He was so young, so vulnerable, so sheltered and stupid. Often she couldn't help but manipulate him. It was so easy, like molding a chunk of Play-Doh. Over the few weeks they spent together, their relationship growing deeper, she never told him who she really was. She leveraged his innocence against him. She was Sophia Harding, the administrative assistant in the admissions office, new to Sutter Point and isolated like him, jaded like him. He was too trusting, too susceptible to flattery, but that wasn't his fault. What twenty-year-old boy wouldn't want to believe he had enchanted a pretty older girl? That the campus was nearly empty made the charade easier—it all felt like a dress rehearsal, with no audience to mete out judgment. And Jake didn't have much of a social life to compete with; he told her about a group of kids he'd met last year, all part of some secret society they'd poached him for late last semester. ("Not so secret anymore," Sophia said, when Jake told her about it one night over burritos and beer.) But they'd been ghosting him all summer. The only friends of Jake's who remained on campus were a girl named Sasha and a boy named Rex, and Jake hardly talked about either of them, let alone offered to introduce them. Sophia suspected that they didn't even know that she was a part of Jake's life— that Jake wanted to keep her private, protected.

Jake developed a crush on Sophia, no doubt, but it didn't feel sexual. It felt like hero worship. When he listened to her, his face became an open target; his misty eyes, his liquid mouth.

———

She began to test the bounds of her power over him. One night in late August, a week before classes began, she texted him at one in the morning and asked if he could pick her up from

Waverley's, a wine bar across town. She'd driven herself there and proceeded to get drunk expressly for this purpose. *Give me 20 mins*, he texted back. He called her in fifteen and told her he was waiting in the parking lot. When she emerged from the bar, drunker than she'd initially planned to get, he flashed his brights twice so she could find him. She got into his car. He was red eyed and wearing flannel pajama pants. He drove in silence.

"Are you mad at me?" Sophia said. She knew he wasn't mad. He was jealous and insecure, and he probably didn't even know it.

"Of course I'm not mad," Jake said.

"Did I wake you up?"

"No."

"What were you doing?"

"Watching shit on YouTube."

"You liar," Sophia said. "You were probably jerking off."

Jake held the steering wheel tighter. "You're such an asshole," he said tightly, but he smiled a little when he said it.

When he made a left onto Presidio, heading toward Sophia's apartment, she panicked. She grazed her hand over his knee, just enough to discover the hard ridge of his kneecap beneath her fingertips, then quickly pulled it away.

"I don't want to go home," she said. "Take me to your apartment. Let's hang out." Jake scratched his jaw. Sophia heard the rasp of his stubble. "Or we don't even have to hang out. We can just go to sleep."

Jake glanced at her. She could practically hear him thinking. "It's really late," he said.

"Do whatever you want," Sophia said. She lay back against the headrest and closed her eyes. "You're in charge."

Beneath her, she felt the car turn around.

Back at Jake's apartment, Sophia took off her boots and her socks and got into Jake's bed. Jake lay down on the couch. Even in the dark she caught him looking at her, then looking away.

———

As the semester grew nearer, Jake began to pull away from her. He became anxious, anticipating his friends' return. He needed to focus, he said. Focus on what, Sophia didn't know. Jake didn't seem to really know, either; he'd carried around a book of William Blake poetry with him all summer—one of the initiation rituals for that ridiculous secret society—and now he seemed to believe he needed to memorize every single poem. So childish. By the final week before classes began, he'd gone silent.

But Sophia didn't care. Sophia wasn't threatened. The bond she and Jake had forged over those few weeks was strong enough to transcend pettiness, and that wasn't even counting the bond of their blood.

He'd come back to her. She knew that he would.

At some point, Jake would need her, and she would be there for him. Because that was what family did.

And of course, she turned out to be right. Jake did come back to her, and there was no one else in the world who could've helped him like she could.

CHAPTER TWENTY-SIX

She said that writing would help. He said that writing it all down would only make it worse.

"It'd be like an ouroboros," Jake said. "Like I'm sticking my tail in my mouth."

"You can't think of it that way," Sophia said. "Think of it as a purging. An exorcism."

"It won't work," he repeated. He couldn't adequately explain to her all the ways it wouldn't work.

"Then tell someone at school about what happened. Someone who can do something about it, I mean. I can help you get in touch with the counseling department."

"Please, don't do that," Jake said. He'd made Sophia promise not to use her authority against him, and he believed her when she said she wouldn't.

But now he understood that people could not be trusted, even the ones you thought you loved.

"Why do you think you owe these people anything?" she said. "It's not like you took a blood oath."

Jake gestured down at his ruined shoes, splattered in his

friends' blood. After Nic had dropped him off at his apartment from Dr. Lowman's house, he'd run straight here, to Sophia's. She'd answered the door immediately, no questions asked, then handed him a glass of water and sat him down on her velvet couch. It was a particular shade of gold, that couch, with a hint of mossy green if you rubbed it in a certain direction. She'd waited for minutes while he'd prepared himself to speak. When he did, she remained quiet, holding him lightly with her steady gaze.

"I might as well have," he said now.

Then Sophia took his hand. It was the first time they'd made physical contact—not counting the time she'd drunkenly put her hand on his knee, which he knew had meant nothing—and her skin on his was like an electric shock, bolted through his hand and straight to his heart.

Jake wondered, not for the first time, why Sophia liked him so much. Why she even bothered with him.

"Even if you lose them," she said, "you'll still have me."

Tanya had said something like that to him once, and Jake had believed her with his whole entire heart. But he'd lost her tonight. He didn't blame her for what had happened. He only blamed himself.

After what he saw, and what he should have done about it and couldn't for the life of him seem to do, he was fully confronted with his own worthlessness. And that made him hate himself more than he could ever hate her.

And all this hatred, all this anger, this stagnancy, this fear—it was just too much. He couldn't possibly hold all of it.

There had to be a breaking point.

"Why should I believe you?" Jake asked. Then he slid his hand out from under Sophia's, and it was like he'd pulled a brick loose from her foundation. Something crumpled behind her eyes, then rapidly hardened over, gleaming with an intent

Jake had never seen in her before. There was always something about Sophia's face that felt familiar to Jake—something in the way her features were organized was instantly recognizable—but now it was as if he had never known her.

Suddenly she stood from the couch, looking at him with that cold expression he was too stupid to understand. He expected her to kick him out of her house, and probably out of her life, too. Finally, she was understanding just how useless he was, how unworthy of knowing.

But that wasn't what she did.

"Because I love you," she said.

"Why?" Jake felt his face flush with anger. Or confusion.

"Because you're my family."

"How can you say that? You barely even know me," Jake spit out.

Sophia reached up, as if she wanted to touch his cheek. Reflexively he leaned away.

She dropped her hand. "I know you better than you think," she said.

Her affect iced over again, but she didn't seem mad—only distant. She became a stranger again, some older woman from New York whom he'd met only a few weeks before, whom he'd forced himself upon now, having invented some connection that never existed.

Or maybe she had forced herself upon him.

He got up from the couch and headed for the door, but she caught his hand and gave it a tug, holding him to the spot. For the first time since he'd met her, she looked scared.

And he couldn't help but feel that it was him, Jake, whom she feared.

"I need to tell you something," she said.

And that was where the break happened.

CHAPTER
TWENTY-SEVEN

J: u got on signal ok?

S: Yeah, hi

J: remember what i told u yesterday?

S: Which part?

J: the important part

S: Yes

S: Why what's up

J: i can't stop thinking about it

S: In what way? Like you're making plans?

J: making plans yeah

J: options

J: the fuckd up thing is that i don't even care about the pain. like i would just do whats easy and accessible, not necessarily whats not painful

J: thats when u know its bad lol

J: idk maybe i should call my mom or dad

S: Why would you do that?

S: What would you even say to them?

S: They lied to you. They turned your life itself into a lie. What makes you think they're going to help you now?

J: thats fucked sophia

S: Don't blame the messenger

S: I know it's painful to hear but it's the truth. And you're not going to hear it from anyone else

S: See what I'm doing here? I'm telling you the truth because I love you

S: What are you going to do now?

J: about what

J: oh. idk

S: You know I'm here for you. Whatever you decide to do

S: Just please don't hide anything from me

September 17th, 9:30 a.m.

S: Hey, you okay?

J: yeah all good. sorry for the silence just been trying to focus on work

S: Ok

S: Have you thought any more about it?

J: honestly yeah

J: the work thing was a lie lol idk why i told u taht. literally cant focus on anything

J: i cant be in my body

J: i dont even know how to explain this feeling

S: And you still don't want to get help?

J: why do i need help when i have my sister

J: i have a fuycking sister

J: wtf

S: I know

S: Well

S: Then let me help you

S: Want to come by today? We should talk in person

J: yeah its not like im going to class today lmao

J: can i come over now

S: Of course

September 20th, 5:23 p.m.

J: so

J: i called my dad

S: You mean our dad

J: yah him

J: i just wanted to hear his voice

J: sad but true

S: What'd you say to him?

J: well he asked me how i was doing and i wasnt gonna be like oh im fucking great never been better

J: so i was like you know, im not having a great time

J: he said why and i said some bullshit about how my workload is a lot heavier this semester than last one and its been hard to balance school w work w social life

J: and jhe literally said, well thats life and it doesnt get easier so you need to learn to deal with it

S: Is he fucking serious

J: yeha

J: then he said he had a meeting

J: said bye and hung up

S: This fucking guy

J: its so pathetic but i still want his approval

J: love him unconditionally

J: its hard not to take everything he says to heart

J: and not think that hes right

J: like i should just deal with it and move on

J: get over myself

S: Jake

S: What you're feeling is real pain

S: And we need to find a way to get you out of it

S: Call me

September 22nd, 6:33 p.m.

J: sorry to bother you btu im feelinglike a real waste of space rn

S: I understand

S: You know there are ways to fix that

September 27th, 1:31 a.m.

J: yeah so im not talking to anyone rn

S: What do you mean?

J: all the s&s people

J: i texted tanya to see how shes doing and she iced me out

J: i was so scared to reach out to her but i figured i couldnt feel any worse than i am now so what is thereto even be scared of

J: a silver lining

J: i dont feel scared anymore

S: Do you think she's hurt by what you said to her?

J: probably

J: and she knows i didnt do anything to help her

J: i mean i think she knows that i know what really happened to her and didnt do anything

S: Well, it was a hard situation for you

J: it wouldnt be taht hard if i was a different kind of person

S: I guess so

J: the funny thing is that i didnt tell bc iwas so scared they would leave me

J: and guess what they did anyway

S: Well

S: Joining that society in the first place wasn't the best choice you've ever made

J: ckealry not

J: im so dumb

S: 😶

───────── October 2nd, 5:00 a.m. ─────────

J: do yo uthink i should tell my parents that i know about you

S: What would be the point?

J: to clear the air

J: one last hurrah before i go

S: Don't tell them

J: ok

───────── October 7th, 8:13 p.m. ─────────

J: can i come over in a few? need to run this by you

S: Of course

S: Run what by me?

J: i think i know what to do now and i think it will work

J: its actually poetic

J: but i want to know if you think its a good idea

S: Oh

S: Yeah come over

October 9th, 4:44 a.m.

J: are u up?

S: Yeah. I'm not sleeping tonight

J: starting to get really nervous

J: idk if i can do this

S: I'm not going to tell you whether you should or shouldn't do it

S: But I know that you can't live with this pain any longer

J: yeah

J: im scared thogh

S: Didn't you just tell me that you're not afraid of anything anymore?

J: thats true of some things

S: It's inhumane to allow yourself to live like this and it's up to you to make a decision about how to help yourself, one way or another

S: If you can't help yourself, then I can't help you

October 10th, 4:33 p.m.

J: can you come with me tonight

S: To the wayside?

J: yeah

S: Jake

S: No

J: i might need u to push me

J: im not even kidding

S: Please don't ask me to do that

J: ok im sorry

S: It's okay, you don't need to be sorry

S: Calling you now

October 10th, 7:45 p.m.

J: leaving my phone at home

J: thank you and i love you

S: Hang on

S: Just tried calling you

S: I know we talked about this before and you have your heart set on this now but I don't know if you should do it

S: Did you leave yet?

S: Tried calling you again

S: Please pick up

S: Are you doing it?

CHAPTER
TWENTY-EIGHT

The light had diffused across the dirt, the dense pines sheathing the cliff face across the ravine limned in a honeyed glow. The sun was behind them, close to setting. The other hikers were gone. At some point, the three of them had slunk down to the ground, arranged in a tight circle. Kate held her pebble-studded palms upright on her knees. She braved a glance at John; she'd been fixated on Luna—Sophia—as she spoke, unable to look away, every now and then catching the briefest flashes of John, of Jake, and even of herself, even though that was technically impossible, and when a wave of nausea threatened to double her over, she reminded herself of that. She did not share blood with this woman. (But John did. Jake did.)

John's expression was unreadable, his anger settled into stillness. If she clawed at his face, slashed a knife across his eyes, would he react then? Would he yell? Would he fight back? Possibly not. He was not the type to lash out. Kate had always thought that was the most dangerous thing about him.

From her other side, she sensed Sophia staring at her. But Kate would not turn. She would not look at her again.

"I keep going over and over that last conversation that we had," Sophia said now. The sound of her voice made Kate want to retch. "I tried to help him; I really did. But he was beyond help."

It would take Kate forever to catch hold of her reality. But it was possible—likely, even—that she never would. That she would continue to exist in this state, a universe only minimally divergent from the other one. It wasn't so bad here. Maybe she could finally find Jake here, too. No one would even need to know that the real Kate had ever left.

Kate opened her mouth, then closed it again. Her tongue felt heavy in her mouth.

"This last conversation," she managed to say. "What exactly did he say to you?"

"What I just told you," Sophia said. "He wasn't positive that he would go through with it. I told him to hold on for just a little longer, that I would be there in an hour. But when I finally got up here, he was gone."

Kate knew she shouldn't believe her. But what choice did she have? What was the alternative?

"Was Luna Kline even a real person?" she asked.

Sophia nodded. "She's really Jake's Brit Lit TA. I found her name on his class schedule."

"But I saw you in the lecture."

"I'm a staff member," Sophia said. "I can get into university buildings."

"And you wanted to cover your tracks."

"It's not as calculating as it all seems. I really did want to get to know you. I wanted to make amends somehow, but I couldn't tell you who I really was." She shot a glance toward John, who offered nothing. "It wasn't my place to tell you."

"Getting to know me and sleeping with me are two very different things," Kate said, her anger returning. Something dangerous flashed behind John's eyes, mirroring hers, but still he remained silent.

"I couldn't help the way I felt about you," Sophia said. "I just felt this . . . pull toward you."

Nausea surged through Kate again. She leaned her head over her knees, taking deep breaths. She knew what she had done, but she was too disgusted to put the name to it.

When she lifted her head, she found John standing over them, swaying slightly, his arms hanging loosely at his sides. It brought to mind the peculiar way idle video game characters rocked back and forth, comical but also menacing, cueing to their director a willingness to be sprung toward any whim.

"How can you live with yourself?" John said. He addressed Sophia—his sneakers, dusty black, were angled toward her—but Kate knew his words were meant for them both.

His daughter. Luna—Sophia—was his daughter. A daughter he had neglected in every way that mattered, and of whom he had uttered not a single word to Kate, left not a single clue for her to find.

No, Kate thought: *that* was the most dangerous thing about John.

Sophia stood then, too, leaving Kate staring up at them both. They had the same ears, Kate noticed; the cartilage bent slightly inward along the top, like a small creature had rested its pinkie finger into the curve.

Sophia was saying something now, but Kate couldn't hear it. Now she was looking at their thumbs and their kneecaps, and also the posture, the dip in the lower back and the wide set of the shoulders, and the deep, bifurcating groove in the philtrum. Their eye levels nearly matched up. Sophia's mother must have been tall.

Then the energy changed; Sophia had uncovered John's

switch, long buried or carefully hidden. Kate stood, too—she
felt too exposed on the ground—but she kept a careful distance
away from Sophia and John.

"My entire life, you've treated me like trash," Sophia was
saying.

That was the flick of the switch. John animated into anger,
stalking closer to Sophia, his hands curled into fists at his sides.

"I paid your entire college tuition," he said. "And I helped
your mother pay her mortgage. I bet she never told you that."

"Why do I give a shit about a mortgage? You didn't come
to my mother's funeral."

John was moving forward, step by step, driving her closer
toward the edge of the cliff. Kate stayed back, kept her mouth
shut, watching the dance unfold on the screen before her.

"Your mother hated me," John said.

"That's not true."

"It is, actually. When you were around four or five, she told
me not to contact you. No visits, no phone calls. Other than
child support, she wanted nothing to do with me. She wanted
you to have nothing to do with me."

"But you still sent me birthday cards."

"A small rebellion."

Sophia scoffed. "So you did it for yourself. Not for me."

"I wanted you to know that I was a real person. That I was
a part of your life, despite what your mother might have told
you about me."

"If you really wanted to be a part of my life, you wouldn't
have blindly assented to whatever my mom said to you twenty-
five years ago. You would've fought for me." Sophia shook her
head in disgust. "You're pathetic."

The words bored straight through Kate's gut. Sophia was
right. For all John's posturing, for all the money he'd amassed

and bravado he mimed, he was a coward, right down to the core. Kate had always known it, but she'd been too ashamed—for John, for herself—to admit it.

"I'm pathetic? You fucked my ex-wife!"

"You didn't even tell me when Jake died. That's how little you care about me."

"You didn't need to know about Jake."

"How can you say that to me? How can you hate me so much?"

"I don't hate you, Sophia," John said.

"But you wish I never existed."

John just stood there. His silence said everything.

"You're *hurting* me, John," Sophia said then. "My entire fucking existence has been one long, continuous kick in the teeth."

"Is that why you killed my son? To exact some petty revenge on me?"

Sophia paused, breathing heavily. "I didn't kill Jake."

"You weaseled your way into his life, made him trust you, then exploited him when he was at his most vulnerable. That's as good as pushing him off that cliff."

"The same could be said for you." Anger glinted in Sophia's eyes, a tiny, vicious knife. "Jake called you before he killed himself. He tried to ask you for your help. Do you even remember that conversation? Do you remember what you said? You told him to *deal with it*."

Jealousy lodged in Kate's throat like bitter fruit. Jake hadn't called her a week before he died. He'd called John. If he had called her, Kate told herself, she would have known he wasn't okay. She would have gotten in the car right then and there. She would have driven up to his apartment and cradled him in her arms until he felt better. She would've moved heaven and earth to help him.

She would have she would have she would have.

But John—he had done nothing.

Worse than nothing.

He had fed into all of Jake's greatest fears.

"Why?" Kate said now. Sophia and John both looked at her like they'd forgotten she was there. Louder, she said it again: "Why? Why didn't you do anything? Why couldn't you get out of your own way and save our child's life?"

John bounced his hand against the air in a placating gesture, but she could see the wildness in his eyes as Kate moved closer to him.

"I would have helped him if I could," John said. His voice broke into a sob. "I would have. I would have. I would have."

This was the moment Kate would later replay the most. In retrospect, she mined the scene for evidence of what was to come: The way John covered his face with his hands and, in so doing, lowered his guard. How he flinched when she and Sophia stalked closer to him, until she and the other woman were both only inches away from him, so near Kate could smell them both against her skin. Sophia's leather-and-flowers scent, John's sharp peppermint soap. (It was the same soap Jake had used, she'd realized; how was that even possible?)

And in retrospect, Kate fought to reenter her own mindset, so that she could pinpoint the precise moment that she decided she would not attempt to quell Sophia's anger, and then not to pull her away from John, and then, at the very end, not to reach out a hand to him, even though she knew that if she had, he would have pulled her right down with him.

She wondered, too, whether she would have been better off that way.

"That's a *lie*," Sophia said.

Kate still heard the way Sophia emphasized the word with a

single hard push against John's chest, leveraged with both hands
and a back foot in a Sisyphean stance.

Kate remembered that it only occurred to her later—seconds
later, but too late nonetheless—that John's anger, physicalized
into movement, had forced the three of them to the edge of
the cliff. It was four feet away from the drop at most, but those
four feet were covered instantly, seamless as practiced choreog-
raphy, when John first stumbled backward—one foot—then
caught a heel on a gnarled root that thrust upward from the
earth—another foot—and then pushed backward still, his arms
cartwheeling around him, fingers flexing to grab the formless air,
the momentum going and going, unstoppably, forcing him over
the edge of the cliff, the end of the known world, and soundlessly into the ravine below.

CHAPTER
TWENTY-NINE

Sophia's body betrayed her. She was trembling so violently she slunk to the ground. This shaking implied that she had done something wrong, that she was guilty, but she wasn't. This, she reminded herself, was a somatic response to shock. It wasn't her fault that John fell over the side of that cliff, just like it wasn't her fault that Jake had thrown himself over it. It was John's fault for luring her over there, taking her with him. It was his fault for spewing such hateful things at her. It was his fault for turning his back on his child when he needed him. (It was his fault that he'd turned his back on both of his children. And look at how they turned out.)

Really, it was his fault that she was even here in the first place—that she'd been made to orchestrate the meeting among the three of them, and then to force his secret into the light.

It would've been better if John had never even sent her mother that money, never even attempted those half-assed birthday cards. That he'd done so had made him think that he was doing the right thing. Worse to be a bad person and think you were a good one. Better to be bad and to know it.

"Get up."

Sophia looked up to find Kate, reduced to a silhouette by the sun sinking behind her. She reached a hand toward Sophia. Sophia took it and leveraged herself to a stand. Inside Kate's cool, dry hand, her own was damp and still shaking, a seizing little fish.

For a moment they looked at each other. Kate had a peculiar expression on her face. It was empty, unblinking, as though she were considering a blank white wall. Like John's had been, before he'd snapped.

"Are you going to tell anyone about this?" Sophia finally said.

Something flickered over Kate's face—a wave of recognition, even of fear—but it quickly vanished, a curtain snapped closed.

"I don't know," Kate said. "I just want this to be over."

"I want this to be over, too," Sophia said.

But it wasn't over. Sophia knew that.

What would happen when she came down from this mountain? Sophia couldn't grasp it. She wasn't guilty—she *wasn't* guilty—but Kate might think she was, probably she did, and so there was the possibility of pressed charges, a lengthy trial, prison or an excruciating settlement. But even if Kate extended to Sophia some saintly goodwill and she was spared legal repercussions, there was still the question of how to live. How to just keep doing this, after what had happened here.

Here, where she had been orphaned.

Clarity pressed upon her then.

She could not come down from this mountain.

And Kate—she might as well have been dead. The other woman nodded at something Sophia had just said, though Sophia couldn't remember what it might have been. Kate's lips were cracked and dry. She darted the tip of her pale-pink tongue against the corner of her mouth, licking it wet. Sophia had the sudden urge to grab it between her fingers and tug, just to make her scream. Why wasn't she screaming?

A black bird soared overhead, cawing.

Finally, Kate said, "If I'd allowed myself the option, I don't think I would have had a child." A glance toward Sophia, cutting and accusatory; then her gaze softened again, turned milky. "But I thought I couldn't deprive my husband of a baby. I thought it would be cruel."

"We talked on the phone once," Sophia said. She'd been wanting to tell her this from the moment she'd finally drummed up the nerve to approach Kate in the library, after days of watching her from afar. Now was as good a time as any to air any lingering memories, impressions, grievances. "I called John on my sixteenth birthday and you answered the phone. You said you'd just found it in Jake's toy box."

"That was you?" Sophia nodded, but Kate's expression continued to reveal nothing. "I never told him you'd called. I'd thought he was having an affair. Why wouldn't I think that? How could I ever imagine that he'd had another child?" Kate looked away. "I'm having a very hard time squaring the two of you."

"John and me?"

"You and you."

How to explain this? Sophia couldn't really explain it to herself. It wasn't her intention to become romantically involved with Jake's mother. She'd never even technically been with a woman before. But when she met Kate, and the voice that had haunted her for over a decade had snapped into its physical form, she knew, instantly, that she needed her. In any way possible.

Grief had a funny way of unfolding. Where it suffocated some people, others used it like a honing steel, sharpening their edges against it. Kate was the latter, and Sophia fancied herself that way, too. Sophia liked Kate's bluntness, recognized herself in it, but she also liked the sweetness hidden at the core of the blade. It'd been so unfamiliar to her. She'd wanted to know what it tasted like.

And what she'd said to Kate earlier was the truth—you couldn't help how you felt about some people. It wasn't right to act on her feelings; she knew that. But she couldn't *not* do it.

"The only lie I ever told you was about my name," Sophia said now. "Everything else was real."

"Your mother?"

"She's dead."

"Your job."

"Okay. That, too."

"Your tattoo. That's not John's handwriting."

"It was an ex's."

"My Girl." Shane had declared it their song, his and Sophia's, but then it had been his and Shayna's first dance at their wedding three months ago, per Shayna's gloating postnuptial Instagram post. After Sophia saw the post, she'd spent a long couple of minutes holding a pair of sewing scissors over the words inked into her inner wrist, considering cutting them out, but she couldn't go through with it. She'd been afraid of the pain.

Look how far I've come, she thought now.

"I think you lied about more than you even know," Kate was saying.

Sophia nodded, because it was right. What was real? What was not? She pressed a hand to her belly, where a deep, aching pain blossomed inside her core, emanating up through her eyes, her teeth, every cavity in her face, and the pressure obscured her vision, like a clear film had been laid over her eyes.

This body was real.

And over there, that black bird that had landed on the jagged chimney of that godforsaken ruin: that was real, too.

And her father's body, heaped on a bed of rocks very far below, only just visible to her naked eye: somehow, that was also real.

Sophia dragged her gaze up to Kate's face, which had devolved into a smear of fleshy pigments.

"What was he like?" Kate said.

Sophia understood, abstractly, that she should have been afraid to be standing here like this, with the end of the world at her heels and her father's ruined body far below, and her terror—messy, jagged, wild—honing into resolve.

But she wasn't.

A silver lining. I don't feel scared anymore.

Sophia conjured the memory of her brother. The one she had imagined, and the one she had known. In the end, they weren't so different from each other. Both had haunted her in their inscrutability. She had been so desperate to know him fully, for his presence to be the material answer to a lifetime of ephemeral questions.

If she could've absorbed his spirit, she would have. If she could've eaten his soul, she would have.

"Quiet, right down to the soul," Sophia said now. "Insecure. Sincere. Lonely. Sweet. Gullible. An escapist. A deep thinker. Curious. Naive. Unambitious. Thoughtful. Lazy. Resistant to change."

"I don't know who I am anymore," she heard Kate say.

"I don't, either," Sophia said. She tried to say it. She thought she said it. Slowly she stepped backward, chased by the sensation of moving through a basin of liquid. It was heavier than water, and cloudier, too, but with the muscular pull of a retreating wave.

The current grew stronger. It lapped against the backs of her heels, coaxing her balance to falter so that it might bear her away on her back, so that she might reveal her face to the shy sun and the stars in hiding, and beyond all that to the heaven that Sophia was sure, now, did not exist.

She was so close to it all, her boat casting swiftly off the shore, but then there was a counterweight—a violent tug—in the equal and opposite direction.

It took Sophia a moment, an eternity, to register what had happened.

It was her body that tipped her off. The red dirt was embossed upon her hands and her knees, and the imprint of a fist, encircling her upper arm beneath the cuff of her T-shirt, was already beginning to bruise. Her jaw ground and ticked, her head swayed lightly on the stalk of her neck, and inside her chest her stubborn heart punched out a punishing beat.

And there, on the ground before her—there was Kate. She had fallen backward into a crouch, bracing herself with one hand while the other shook itself free of its heavy weight. The weight of Sophia's body, hauled out from the current.

Kate raised herself to a stand. Her dazed look had given way to a sort of fixed determination. It steadied her as she brushed the dirt from her knees and her red palms. Plumes of dust withered in the air between them.

"I did this for my family," Kate said, over the hard pants of her breath. "Do not ever think I did this for you."

It was then that Sophia could understand what had just happened: Kate had tugged Sophia back from the edge of the cliff before she could hurl herself over it.

Kate had saved her life. As if it were hers to save.

CHAPTER
THIRTY

Nighttime, the dead of it, the sky not quite black but a velvety, opaque blue. Up here, at the Wayside, Jake lingered near the ruins of the mansion. The light of the moon cast over him, revealing the rectangular bulge of the cigarettes he'd tucked into his front pocket.

What the moon didn't see: That his brain couldn't register the taste of food anymore. That he'd had to throw away his Nike Air Force 1s, the stark-white ones his dad had gotten for him, because the blood wouldn't come out of the leather, not even with the internet's suggested stiff-bristled brush or abundance of suds, and the pettiest part of him was still upset about it. That the song stuck in his head was "All We Ever Wanted Was Everything" by Bauhaus, the saddest, slowest song that band had ever made.

Had he wanted everything? He hadn't thought so. Freedom, safety, to be good. But that had proved impossible, so then he'd stopped wanting anything at all.

The lip of the incline was a few yards away. Ten, if he'd had to guess, but he'd never been much good at those kinds of guesses. He couldn't even parallel park.

When he approached the edge, that final maybe-yard, he heard something rustling in the woods behind him.

"Hello?" he said. His voice, unused for so long, emerged with a crack like dried earth.

And the rustle—it answered.

"Who's there?" he asked.

This was by rote. A final kindness. Because if that really was a person harassing the bushes, signaling their presence, then he knew exactly who that person would be.

It could only be the one.

And if it was that one person, he wondered if that person was here to help him, like he had asked them to. Or maybe they were here to finish off what he'd started.

Then the rustle grew louder and closer, as if the thing—the person—had broken into a run.

He closed his eyes, opened his arms, and waited for the impact.

He waited like that, eyes closed and heart wide, for a minute, maybe two, even after the rustle in the woods crescendoed with a great flap, then released into a caw denouement.

A bird. It was a huge fucking bird in that tree. It was absurd enough to make Jake laugh.

He dropped his aching arms and turned himself around, craning his neck for a better view of the river below. It looked like little more than a black mass—the kind of rich, chewy nothingness you could sink your teeth into—but the full moon had shaken the skin to a glitter.

He didn't feel fear, looking down at the drop. Not anymore. The fear had shaved his nerves down to the quick. But if he had to detect any emotion—which he was compelled to do now, in the spirit of reflection—it might be a cross between relief and exhaustion. He imagined the darkness as a blanket.

It would swaddle him, swallow him, and in its endless folds he would finally be free.

He turned his face to the harsh caress of the wind, which was strong enough to nudge him slightly sideways. He wouldn't miss this sensation. It was like the world itself was bullying him down to a kneel.

Then he righted himself, pressed a hand to the cigarettes, considered one last smoke, and realized he was stalling. The song that was stuck in his head ran out.

Oh, to be the cream. Oh, to be the cream.

Oh, to be sweet. Oh, to be wanted.

Jake was not sweet, and he was not wanted. His very presence was a nuisance. He felt it, the lumbering itch of himself, where it stuck from the skin of the earth like a burr.

He had always known this about himself, this fundamental wrongness, but there was only one person who seemed to understand it, and then to encourage him to finally do something about it.

Sophia. The sister his father had hidden from him.

He thought about their conversation yesterday, the last they would ever have. The last Jake would ever have, with anyone. (This thought, too, prompted a wave of cleansing relief.)

This conversation was not so different from the ones they'd had since she'd revealed herself to be his sister, which, as fate would have it, was also the worst night of his life.

But the crux of that conversation was different than before, because this was the conversation that had instilled in Jake the bravery to commit to what he'd been wanting to do, in varying degrees of seriousness, for a long time now.

I don't know what to do, he'd said to her.

I can't tell you what to do, she'd responded. *But I know what I would do.*

So if you were me, he'd said, *what would you do?*

Now, Jake remembered the expression that came over her face, a combination of pity and defiance that did not typically fit together.

Let me put it this way, she'd said. *You didn't have a choice to be born into this world. But you have a choice in deciding when to leave it.*

Then she'd gathered him up in a hug, pressing his mouth into her shoulder. He breathed in her special scent, a potent combination of her soap and perfume and skin that would always linger on his clothes well after he left her apartment.

Into his ear, she said: *If I were you, I wouldn't be able to live with myself.*

This was when everything clicked into place. This was when the fear rushed out of his body and was replaced by acceptance, followed closely by determination.

When he'd returned home, he'd pulled out his journal, mostly neglected, and written down as much as he could. Then he'd ripped out the page, folded it up, and thrown it in the trash. It hadn't been good enough. He wasn't smart enough to come up with the words that correctly mirrored the stuff in his head. But tonight, before hiking up to the Wayside, he'd pulled the page out of the trash and stuck it back inside his journal.

He did this for his mother. He knew that she would find it.

Now Jake threw a final glance up toward the moon—a ragged cloud passed over its face, dimming its light—then harnessed his newfound purpose to step forward, and forward, and forward again, until he no longer felt the ground beneath him.

EPILOGUE

SIX MONTHS LATER
The house was calm and quiet, and the trees kept it cool. Her nearest neighbors were over a mile away, a grocery store ten, a mall twenty. Kate liked it this way.

She used to be so afraid of the quiet—that way madness lay. In the quiet she heard the dirt thudding onto the coffin. The choked sob from Sophia's throat. The nothingness of John falling over the edge of the cliff. Not a scream, not a cry, not a plea for mercy or forgiveness. That particular silence haunted Kate the most. It was more horrific even than the silence that followed her decision not to let Sophia die.

After it happened, after she brushed the dirt from her palms and caught her breath and secured Sophia safely away from the edge, propping her up, marionette-like, against one of the ruin's low walls, Kate had numbly called Wachs's extension and asked him to come up to the Wayside alone. Later she'd found him kneeling over her with a hand on her shoulder; apparently she had lain on the ground and closed her eyes, fallen asleep, disappeared from her body entirely; she didn't know. She could barely keep her head in the upright position. She was so soft and fetal, blinking her eyes open to a world in which the light was too sharp and she could not parse the language.

How could she have explained the two bodies? How could she navigate the process of pressing charges against Sophia?

Easier to share with Wachs the half-truth explanation of why John was dead. ("Unalive," as the kids were saying on social media now, skirting prudish censorship traps.)

John had tripped and fallen. It was a horrible accident, beyond comprehension.

Trip and falls happen all the time, she'd told Wachs, repeating his own words back to him. ABC. 123.

There was a sharp look from Sophia, stunned like an animal grazed by a passing car. By the time Wachs had turned to her to ask for her account of the events, she had picked back up her expression of shocked dumbness.

Sophia corroborated Kate's story. It was an accident.

The girl was all kinds of things, but she was not stupid.

On the endless trip down the trail Kate studied a small navy stain on the back of Wachs's shirt. It was shaped like a shriveled lemon in some moments; in others, when the dappled light splattered discordantly across it, the entire continent of Antarctica. Sophia lingered somewhere behind her—she didn't know where—her breath wouldn't leave her alone. But at some point on that endless descent, the other woman approached Kate, just close enough so that she could hear her say, across the brutal whipping wind: *You won't see me ever again.*

This was what the silence uncovered.

But Kate was no longer afraid of what she heard. She wasn't afraid of madness, its contaminating spread. When she felt it creep along the floorboards of her cabin, she would simply get up from whatever she was doing—not that she was doing much of anything, but her therapist assured her that this was okay—and put on her sneakers (her own, this time) and hike deep into redwood territory, where the quiet was purer, and not so lonely. How could she feel alone in the presence of those mammoth creatures? They cradled her in their indifferent power. Sometimes she lay on the ground and listened for the roots colonizing the deep earth.

It was here that the wound callused over. Here, she forgot that she had nothing, because at least she had this: An ear to listen. A heart stubbornly beating. A mind that remembered.

And she had a pair of friends, her fellow mourners. It was the Deilys who had found this cabin for her, the wilderness equivalent of a stone's throw away from their own. Kate visited them weekly, bearing the kinds of simple, nourishing foods that Richard had once fed her—crocks of lentils, trays of butterscotch fudge, buttered noodles. The Deilys were even kind enough to get Kate her own rocking chair, which they kept right here on their porch.

Together, the three of them would rest in their own silences, summoning their own demons, their plates full and resting on their laps. They would tilt their faces to the sun and step so briefly inside that other world, the better world—the world perhaps not so distant from this one—in which their children still lived.

And it was there, in that world, that she felt, finally, free.

ACKNOWLEDGMENTS

Writing is a solitary activity, but it takes a community to get that writer to actually sit down and write—let alone to make a book.

First and foremost, I am infinitely grateful to Caitlin de Lisser-Ellen, who trusted me to bring her idea to life, and to Steven Salpeter, for shepherding this project through the finish line. Also at Assemble Media, thank you to Jack Heller, Madison Wolk, and Jiayun Yang.

Thank you to Brendan Deneen, who first gave me a shot at writing this novel and then took it under his wing as its editor. Thanks to the rest of the team at Blackstone Publishing, including Alenka Linaschke, Tatiana Radujkovic, Brianna Jones, and Ember Hood. You have been a dream to work with.

Thank you to Deborah Landau and the NYU Creative Writing program. Endless gratitude to my graduate professors, as well as my brilliant peers in workshop, for forging me into a true writer. Thank you to my undergraduate creative writing teachers at NYU, who instilled in me the belief that

I could do this for real. And thank you to my high school English teacher, Gus Young, who recognized and nurtured my potential.

I'm lucky to have had wonderful professional support as I worked on this book. Thank you to my former colleagues at BDG Media and current coworkers at theSkimm. You are all class acts.

Thank you to my family and friends, my greatest cheerleaders. A special thank-you to Maddie Shepherd for connecting me to Assemble Media, and to Joanna Margaret for your support on this novel. Thank you to Sarah Bird and Meredith Turits, my writing fairy godmothers.

Infinite thank-yous to Tara Rosegarten, my guardian angel in this lifetime—and probably several other lifetimes before this.

Thank you to Jon, my partner in everything. It's so cool that we fell in love while I was writing this book. I love making art with you in my corner.

Thank you to Dad, for your unwavering encouragement. To Mom, for reading every word I've ever written and having deep insight into all of them. Look up *stalwart belief* in the dictionary, and you will find my parents' names re: their daughter's literary aspirations there. And to Alex, my soulmate, my Favorite Person™, and forever my first and best reader. Everything I do, I do for the three of you.

Finally, I would like to thank Meg Murray and Ivan Maisel, our family's dear friends. Telling a story from the perspective of a parent who has lost their child to suicide is a delicate matter, and not one that I took lightly. Throughout the writing of these characters, I turned toward Ivan's memoir, *I Keep Trying to Catch His Eye: A Memoir of Loss, Grief, and Love*, in which he gracefully reflects on the loss of his and Meg's son, Max, to suicide in 2015. It is my sincerest hope that I depicted Kate's and Jake's experiences with respect and integrity.

I would also like to highlight the work of the American Foundation for Suicide Prevention, introduced to me by my friend Joe Fontana. The AFSP provides vital resources for survivors of attempted suicide and those who have lost loved ones to suicide, prevention education, and crisis support.